"Open up," he demanded, inhaling her scent, drawing her taste deep inside him as she gasped in reaction. Her lips parted, let him invade her hot sweetness and he was lost, his Cat purring with a sensual recognition he'd never found before. His *femi* wanted him, even if she wouldn't admit it.

He could live with that.

For now.

Later, later he could teach her to revel in his dominance. Hear the whispered pleas she'd give him for her own sensual satisfaction. In time, she'd give him that. Right now, he wanted just one word.

"Give me your name."

THE HUNT

ANNE MARSH

LOVE SPELL NEW YORK CITY

LOVE SPELL®

October 2009

Published by

Dorchester Publishing Co., Inc.
200 Madison Avenue
New York, NY 10016

Cover art by Anne Cain

ISBN 10: 0-505-52824-X
ISBN 13: 978-0-505-52824-7
E-ISBN: 978-1-4285-0743-2

Visit us online at www.dorchesterpub.com.

ACKNOWLEDGMENTS

My gratitude to my family, who looked me in the eye and said: yeah, you can do it. Thanks Mom and Dad, Beth and Amy, Marge and Lou and Louis. Plus, it never hurts to have the kids add kisses when you send the book off into the big, wide world to meet an editor: see what happened, Zoe and Ethan? I told you your good-luck kisses would work.

Special thanks as well to the fabulous women of the Orange County Chapter of the RWA, whose annual contest introduced me to Dorchester Publishing, as well as bottomless thanks to my agent, Roberta Brown, and my editor, Alicia Condon, who not only saw past the sticky bits in the book (good-luck kisses can be messy!), but helped me work through them.

THE HUNT

CHAPTER ONE

Great gold statues of fearsome cats guarded the Temple of Amun Ra, carvings that were said to take on lives of their own whenever a thief entered the treasure-laden tombs below. Whatever the truth of the tale, it was certain that Guardian warriors roamed the catacombs beneath the temple, mysterious males that the simple farmers of the nearby Valley both feared and envied. They had been summoned to protect, to pursue—and to hunt. For once a year, the Guardians claimed their price for the protection that they afforded to the Valley and its inhabitants—the right to hunt the Valley's virgins for mates.

Miu's knees were shaking so badly that she thought she'd have to drop on all fours and crawl up the broad limestone ramp that disappeared into the dark, cool depths of the temple. Heqet help her, she'd been sun-crazed to think she could pull off this job. The red rays of the late-afternoon sun blazed a heavy path across her shoulders.

She straightened and walked faster. She would do this. She had to do it.

Two massive pylons marked the temple entrance. A stonecutter had carved an elaborate depiction of two Cats shifting from Cat form to warrior form, their massive claws morphing into steel daggers that bit mercilessly into the thief the two beings had just run to ground. The thief looked backward in horror, his mouth frozen open in a soundless shriek. *You can do this*, Miu told herself. *You won't end up like him. Ninety-nine successes and you think this will be your first failure?* No, Heqet willing, she'd be in and out of the temple long before those lethal claws scored her shoulders. Before its feline guardians realized they'd let a thief wander loose in their midst.

The row of white-clad virgins in front of her stepped over the threshold and disappeared into the dark shadows of the interior. The woman next to her sobbed audibly, the small mounds of her breast heaving wildly beneath her silk robe—she was barely more than a girl, Miu realized with disgust. It figured that the Cat warriors would prefer children for mates. Of course, the woman on her other side was of a more calculating bent—she was rubbing the silk of her robe between a thumb and forefinger, assessing the quality of the weave while she ogled the statues of Cats that filled the room they had just entered.

The Cats were well over seven feet tall and carved from what looked like pure gold. Dark obsidian glittered from the slashes of their eyes. One of those, melted down and refashioned into a series of less memorable ornaments, would have kept Miu and her sister sheltered for months. A pity it wasn't possible. She took a second look—professional curiosity only, she assured herself—and forced herself to move away.

She wasn't here to steal seven-foot statuary.

She was here to steal something much smaller. A necklace. Made from silver and moonstones, and placed in a coffer some fifty years ago. It had other—special—properties, she'd been told, but those didn't matter. Just as it didn't matter that *she* wasn't the one who wanted the necklace. She'd do as she'd been ordered to do. Find the necklace, pocket it, and escape from the temple without being caught by one of the legendary Cat warriors. Then she would be home free. Literally.

Everything depended on finding the necklace.

And avoiding the temple's Guardians. She eyed the frieze again.

Frankly, she wasn't convinced that there was any such being as a Guardian. Warriors, yes. Undoubtedly, the temple's defenders kept watch over its fabled riches. But a special breed of Guardians who could change into deadly felines? No. The stories of the Cats and their annual Hunt for virgin mates were too outlandish to be true. What man would really send the unwed females of his family into a great stone monstrosity of a tomb, to be chased down by shape-shifting warriors on the prowl for mates?

Miu wondered if anyone were checking to see whether or not all the women being herded into the sanctuary were, in fact, virgins. Miu suspected there was more than one poseur in the lot, starting with the avaricious woman to her right. If that one hadn't lain with a man, Miu would do penance for a week.

Patting the trembling girl to her left, Miu did her best to blend in. "It will all be over soon," she promised, not knowing if she spoke the truth. But how could anybody with a conscience keep this child here?

The girl shot her a teary-eyed look and then frowned. "Do I know you?" she asked. Not so simple as she looked then.

Of course the girl didn't. Having prepared for this eventuality, Miu lied smoothly and waited to see if the girl would accept her fabrication. "I'm from one of the outermost farms."

Not looking convinced, the girl nodded and then returned to her weeping.

Miu slipped away in midsob. There was no point in being careless; if the girl decided that she really didn't know Miu, she might complain—and there was always some male, somewhere, who was willing to entertain complaints. She shrugged. The Valley was inhabited by farmers with carefully tended fields, an isolated group who did not welcome strangers.

The yearly visit of the traders, who entered the Valley leading pack animals loaded with whatever the townspeople could not grow or make for themselves, had provided the perfect cover for Miu's arrival. In the flurry of excitement generated by the traders, no one had noticed Miu slip away from the group. The following evening, no one had objected when she joined the procession of virgins trooping toward the temple for the Hunt.

Up until now, it had been easy.

The men herding the women into the temple stopped and retreated. Miu tried to look virginally distressed rather than desperate, as the temple priest appeared and launched into a long-winded address about the honor that would be paid to a select few of the assembled women.

A pontificating fool, she decided long minutes later,

who enjoyed the sound of his voice and the delicious echoes of the high-ceilinged chamber in which they waited. The rows of Cat statues stretched away on both sides of them, but she saw no guards, no weapons here inside the temple.

Still, she had the strangest sense of being watched. Then she happened to glance up at the galleries above. Heqet help her, the galleries were crowded with dark figures who almost tempted her to believe in the preposterous legends of the temple Guardians: impossibly tall, broad-shouldered males shrouded in long black robes, their hair bound back into disciplined queues that flowed halfway down their backs.

Her head shot around as she caught the priest's last words. ". . . virgins, of course," he declared. The man's words felt like a slap across the face. Miu was not a virgin, but unless she missed her guess, neither were many of the other women. Now the priest moved on from his self-congratulatory words on their well-preserved virginity and explained how the Hunt would be conducted.

No woman had ever outrun the Cat lords, he assured them. Miu wanted to scoff, but she kept her expression blank and her eyes demurely cast down. "When the signal is given," the priest said, "the hangings will be drawn back from these walls. You will each choose a tunnel and enter it. Run. You have a night's span to reach the standing stones on the other side of the Valley. Any woman who makes it there is free to choose whether she wishes to remain with the Cat lords or to return to her own kind in the Valley." The priest smiled with a false benevolence. "No woman who makes it to the standing stones will ever run again, and the dowry provided to each of you by the Guardians will be hers to keep."

Ah, yes. Money. A perfectly understandable explanation for why there were so many women in the room and why their families had offered them up for the Hunt. Without money in hand, scruples were a luxury most could not afford.

The priest eyed the assembled women sternly. "Of course, there is another possible end to the Hunt, when a hunter catches you as his mate." The details of what happened then—the ritual taking of the girl's virginity—had been a popular topic in the Valley's taverns. The legend had a savagery about it that impressed even the visiting merchants, who had seen a great deal of the outside world. Once again, Miu had her doubts about the truth of the tales. The Cat warrior would bell his mate—and mark her as his so that he would always be able to find her? Poppycock. She didn't know what *belling* was, but it was undoubtedly some romantic euphemism for a sex act.

The priest was concluding his speech now, and his final words brought her head up in disbelief.

"You'll go, one by one, into the audience chamber and be examined by the Amun Ra," he said. Interview with the lord high ruler of these Cat people? Not if Miu could help it. This Amun Ra would spot her for a phony and she'd end up like the thief on their ghoulish door frieze before she'd even had a chance to do any plundering of her own.

Decisive action was called for now.

Her voice brought the proceedings to a standstill. "No."

The old priest just about choked. Red suffused his face and one of his acolytes had to rush over and pound him unceremoniously on the back. He stared balefully at her. "It's not a choice for you to make, girl. The Amun Ra has spoken. He has made his wishes *quite* clear." Apparently the wishes of his supreme high holiness trumped those of a mere female.

The priest tried to continue, but she cut him off. "Yes, yes"—she gestured toward the rows of feline statuary—"I realize that I'm merely prey for this charming Hunt of yours, but I never agreed to any examination. That kind of humiliation?" She shook her head. "Not what I signed up for."

He stared at her, nonplussed. One or two of the women nearest her began to draw slowly away. Obviously no one had ever challenged the priest.

"I don't see why you—or anyone else—needs to inspect me. Clearly"—she let one hand slide down the front of her robe, deliberately pressing the thin silk against the round, firm curves of her thighs—"I've got two legs that work perfectly well. I've sufficient wind to run. And I don't"—she cocked an eyebrow at him just to see if that would set him off—"plan on getting caught."

She waited to see if the males watching in the gallery would take the bait. They were hunters. They would revel in the challenge she had so blatantly issued. And, being men, she doubted that they would stop to wonder why she had issued such a crude challenge.

The priest made the mistake of arguing with her. "You agreed." He pointed an accusing finger at her, stalking toward her in a self-righteous swirl of expensive robes. "Your family took the dower. You came here."

She smiled soothingly. There was no need to tell the man that she had simply ordered the appropriate clothing from a seamstress back in Shympolsk and then slipped into the ranks of the women marching toward the temple. No dower had been paid for her and no family had agreed to send her.

"And if some shifter decides that he can drag me off as his mate, he'll need to catch me first." The intense interest from the galleries above grew stronger. She could smell the heady scent of well-cured leather, masculine bodies, and a goodly amount of sexual interest pouring from the watchers above. It was a very good thing she had no intention of getting caught; she suspected that, legends or no legends, what those men took, they held. Under other circumstances, she would have applauded that sentiment.

The man who strode out of the darkest shadows of the chamber was as impossibly tall as the hunters who crowded the gallery above, but he wore the black robes of a temple priest. His bare feet moved silently over the mosaic tiles with all the grace of a fighter. A match for her skills indeed. This one would be harder to fool. The deep cowl hid his face, but she could just make out firm lips set in a stern line.

He took her arm and she allowed him to steer her deeper into the cool, scented depths of the temple. "Come," he said in a voice of liquid darkness. Behind her she could hear a muted roar. For a moment, it seemed as if the stone statues of the cats stirred, shimmering into eerie life.

Impossible.

They stepped into yet another high-ceilinged, cool room wreathed in smoky shadows. A lintel carved with unintelligible glyphs decorated the entrance and the walls were carefully pieced together from the vast limestone blocks that had been brought at some point in time from foreign quarries—no one in the Valley could remember how or when the temple had been constructed.

The man shoved the cowl back from his head with an impatient hand and she realized that he had more than just the build of a Guardian. He had the face of one as well. Three dark gold bars striped the left side of his face and black eyes regarded her unblinkingly. If what she'd been told was correct, those three bars meant her escort was none other than the Amun Ra, the temple's leader and the first of several obstacles on her path toward the necklace.

He sprawled on the low divan that occupied the center of the room and, for the first time, she realized they were not alone. A stunningly lovely woman, wrapped only in a fragile, transparent silk chiton, reclined on the couch. She wore elaborate gold armbands on her upper arms, which chimed with a small shimmer of bells whenever she moved. Her eyes narrowed as she stared at Miu.

"Why have you brought this one here, my lord?" She ran a small, caressing hand up the powerful bulge of muscle in his forearm. A red flush colored her cheeks and her eyes glittered feverishly. She looked, Miu decided, as if she wanted to consume the Amun Ra whole.

"She threatened chaos, love," the Amun Ra replied

absentmindedly. He splayed one dark gold hand possessively against the woman's bare thigh, opening her to his gaze. And Miu's.

To her own disgust, Miu made a choked sound of amazement. The Valley dwellers might be simple farmers, but these people inside the temple were more sophisticated than she had ever dared dream of being.

"You wish to join our Hunt." Without dropping his hard gaze from Miu's, he spoke softly to the belled woman. "Spread your legs, my love, and show our guest what she may expect when she fails to escape from my hunters. This is Halilah," he said, not taking his eyes from Miu's. "My lover for today."

The dark finger pressing into the bare flesh of the woman's sex aroused a throaty moan from his companion—and Miu's unexpected fascination. She should be angry or shocked or taking advantage of the couple's display to search the room for escape routes. Instead, she stared as mesmerized as a chicken before a snake, feeling an unfamiliar slick of wetness between her own thighs. The thin gold chain that circled the woman's waist dipped between her thighs and disappeared. Miu refused to pursue the thought. The woman did not merely wear the bells—she contained them. With every step she took, the small brass balls would remind her of the Cat that had captured and belled her. Small sparks of electric pleasure would chime in the moist delta between her thighs, building into a helpless ache that only the Cat could—and would—assuage.

"Belled," the Amun Ra said darkly. "Hunted. Taken. My hunters will track you through the passageways and they will show no mercy when they run you to ground." He smiled coldly, but his fingers stroked his own mate's liquid flesh with a tender discipline. "You posed them a challenge and"—he frowned inquisitively—"you did so purposely. I would not have thought you the sort of woman to take part willingly in the Hunt."

"But I am." There was too much at stake not to convince him that this much was truth. "I merely prefer to play your games in my own way."

"It is not a game we play."

She knew that now, but the realization could not change her decision. She would not allow him to frighten her off with this dark passion.

The Amun Ra regarded her levelly and then made an imperious gesture with his fingers. The silk hangings covering the far wall fell in a soft whisper of impossibly expensive fabric. She counted at least a dozen dark passageways leading away from the audience chamber; the entire temple must be riddled with them.

"Choose," he said simply. "Choose. And run."

The Guardian standing in the shadows shook his head as the female sauntered toward one of the passageways and disappeared into the blackness. Strong, sensual, and cunning—all traits his Cat admired. And yet she was almost too confident to be one of the Hunt's usual runners. Too different from the other females he'd watched run over the years. "Who are you?" he asked under his breath.

For the first time in decades, he felt an intense interest in the outcome of the Hunt. If he had possessed even the slightest desire to take a mate, the tempting feminine morsel that the temple had swallowed up would have been high on his list of candidates. He wanted to chase the honey-and-apples scent of her up the line of those surprisingly long legs. Bury himself in the creamy, gold-colored skin that had his Cat demanding to lick her from head to toe. Concentrating, of course, on all the creamy pink bits.

He suspected that she'd have a good many of those.

And that she would protest vociferously if he so much as laid a paw on her.

Persuading her to explore a little passion—with him—would have been intensely pleasurable. Unfortunately, she'd picked a passageway that was likely to drop her square in the middle of the Guardians' personal chambers. Most of the passageways led through that particular area; it made the Hunt simpler if the Guardians didn't have to spend hours combing the miles of dark, dusty passageways for lost females. One of his brothers would choose her and chase her; the next time he saw her, she'd be wearing another male's bells.

He knew, too, bone deep, that she was no match for either Guardian or Ifrit and yet she'd be throwing herself into the path of both in his temple. He didn't like the idea of her getting hurt. But that was wrong. He tested the thought warily. If she broke the rules of the temple, she wouldn't get any more than what she had coming to her. That shouldn't have bothered him. But it did.

He bit back the feral growl that threatened to erupt from his throat. He didn't want a mate. He shouldn't care who had her. Or who hurt her.

But he did, on a completely primal level. His little

interloper smelled like no female that had come from the Valley. She had an exotic, wild scent—and a purpose clearly at odds with that of the other, mate-hungry women around her. He wanted to know what that purpose was. He wanted *her*.

"She's no bride," he said to the man lounging on the divan. "She's up to something." His hard gaze was trained on the shadowy passageway where the female had disappeared. He swore he could still smell her scent.

"Perhaps." Amun Ra's air of sensual insouciance fell away as he smoothly rose from the divan. "Quite probably. And *that* is why I summoned you here."

Pulled him away from watching for signs of Ifrits. Fortunately for Amun Ra, Jafar was very good at what he did. His werecat senses let him see in the dark depths of the temple. They made him strong. Fast. A lethal welcoming committee of one for any Ifrit foolish enough to cross over from their realm to *his*.

He swallowed his displeasure at being called away from his post. Amun Ra would have had a good reason.

"You follow her." Amun Ra gestured after the fleeing female. "Track her. If any of my Guardians can find out what she's up to without his cock doing his thinking for him, it will be you."

True enough. It was an accepted fact. He didn't want any female. "The lower levels are unguarded," he growled. He wasn't going to leave those tunnels unattended, not with the recent uptick in Ifrit activity. Those bastards would seize the opportunity to cross over if they knew no Guardian was waiting for them.

"For a short while only, Jafar." The eyes of the Amun

Ra examined his Guardian. "One of the other Guardians can take your place for today. Once you've learned what she's up to, report back to me. And then you can return to your post."

Handing off his responsibilities didn't sit well at all. "I'm the best." He was.

Amun Ra smiled, but it was a smile that didn't quite reach his cold eyes. "Precisely. And I want my best following that female. She's your priority now, not the Ifrits. Keep her from getting loose in my temple. Find out what she's after. That's what I want you to do."

That's what he was *ordering* Jafar to do. "You want me to babysit this female?"

"Make sure she doesn't get lost; that's all I'm asking." Amun Ra's voice was cold. "Call it babysitting if you want, but you stick to her like a leech. I want to know where she goes, what she does."

"She's that important." He didn't protest again, but it burned him to know he was going to have to follow this female around.

"Maybe. Maybe not. Find out for me."

He didn't run errands. He was a Guardian, a warrior. He fought battles. He did *not* slink around the passageways like some spy. Amun Ra must have sensed his resentment, because he continued, "You do this because I'm telling you to. Because I say it's important. You don't call me on it. Understand?"

Jafar did. He didn't have to like it, but Amun Ra had given him his orders. Follow the female. Find out what she wanted. He only had one question. "You want me to kill her?" He would if he had to.

"No," Amun Ra said thoughtfully. "Not yet. Maybe she's not up to anything."

"And maybe she is." Her scent still teased Jafar. "You giving her the rope to hang herself?" He didn't wait for an answer, instead angling his larger frame into the passageway that had swallowed up the female runner. The sooner he completed his task, the sooner he could return to the Doorways. The sooner he could go back to taking care of the business that really mattered.

"Why not? Discover what she wants here. Be careful, my brother," the Amun Ra called after him, knowing laughter coloring his voice. "That one will run, Jafar—and run hard."

Didn't he know it? Too bad the Cat in him was intrigued.

If she were up to no good, he would bring her down. If she were in the market for a mate, she would find one. That possibility still teased him. She was pretty, for a human, impossibly *alive,* with a warmth that made him want to wrap himself around her. Her long, chestnut-colored hair had spilled about her shoulders in deceptively soft curls and waves. Her face was heart-shaped, the eyes demurely cast down so that the long lashes rested like the shadow of Thoth, the moon god, against her skin. She had looked sweet. Innocent. An unexpected smile creased his dark face. And she'd looked as if that pose of innocence were killing her.

Perhaps the little *femi was* looking for a mate. Perhaps she would be delightfully eager to be hunted.

Erotic images flooded his mind. He would enjoy the pleasures of mastering her. Already, his cock was thick and hard, demanding to be planted deep in her wet sex. It was just the summer heat, he told himself: the mindless mating frenzy that seized them all when the sun blazed relentlessly in the abovelands, beating down on their stony world, heating it—and their blood—until they found temporary release with their sex partners.

Unfortunately, there were few sex partners belowground. Only those women the abovelanders had cast out or had marked for punishment. Or had sent to the Guardians for their Hunts. The Guardians had no females of their own, no hope for release from the burning heat that built remorselessly in them unless they found mates.

And now—completely unexpectedly—here was a female who called to him. One intended for the Hunt. A feral possession welled up in him. *His.* His mate. She could be.

Dropped in his lap as if by the gods themselves.

It was impossible. He knew as well as the Amun Ra that there was no female in his future. Not given his past.

"Good hunting," called one of the other warriors as he passed. They glided smoothly out of the shadows, as drawn by the female's presence as he was. He must find her first.

Loosing his senses, he let himself shimmer from man form into the sleek, muscled body of his hunting Cat. He would follow her. See what she was *really* up to in the temple.

He didn't *have* to make her his mate.

Chapter Two

Miu set off down the tunnel. Lickety-split. This Amun Ra had apparently bought into her eligibility and was going to allow her to participate in their Hunt. She had the access she needed to the catacombs beneath the temple and only a complete fool would wait around for him to change his mind.

Once around the bend and out of sight, she stopped and assessed her position. Would she be able to sense the necklace in the tomb far below her?

The item she'd been sent to steal was one ancient necklace of unknown *mazhykal* provenance and powers. Made of silver and set with at least one large moonstone. Last known owner: an alleged princess who had met an untimely end at the hands of the Guardians. Right here in this temple, where she'd been laid to a hasty rest. Since the princess had died wearing the necklace, presumably she'd been buried with it. All Miu had to do was find the casket, pop open the lid, slip off the necklace, and then make a fast run topside.

Mission accomplished.

Fortunately, one of her ancestors had been a randy moon daemon who'd hooked up with a human great-grandmother. Though Miu's mixed blood put her way down on the bottom of the daemon pantheon and she generally didn't have enough *mazhyk* in her to boil water or cook an egg, she did have an affinity for the moon.

And all things moon-related.

That meant she had two things going for her on this mission. First of all, two of Egip's three moons had just entered their full phase. Even inside the temple and moving rapidly underground as she jogged along the downward slope of the passageway, she could feel the warmth of the moonlight tugging at her. She'd be able to find her way back to the surface—and the moonlight. It was a nice little insurance policy against being immured alive in the catacombs.

Secondly, the damned necklace just happened to be sporting a particularly large moonstone in the center. If she centered herself, she should hear the stone's call.

She had one other advantage: a map. She had no idea how the thief master had procured it, but she would gladly use it. She mentally followed its shadowy curves out of the temple, fixing the twists and turns in her memory. That was her escape route.

But instead of the maze of passages she should be focusing on, the starkly sensual scene she had just witnessed replayed itself again and again in her mind. The Amun Ra's stroking had been intensely sensual. Even though the last thing she needed right now was a possessive alpha male, she couldn't forget the look of pleasure on his face as he touched his partner. What would it be like to have a male look at *her* that way?

Focus on the map. She wasn't here for sex.

A soft, unfamiliar sound came from behind her and the hair rose on the back of her neck. She might be a minor daemon—and only a half daemon at that—but she could still recognize *mazhyk* forces when they were unleashed. Somebody much stronger than she had entered the passageway behind her. She didn't need special senses to know that boded ill for her.

For a brief moment, she considered abandoning the necklace. The Master could find himself another treasure for her to purloin; her moon daemon senses were tugging her violently to the left, where a small, narrow passageway crept almost vertically upward. Take that passage and she'd find herself on the surface within minutes. Without the necklace and still in hock to the Master for one final theft. But she'd be alive. Whatever was hunting her—and somehow she was certain that she *was* being hunted—would have to settle for going to bed hungry.

The thief's mark burning on her forearm jerked her out of her fantasies. The Master was growing impatient. He'd sent her to steal the necklace. And he'd made it very, very clear what price he would extract for failure. She blinked away the unwelcome image of Lore's sugar-sweet face and the betrayed look in her sister's eyes when Lierr—the Master, she reminded herself deliberately—had taken her away. If she made this last theft, Lierr could never again hold Lore's safety over her head.

She could not screw this up.

So she quickened her pace, stretching her senses. Ahead, she sensed a vast cavern. If her map were correct, there would be a large room up ahead. Undoubtedly, it would be filled with Guardians or their servants. The faintest clink of metal weaponry reached her. Not the way she wanted to go.

CHAPTER THREE

Jafar moved swiftly through the temple passageways in his Cat form, padding down the ever-darkening corridors without hesitation as he picked out a path that would put him on a directly intersecting course with the running female.

Her scent called to him, but there was some other attraction as well. Although there was no denying that the woman was pretty, he had seen human women possessing greater beauty. He had never, however, seen one who seemed more alive. She vibrated with a delicious energy. Beneath the concealing folds of the silk cowl, thick curls tumbled down her bare back. Her skin was a creamy gold, the color of the exquisitely expensive honey pots that the southern traders brought through the well-guarded passes and down into the Valley below. However dear those sweet, viscous strands of liquid gold, Jafar would have offered far more for this woman.

It seemed unlikely, however, that she would welcome his advances. Despite her obvious curiosity at the Amun Ra's display, her expression had been reserved.

Hostile even.

If she had come here to participate in the mating

Hunt—and he doubted it with every fiber of his being—she had not wanted to do so. No, his senses screamed that she was here for some far more nefarious purpose. What did she really want inside his temple? He'd find out—and then he'd stop her. His Cat came to a sudden halt, raising a velvety muzzle from the stone floor of the passageway.

The trail ended.

Abruptly.

His quarry had skipped the obvious side passages along the route, and he'd been convinced she was headed for the Guardians' chamber just up ahead. Most females ended up there, saving a great deal of work for everyone.

He sniffed again. Her scent was still strong, so she had been here. The question was: where had she gone?

His pupils widened to accommodate the lack of light in the tunnel. Golden eyes shone, flicking over the empty passageway.

There.

The narrow tunnel overhead was almost invisible, the opening half tucked behind a stone beam.

Now that was interesting. His little *femi* had chosen a most unlikely direction. Straight down into the catacombs where the Valley's dead were buried and where the Doorways lay. When he'd received the summons from the Amun Ra, he'd been following the almost invisible trail of an Ifrit recently escaped from Qaf, the daemonic lower realms that lay on the other side of those Doorways.

Although almost none of the mortals could see them, the Ifrits were well over seven feet tall, massively built and strong, with powerful wings. Worse, they were brutal, indulging in a casual violence that had decimated the local population before the Valley's inhabitants had made their deal with the Guardians: virgins in exchange for protection.

Leaping lightly from the ground up to the round opening, Jafar crouched inside the lip of the passageway. Empty. So far, she was fulfilling his expectation that she would be quite different from the usual run of females. She'd disappeared down the passageway as if she knew where she was headed. As if she had a particular destination in mind.

But not escape. If his *femi* had wanted simply to evade the Guardians and claim the dowry for herself, she would have chosen either of the two passageways on the left that led up to the surface. He was suddenly sure of that. She would have recognized the scent of fresh air for what it was.

What did she want then, if she did not want her freedom and she did not want a mate? Padding forward on silent feet, he ran swiftly after her.

Miu ran lightly down the passageway for about a quarter mile before she paused. With sure hands, she untied the satchel of supplies that she'd fastened around her waist beneath the silk tunic. Reason number two for not wanting to submit to a virginity test at the hands of his arrogant highness, Amun Ra. He'd have questioned the presence of several shortknives, a flarestick, and a small scrying bowl lodged between her thighs. Not your typical wedding fare.

In fact, it kind of highlighted her lack of sincerity in the offering-herself-up-for-marriage department.

Striking the flarestick against the wall, she waited

for her eyes to adjust. The light flared to orange life, the glow shocking in the Stygian darkness of the passageway. Fortunately, her moon daemon genes meant outstanding eyesight even in the absence of light, but her other senses were not as well honed. She didn't want any sand snakes or—Heqet forbid—a tomb spider dropping unseen out of the darkness. The sand snakes were particularly vicious, burrowing into any warm, wet spots they could find. She shuddered.

All she could see was two walls. A ceiling. A floor. Darkness surrounded her, broken only by a perfect pool of light from the flarestick. Beyond the reach of her arm, the corridor dissolved into inky blackness. It couldn't have been any darker if she'd been shut into her own tomb. If she weren't careful, this would become her tomb.

With her daemon eyesight, she could see farther into the darkness than most. The shapes of individual limestone blocks, capstones, and lintel markings loomed out of the darkness as she slipped past the darker rectangles of branching passageways.

Even without consulting her memories—or the map tucked into her bag—Miu knew she was going in the right direction. When she stopped to focus, opening her senses to the still, hot air around her, she could *feel* the call of the moonstone. It sang to her. Teased her. Waited for her. She'd thought the temple was dead. It housed dead people, after all. Dead people and the Guardians who guarded its treasure. But instead, the very structure seemed to seethe with quiet life.

She could hear the soft slither of snakes moving within their burrows in the porous limestone, while the hot breath of unfamiliar breezes trickled through the still corridors from unseen air shafts cut deep into the core of the temple by its builders. Scorpions and spiders moved in a clicking scuttle, sure-footed and graceful as they climbed over the smooth walls. And, of course, there were other, more supernatural inhabitants of the temple.

The temple had stood for more than a thousand years, she'd been told. During those years, it had seen its share of deaths—accidental, gruesome, and otherwise—and sometimes spirits had lingered, taking up residence as and where they pleased. In these subterranean stretches, there might be death spirits; farther down still, there would be ghouls and ghosts. Rumor had it that there were Ifrits loose in the catacombs; she could only hope those rumors were untrue. Not even she had a chance against an Ifrit.

Listening for pursuit, she heard nothing. She hoped her little volte-face had thrown off her pursuer. She didn't think she had been hearing things; you didn't survive as a thief without learning to trust your instincts. Although she had a couple of portable spells in her bag, she preferred to save those for later. Once the spells were gone, the spells were gone. *And you don't know what sort of creatures you're going to find down here*, she told herself. Sand snakes could end up being the least of her worries.

Just ahead, she spotted a hole in the floor of the passage. Could it be a shortcut to the level below? There was only one way to find out.

Impatiently tying back her hair, she fashioned a smooth tail from the bushy mass of curls. She no longer needed the charming maidenly appearance she'd been affecting in the temple overhead.

Shoving the remaining items back into her bag, she slung the satchel over her shoulder. With the flarestick clenched in one hand, she checked the shadows below her one last time for lurking tomb spiders and prepared to lower herself through the hole in the floor to the next level of the catacombs.

"Sometimes," she muttered, "you just have to jump." If she didn't jump down, she couldn't find the necklace. If she didn't find the necklace, it didn't matter what else found her. *See?* There really was no other option.

Sitting on the edge of the hole, she swung her legs into the black pool of darkness, raising the flarestick over her head. A large dark shadow lunged out of the darkness. Behind her.

Stupid, stupid, stupid. Without turning, she lobbed the flarestick over her head—there was the satisfying smell of singed fur—and slid into the open hole.

A feral roar shook the tunnel. And, *Oh shit*, she thought. Perhaps there was more to the Cat legend than she had thought. The next moment, a shimmer of gold light spiked through the sudden darkness and hard male hands seized her about the waist.

She was pulled ruthlessly back through the hole, onto her feet, and up against a hard chest. A hard, naked chest. Stomping down with her foot, she sought for her attacker's vulnerable arch. There was a satisfying grunt of pain. *Take that.* Snapping her head backward, she tried to aim for his nose. This time, the results were less satisfying. The man pinioning her shifted smoothly, making her head ring as it struck the muscled shoulder he twisted into her attack. Stars ex-

ploded behind her eyelids. A hand twisted hers up behind her back until moving meant a painful gasp for
breath. His other hand wound around her long pony-
tail, rendering her immobile.

"Pax," a rough voice growled in her ear.

She wasn't that crazy. Or that trusting.

Instead, she kicked harder, trying to buck her attacker off. Her breath sounded harsh even to her own
ears, but she hadn't heard a sound from him after his
initial protest at having his foot crushed. *So* not good.
If only she could get her head around to see her attacker, she'd have a better idea of what she was up
against.

Damn. Damn. Damn.

The warrior restraining her was hard bodied and
harder eyed. Tilting her head back against his chest,
she looked up into a face that was almost alien in its
handsomeness. Gold eyes glowing at her in the darkness. Dark hair woven into hundreds of braids, each
fastened with a small topaz. Tawny-colored skin that
was eminently lickable. A firm mouth. No. There was
nothing soft about this male at all.

He pinned her effortlessly against all that hard, hot
flesh.

"Be still," he grated. A note of impatience crept into
his voice. Good. She was going to make killing her as
difficult and annoying as possible.

"I don't think so," she gasped. "I haven't done anything. Haven't taken anything." When he eased up on
his grasp of her arms, she gulped air frantically. The
smell of him was wild, intoxicating. What was he?

"I'm not here to hurt you," he protested against her
ear. With his mouth pressed almost against her skin,

the words seemed like a lover's caress in the darkness. To her surprise, her body considered the erotic possibilities of her position. That this man's hands had full access to her body. Could explore where and how they pleased. Wetness slicked her sex and she kicked her legs against his shins. Hard. How dare he be so damn attractive?

"Not nice," he grunted. His leg hooked around hers, immobilizing her. Pinning her against his body. Helpless. "I'm here to help. Consider me a rescuer."

"That would be more believable," she grunted, "if you let me go." Gods, could one of the Guardians have caught up with her so fast? "You're a Guardian, aren't you?"

She wasn't surprised when he didn't answer her, but merely tightened his grip.

"I'm not interested in being a mate." She tried again to throw his body off, but it was like trying to shift a damn mountain. She had all the effect of a gnat pushing against a boulder.

To her surprise, however, he said, "Very well."

Her eyes narrowed. "No mating," she repeated.

"No mating," he agreed. "Look, all I want is to talk." She doubted that. If he weren't one of the Guardians, he might be another thief after the same prize as she. It would be just like Lierr to send two of his minions after the same treasure.

"Let me go," she said again. This time, he did, although he kept her trapped between his body and the wall. No diving down into the hole or sprinting up passageways for her. Even if she had tried, she suspected that he would have caught her with humiliating ease.

He bent down and retrieved her flarestick. For a brief moment, as he struck the thin tube against the flinty wall, he was vulnerable. One quick chop at his neck and she'd be free. Why was she hesitating? It was him or her.

"You resisted temptation," he said, straightening up, and she knew he wasn't referring to the wrestling match in which they'd just engaged. Now she was just glad that she hadn't given in to the urge to land a blow on his exposed nape. He had been expecting it.

He had been ready to stop her.

In the orange light of the flarestick, she examined her opponent more closely. He was tall. Broad shouldered. Overwhelmingly masculine in the small confines of the tunnel. The strong line of his jaw and cheekbones gave him a face as harshly beautiful as Amun Ra's, but the sable-colored eyes and the dark hair that spilled loosely over his bare shoulders made him seem less civilized. More feral. She didn't doubt that the Amun Ra could kill if he wanted to, but this man would do so without hesitating.

She pursed her lips, considering.

And the man couldn't be much more naked. A pleated, loose linen cloth was wrapped around his lean hips, and he wore a leather weapons belt stuffed with an impressive array of knives and throwing stars. So, in addition to being practically buck-ass naked, the man was a walking arsenal. He looked tough. More like a mercenary than some sort of honor guard for temple valuables, she thought, eyeing the long pale scar cutting from one cheekbone down to his jaw. The only other items that he wore were simple gold cuffs fastened around his wrists.

No, he didn't look like the Guardians she'd seen, despite the similarity in size and high-handed arrogance. And the only tattoos he had were dark marks inked onto the golden skin of both forearms. Unlike the Amun Ra, however, his face was bare. None of the telltale markings that Guardians reputedly sported. Nope, no bars cut across the golden splendor of his face.

Maybe he wasn't a Guardian. Maybe he *was* another thief.

But he was still standing between her and the necklace. Taking advantage of his relaxed stance, she dove for the hole.

CHAPTER FOUR

Her attacker reacted more quickly than she'd thought possible.

Reaching out a hand, he yanked her back from the edge of the deep hole, his body crowding hers back against the wall, trapping her in a prison of his hot flesh and arms. His anger was almost a tangible thing. His large body shuddered with tension as he inhaled, first one breath, then a second. Deliberately calming himself. He was primal, dangerous, and deadly.

Resting his forehead against hers, he groaned. "Look before you leap, *femi*." One callused thumb stroked the nape of her neck.

"So say you." Wasn't he going to snap her neck now?

"Do you have any idea what's down there?" Was he upset? Why would he care if she broke her neck? One less competitor for the necklace that way.

"Sure. Another level. More stone walls," she bluffed.

"You know this for a fact?" His eyes were glowing. "You've been down there before?"

He must know she hadn't. "Research. Did some

asking around before I popped over here. You should try it," she said sweetly.

Were those his teeth she heard grinding? Good. He seemed very different from the Master's usual brand of thief. Not only was he larger and more brutal, but he seemed too direct. As if he were more at home letting his blades speak for him than his tongue, Heqet save her.

"Look," she explained, "we're likely after the same thing here. And there's only one prize. Winner takes all. No splitting." The Master's thieves rarely worked together. Vacancies tended to occur when multiple thieves were assigned to the same task. Cheating was a prerequisite for success and all of them fought dirty. Her eyes narrowed. Was he trying to disarm her? Get her off balance so he could push her through the opening and break her neck? All possibilities.

"So you *are* going down there after something." He paused, but she didn't fill in the blanks for him. "And it's not a mate. You made that perfectly clear. I'm here to make sure you find what you're after. In one piece." He shrugged, putting a little space between her body and his. "Why not team up? You go on down there alone and I guarantee you're not coming back up. Not whole. This temple is a dangerous place and I can protect you." Hard eyes stared at her. "Keep you safe."

"For a price," she countered, testing the waters without agreeing to anything. He wasn't going to do this for charitable purposes. "Who sent you?"

He gave her a small half smile. "I'm independent."

She gave in to the temptation to examine those broad shoulders with her eyes again. Yeah, she'd just bet he was an independent. The man screamed *alpha* and imagining him taking orders from Lierr was damned difficult to do. She revised her original guess at his identity.

"Merck?" she asked. It made sense.

Mercenaries were notorious, for both their brutality and their greed. They happily switched sides—even in midoperation. Coin was their only recognized code of honor; once payment changed hands, mercks finished the job. No matter what. That was why most folks paid their mercks up front—to reduce chances of a double-cross.

If he really were a merck, her best bet would be to get him on her side. Immediately. Unfortunately, she was light on cash at the moment, not having expected much in the way of shopping opportunities inside the temple.

She eyed the muscles in his arms. She'd already spotted the blades; the question really was, how much *mazhyk* did he pack?

"Are you strictly a weapons-grade merck? Or do you do *mazhyk* as well?"

The little *femi* had courage, Jafar had to admit that. Up against a wall, literally, and she was still asking questions.

"Both," he bit out. She'd sense the *mazhyk* in him; better she thought it was part of his stock in trade, one more weapon he sold for cash.

"Right. Well." When her gaze moved down his body, cataloging what she saw, he suddenly knew precisely what a side of beef felt like.

The obvious approval in her eyes roused the Cat in him again. She was aware of the heat between them, too. He could tell, but he couldn't give in to it. He'd done that—once—and Guardians had died for it. Trusting a female who appeared inside the temple out of nowhere was criminally stupid and he wouldn't do it again. Nevertheless, for just a moment, he allowed himself to imagine taking her mouth with his, sliding his tongue against hers as he learned her taste. His cock stirred.

Her eyes held unease. Good. She was supposed to be scared of him. She was supposed to follow the rules. Maybe she was just lost. Maybe she'd taken a wrong turn and she meant to behave herself and participate in the Hunt. But her own half admission condemned her, and every instinct he had screamed she was trouble. Hot, luscious trouble.

"You need me," he urged. "Need my protection. Aren't you afraid of the Guardians?" he demanded against her ear as heat tore through him, thickening his cock still further. Would she be able to take every inch of him when he crammed himself into her sex? Or would she whimper with the agonizingly sweet pleasure of just the thick tip of him, thrusting in and out of her greedy, wet sex until she howled for more—and he gave it to her?

Her breath huffed out in a small sigh. "Absolutely not," she declared, shaking her head.

"Do not be stubborn, *femi*," he crooned into the smooth shell of her ear. She shivered. Good. She was deliciously sensitive. Delicately, he licked the curve of her ear, tasting her flesh and giving her just the smallest hint of pleasure. Stubborn female.

"No," she protested, squirming in his grasp.

He couldn't help admiring her tenacity.

He liked that she didn't give up. That she used every weapon at her disposal.

Granted, her petite frame was no match for his larger, harder body. Even if he had been human, she'd have been outweighed. Easily pinned. But she was a warrior at heart and she fought. The Ifrits would eat her up for breakfast, and that was only if his brothers didn't find her first. Fortunately for her, she had him. He'd look out for her. After all, if she were dead—or spread beneath one of his fellow Guardians—he couldn't discover what she'd really come down here for.

Unfortunately, though, he suspected it wasn't for a good fuck.

"Hold still," he warned.

She ignored him, twisting deliciously in his grasp.

"Obey me." He sensed something very hostile moving toward them. And that was to say nothing of the Cats who were just entering the main corridor over their heads. She had no idea of the kind of trouble she was in.

"I don't take orders—"

Whatever she had been about to say was lost in the earsplitting shriek that shattered the silence as trouble launched itself into the air, aiming for his eyes.

The death spirit flew out of the dark shadows of the passage. "Mine, mine, mine," it shrieked in shrill tones as it dove for the mercenary's eyes with the business end of its beak. Not Miu's favorite kind of opponent. In addition to having a face that was half human, half bird, a death spirit could pass through just about anything—and wreak havoc while doing so.

She'd seen one take a nosedive right through a man's midsection once. Although the beak had torn a gaping wound in the man's skin, it was the ghostly passing through that had tied his innards into one large knot. He'd died screaming and sorely regretting disturbing the spirits' nest. For her part, Miu had learned to avoid working in cemeteries. It was almost impossible to spot the death spirits coming until they were on top of you.

"Not supposed to be here," the mercenary roared. Miu could have told him death spirits were free agents, roaming where they wanted as long as there was a dead body somewhere in the vicinity. Since the temple was built atop a deep set of catacombs, the death spirits would have free rein here. Keeping them out must be like trying to keep field mice out of a haystack.

Impossible.

He pushed her behind him and, for once, she was glad to shut up and go. If he wanted to stand between her and the business end of that beak, she'd let him.

Only partly sentient, death spirits retained a few residual memories from their mortal existence and not much else. Sometimes, if the spirits had led particularly happy lives before their deaths, they turned out to make fairly decent companions. Those were glad to show you about a tomb or two, share a few stories, and then wave you on your merry way. Others were so weepy that you couldn't get a word out of them, just sobs and howls that made your flesh crawl with secondhand grief. Miu never asked what had happened to those. The third sort, though—well, those seemed to feel it just wasn't *fair* that anyone else got to live if they didn't. Malicious little buggers. And deadly. This one clearly fell into the third camp.

Tall and thin, it was an almost transparent oily gray that blended perfectly with the walls of the passageway. Correctly identifying the more substantial target, the death spirit dove straight for Jafar's throat.

Time to see what the mercenary was made of. Kind of like a job interview, she decided. After all, if he couldn't handle a death spirit, he wouldn't be much use to her in the catacombs, now would he?

The death spirit certainly was a lively one. Challenging. It zoomed from one side of the tunnel to the other, trailing long gray creepers of rotting fabric behind its transparent body. A musty smell followed in its wake. Dropping to her stomach, Miu minimized her profile.

"Slippery bastard." With a terse curse, the mercenary slammed a clenched fist into the side of the spirit's head as it dove for his throat. In rapid succession, he fired off blows to its crown, temple, and eyes. His thumbs dug into its empty eye sockets, twisting. Howling, the spirit checked in mid-dive, bouncing off the male's knuckles and colliding with the ceiling.

Score one for the living. With an angry screech, the spirit regrouped and altered course. Fists weren't going to stop it for long. Propping her chin on her hands, Miu assessed the spirit's trajectory. Going for the knees now, clever beast. Hamstring the mercenary and then the spirit could finish him off at leisure.

"You got this," she called sweetly, "or you want a hand?"

The merck swung his large body between her and

the death spirit, but his only audible answer was a rasping growl. For a moment, she'd have sworn his eyes glowed in the dim light, but when she checked, they looked normal. Weird.

Then he brought the blades up to his chest and she realized that he did indeed know his way around a knife. He wasn't trying a takedown on the spirit; he was going for the kill.

The spirit was already dead, of course, but there was some bit of leftover life that animated it, something extra that the spirit had squirreled away deep between its bony ribs. Get that bit and you were in business. Presto chango. The spirit popped along to the afterworld and you could relax.

She watched him feint, the blade a dancing silver line in his strong hands. He moved with the lethal grace of an experienced fighter. When was the last time someone else had placed himself in harm's way, to protect *her*? This was something she could get used to. Maybe she *would* let him come with her. Frankly, she wasn't sure she could stop him. Not without calling a whole lot of unwelcome attention to herself. So why not? Why not let him *protect* her, if he was so anxious to do so? She'd be able to keep an eye on him, figure out what he was really up to.

Jafar fought the change. Even though his Cat form would have given him an immediate advantage over the death spirit, he *liked* the way the *femi* looked at him, her eyes following his every movement. He was enjoying the feminine admiration. If he changed, that interest would evaporate to be replaced by terror.

Strangely, he didn't want that. So he fought the feral side of him that wanted to surface.

Fortunately, death spirits tended to count a bit too much on the element of surprise. This one was no exception. When he'd blocked its lunge for his throat, it had retreated to the ceiling of the passageway, buzzing angrily as it darted about.

He moved swiftly, again positioning himself between the angry spirit and his female.

"Hey," the female hollered. "You've got this under control?"

The spirit darted toward her and he shifted positions smoothly.

He growled, tossing a steel shortknife through the air to pierce the ground between them.

"Use it," he snapped, "on the death spirit if it charges. Eyes. Mouth. Heart. Twist hard."

The blade quivered between them, shivering from the force of Jafar's throw. A good two inches of the steel were buried in the ground. Now at least she'd have a weapon to defend herself if necessary. Something told him she knew precisely how to use the weapon. Reassured, he snapped his eyes up, searching for his opponent. He didn't have far to look.

The death spirit floated lazily on the ceiling, all loose, lanky streamers that rippled with rot and decay. One of the younger spirits and a hothead to boot, it had plagued the Guardians a dozen times or more in the last two months alone. Usually, Jafar preferred to simply remove the death spirits to the most remote regions of the temple, but now he didn't have a choice. There was no containing this spirit; bloodlust had consumed it. In his left hand, Jafar idly tossed a second blade up and down, catching and spinning the knife by the haft when it landed. Wait for it. Force the spirit to commit to a path.

Jafar slid one foot into a fighting stance. Had the spirit recognized a Cat—or had it simply scented prey, and easy, female prey at that?

"You don't want to do this." Jafar deliberately met and held the eyes of the spirit, making one last attempt to reason with it.

The spirit's eyes glowed in the soft twilight of the passageway. "Yes. Yes. Yes," it hissed. "Die." So much for reason. Jafar leapt lightly to the far side of the tunnel, drawing the spirit away from his companion. The spirit dove tauntingly near his head, coming close but not within striking distance.

"Fight me," it hissed. "Or shall I take her?"

Over his dead body. Tightening his right hand firmly around the hilt of his shortknife, he deliberately relaxed his wrist. His eyes tracked his opponent, waiting for an opportunity. The death spirit would give him one. Spirits always did. Too simple in their thinking, they did not understand the need to wait. To plot. And then to strike. The spirit's eyes flickered and Jafar's knees flexed, his inside arm rising to protect his vulnerable chest.

Come and get me.

Surprisingly, his companion didn't look shocked by the appearance of the death spirit. No. She looked calculating. Most of the tomb robbers he'd met would have been frightened. A typical Hunt virgin would be shrieking by now. Her calm confused the spirit even more. Clearly, it wasn't used to being met by silence.

"Will you win?" she asked. Running her fingers lightly over his blade, she stared around the tunnel, as though committing her escape route to memory. What was she planning?

"Yes," he bit out. "If you can manage to be quiet for a minute."

She actually laughed.

Perched upside down on the ceiling now, the death spirit growled again. It didn't like the shift in focus. Or the lack of fear on their part. Fortunately, his companion didn't appear to understand the consequences of a loss here. In the unlikely event that the death spirit won, it would rip out her throat without hesitation—unless it was in the market for a human bride, in which case it would settle for planting its razor-sharp claws in her flesh and dragging her off to its lair. There, it would alternate between mating and tearing at her until she was dead.

"Carry on," she said, settling herself back on her rocky seat.

With an earsplitting shriek, the death spirit launched itself from the ceiling, slashing its beak downward with a sharp cry.

Jafar met the descending weapon with his own. Sparks flew as beak and blade met and clashed. Pushing the spirit backward with the force of his own counterthrust, Jafar held the knife close to his own body as he circled. The blade flashed almost invisibly as it streaked along its trajectory.

First one thin dark scratch blossomed on the spirit's torso and then another. Already dead, it could not bleed blood. Instead, it lost psychic energy. With each slash, the outline of the spirit faded a little bit more.

Jafar knew his face radiated a feral intensity that was not quite human, but that couldn't be helped. His companion would eventually understand who he was. What he was.

"Mine," he growled.

The spirit responded with a pithy curse.

Going on the offensive, Jafar drove the spirit toward the wall, delivering another series of brutal blows. Jamming the point of his knife between two ribs, he probed. Twisted. Beneath the seeking point, the spirit's small ember of life popped.

With a sharp crack, the spirit disappeared.

Whirling, Jafar advanced on the second order of business: his *femi*.

One large, hot, *aggressive* male backed her against the wall. His right hand pinned her shoulder to the wall, forcing her to drop the shortknife, while the other traced the curve of her jaw. She wanted to push him away. Redraw the boundaries between them. They were flirting with something dangerous and she needed to retreat. Establish her authority.

"Where were we?" he asked, his voice a low, hot rasp of sound. His legs pinioned hers. One nudge and her thighs would part around his. He felt so good pressed against her. Demanding. Hard.

She licked her lips. "Discussing your employment." Which suddenly seemed like a useful idea.

"Yes. My employment." His lip curled, his teeth gleaming in the semitwilight of the tunnel. "Care to reconsider my offer?"

"Why, yes." A small, sinfully sweet smile curled her lips. "I do. Price," she said decisively.

His eyes snapped to her face. "Excuse me?" You could bottle the arrogance in that voice. Apparently Mr. High-and-Mighty didn't like having a price tag attached to his ass, so she figured she should savor the moment. Keeping his arrogance in check was going to be a full-time job.

"What do you charge for this *protection*?"

His eyes dipped to the shadow of her collarbone but his hands didn't move from where they gripped her. Hard, but not hurting her. She didn't know whether to applaud his discipline—or bemoan it.

"You want to pay me," he said flatly. The heated warmth in his eyes dimmed, and he reached up to capture her face between his hands.

"It's customary," she agreed. "And before you say it, think again. I don't trade sexplay." Although he certainly tempted her to make an exception.

"Money." The hands in her hair tightened, drawing her head backward. "I'm not here for your money."

No money. No sexplay. So why was he really here?

"Consider me bought and paid for." An unreadable look flashed through his eyes. "I'm here to watch after you." His gaze hardened. "That would be the nonnegotiable part of this deal."

Her instincts were flashing a great big "Caution—danger ahead!" warning. Of course, she reflected, that could also be her hormones kicking into overdrive. Something about the big male made her want to take him to the ground in a lip-lock of epic proportions. What would it be like to make him lose control, have all that raw power unleashed on her?

Trading him sexplay for muscle wouldn't be bad at all if a girl didn't mind being dominated in bed. The man bracing her against the wall wouldn't take any-one's orders—least of all in the bedroom. She'd be at his mercy in every way, and she wouldn't enjoy that.

Would she?

Snap out of it, she warned herself. *Focus on the job.* Not on the unmistakable outline of his cock pressing against her hip. "You're a prepaid present. No financial outlay and I don't owe you anything at all when this little journey of ours wraps up. Right." She let the skep-ticism flood her voice. "I'm not that gullible. Who sent you? The Master?"

Instead of answering, he looked deep into her eyes. "I swear you will reach your destination alive."

She remembered the effortless ease with which he'd gutted the death spirit. He'd turn all that leashed vio-lence on anyone—or anything—that stood between her and the necklace. With his help, she'd get out of here more quickly. Be on her way back to ransom Lore before too much damage had been done to her sister. She couldn't afford to look this particular gift horse in the mouth.

"Consider yourself hired."

He nodded curtly. "Tell me your name."

Shaking her head, she shoved free of him. "Unnec-essary."

She realized her mistake instantly. Eyes glowing, he lowered the full weight of his body onto hers, spread-ing her ruthlessly open against the wall before she could so much as blink.

"It's very *necessary*," he growled, using his thighs to part her legs. Her body was deliciously soft, even as she squirmed angrily. Channeling his aggression into a hot, hard kiss, he threaded his hands through her hair, holding her head still.

"Wait," she gasped, her voice smoky with emotion. Good.

"I'm waiting for your name," he bit out. She might have tried to shake her head, but his hands held her still. Her tongue shot out and licked the pink skin of her upper lip, but she did not speak.

His eyes held hers as his mouth descended. Deliberately, he licked a damp path along her upper lip, pressing a firm, sensual stroke against her skin. Demanding an entry. She tasted hotter, sweeter than he'd imagined. The soft skin of her upper lip brushed his, her lips parting on a small, needy breath, and he swallowed the exhalation.

His.

With a masculine growl of satisfaction, he increased the pressure of his lips. Not hurting her, but allowing his larger body to dominate hers. Surrounding her in a heated cage of his flesh. His tongue traced the seam of her lips again and this time he let his teeth nip delicately at her softer skin. He'd take from her the way she'd sought to take from *him*. She'd come down to his temple looking for something, and now she'd get what she had coming to her. He could snap her neck now, end it all, but he wanted more from her.

He wanted satisfaction.

He wanted *her*.

He wasn't good at coaxing. Hell, Amun Ra should have sent Sanur—that Cat was a silver-tongued bastard and his females drove the rest of them crazy, coming back and mooning over the dark-haired Guardian. Sanur would have had the secret out of her in minutes—and never mind that Jafar's Cat growled warningly at the mental image of Sanur wrapping his arms around this female.

"Open up," he demanded, inhaling her scent, drawing her taste deep inside him as she gasped in reaction. Her lips parted, let him invade her hot sweetness and he was lost, his Cat purring with a sensual recognition he'd never found before. His *femi* wanted him, even if she wouldn't admit it.

He could live with that.

For now.

Later, later he could teach her to revel in his sensual dominance. Hear the whispered pleas she'd give him for her own sensual satisfaction. In time, she'd give him that. Right now, he wanted just one word.

"Give me your name," he repeated, letting her retreat a little.

Her breath huffed out in a small sigh. "There are conventions to be adhered to here. Name telling—not one of them." She shook her head. Hell, she wouldn't give an inch, would she? No, she had to make this deliciously hard.

"I'll tell you my name. It's Jafar," he offered, switching tactics and making her a present of his name.

She was unappreciative. "Still no."

"You will tell me," he warned.

"Make me," she dared, holding her breath. Did she think he would not? What were the males like where she came from? His leg pushed hers farther apart. He was bigger, stronger, and wouldn't hesitate to use his body to dominate hers. "Do as I say, little *femi*," he growled.

She shot him a look that seemed to say she would pick her battles.

"You may call me Miu," she capitulated, but there was no surrender in her bold gaze.

Miu. He drew her scent deeper into his lungs, then, responding to the challenge in her eyes, lowered his lips to hers again.

She was a thief, but she tasted so very right. She moaned into his mouth and his cock thickened further with each feminine whimper. She'd lied to Amun Ra and she hadn't been honest with him, but here, in his arms, her body was brutally honest. He could smell the spicy musk of her arousal.

Pressing a last, hard kiss against her mouth, he let her go. She didn't acknowledge his sensual dominance—but her breasts rose and fell more quickly beneath their filmy covering of silk.

His *femi* had enjoyed being dominated.

Or she'd simply enjoyed him.

Without pausing, Miu bent and scooped up her pack from the ground—his eyes followed the delicious curve of her ass, selecting his next point of attack—and shot him a triumphant look before sliding her legs over the edge of the opening in the floor. "Follow me, merck," she ordered, and then jumped down into the darkness.

"Right," he gritted out, lowering himself after her.

She hadn't won their battle of wills yet.

CHAPTER FIVE

She just couldn't win.

Dropping down through the hole, Miu discovered another series of bewildering passageways, but none of them could take her mind off what had almost happened. The hottest kiss she'd ever been on the receiving end of.

She needed to get her libido under control. The merck—Jafar—was a convenient bodyguard. He couldn't possibly be anything more.

Striding down the passageway, she noted fewer exit points. The few shafts she spotted merely cut up toward other corridors, circulating the already stale, warm air through the lower depths. Most were too small to allow anything other than currents of air—and assorted creepy crawlies—to circulate, but you never knew. Maybe one could be large enough to accommodate a female body in need of a hasty exit. Mark your exits. Rule number one.

Her thoughts kept returning to that damn kiss.

The kiss that had left her head—and her body—at sixes and sevens.

Her head knew she needed his protection, but her body wanted much more. And that could be just as dangerous to her well-being as any death spirit lurking in the temple.

When his hand closed over her shoulder, she stared down at it silently, willing him to remove it, willing herself to ignore the thrill of pleasure she felt as he rubbed slow circles over her collarbone. Even as she stared at the offending digit, the large hand whipped away and clapped itself over her mouth. His other hand looped around her waist and pulled her quickly and efficiently into one of the many small storerooms that led off of the main corridor on this level.

"Shhh," the now-familiar voice growled in her ear. Jafar slid the door closed, leaving only a thin crack. "Company," he explained tersely. His hands tightened on her waist as if he didn't want to let her go.

Fine. Her nerves prickled, making his large body a welcome warmth at her back. In the thick ink of the small room, he seemed both larger and stronger than before.

His attention was fixed on the passageway they'd just abandoned.

"Listen," he breathed against her neck.

She fought the urge to stiffen, to betray her nervousness about whoever was approaching.

"Not going to hurt you," he muttered, misunderstanding her apprehension. "Gave my word. Watch." The large hands shifted her forward another step, his body following until she was pinned between the cold stone and him.

The flarestick was abruptly extinguished and she blinked.

The sound of someone running echoed through the passage. The footsteps were light, but erratic. A small body. Female. And not conditioned for that sort of rigorous exercise—harsh panting accompanied each urgent footfall as the runner struggled for breath. Miu heard no sounds of pursuit—and yet . . .

"The Hunt?" she whispered.

She felt rather than saw his nod.

The female burst into the corridor, holding a flarestick. Miu was uncomfortably relieved to realize that the runner was not the young girl she'd stood next to in the procession. This woman was of medium build, curvy, her dark hair intricately braided into hundreds of careful coils. The familiar white silk robe of a potential mate fluttered around her with each step she took. Flummoxed by a split in the corridor, the woman stood indecisively.

What followed her into the corridor had Miu's blood pounding wildly in her veins.

A massive cat, ears flattened against its tufted mane, streaked out from the darkness. Impossibly large, the Cat stood seven feet from its massive paws to its dark, tufted head. Eyes glowing in the light of the flarestick, the animal crowded the woman toward the wall.

Heqet save her, Miu swore silently.

Left, she wanted to howl. *Take the left tunnel*. Or the right. Either choice was futile—the Cat would have its prey in seconds—but just standing there seemed so wrong.

"Good puss," the woman murmured in a throaty voice.

"She likes him," an amused voice whispered in Miu's ear. She bit back a squeak of surprise as Jafar's arms pulled her up against his body, his legs pressing into the backs of hers. He held her still, immobilized between his warmth and the stone.

She wanted to fight those hard arms—no one had held her down since she'd been given her thief mark. Burned into her forearm, the black scars circled her flesh like a lover's fingers, thin enough to cover with a bracelet, if she had wanted to. She never did. She wouldn't hide from what she'd become—or forget who controlled her. As if on cue, the mark burned. The pain, she knew, was merely a warning. A small taste of what the Master could deliver when—and wherever— he wanted.

"Watch," Jafar growled.

Desperate to forget her memories, she did. The large cat shimmered in the air as he leapt toward the woman. She just stood there, arms by her sides, watching him come. The feline shape wavered and then, in the blink of an eye, disappeared. A large, rawboned man stalked toward the woman. His eyes devoured her even as his hands reached out.

"The stories *are* true." She was shocked to her core.

"Of course." Jafar sounded satisfied. Smug. "He's found his mate."

For a moment, the shifter's head swung in their direction. Scenting the air, he growled low and deep in his throat, but then returned his attention to the woman standing before him. "Mate," he growled. And, "Mine." His body flowed with a liquid grace that promised he'd be a deadly opponent in any contest of martial arts or weaponry. He wore loose, dark pants and a longsword in a scabbard across his back. Nothing else but the almost tangible aura of a terrifying power leashed. Miu had seen the claws—and couldn't believe the woman still stood there.

"We should rescue her." Her voice sounded hoarse to her own ears. Desperate. She didn't know the woman out there, she reminded herself. Jumping into the middle of that scene was foolish. It was impossibly stupid. And the odds of her being able to change the outcome were very small indeed.

"He'll woo her," the dark voice behind her promised, and she wanted to turn around and scream at him that nothing could prepare a woman for seven feet of leonine power being loosed on her body.

She'd seen sex acts. Hell, she'd had sex, as unsatisfying as it might have been. But she couldn't even begin to imagine what would happen between the enormous shifter and the delicate woman he'd claimed as his mate. Helplessly, she stared at the erotic tableau.

"He'll be careful," the dark voice promised. Was Jafar aroused? She felt for the seams of the door and wondered if the Cat outside would be too occupied to notice if she tried to sneak away. Were *two* mates forbidden—or encouraged?

Outside, the Guardian backed the female against the wall, inserting his large body between her and the branching tunnel.

"He protects her," Jafar whispered. "His body between hers and danger." She wanted to argue that the only danger was from the Guardian himself. "No one gets to her when he is there."

The Guardian in the corridor lifted his companion's leg and placed it around his waist. The woman's eyes glittered with dark, dazed interest. *She* doesn't *mind*, Miu realized. Not now. White silk fell back, exposing the smooth expanse of pale skin. With this newest discovery, the Guardian growled low in his throat, burying his face in handfuls of hair. His hand moved between their bodies, his fingers rubbing the shy sex through the raw silk of the robe. The pair's breath came in harsh gasps torn from their chests. When her head fell back against the wall, exposing the long pale column of her throat, the man groaned. His dark eyes dropped, fixing on the shadow of her sex where his fingers played.

Scooping his female up into his arms with a dark groan, he cradled her with curious possessiveness. There was a flash of gold in the glow of the flarestick.

The man in the tunnel held a pair of small golden bells.

Regret was not an emotion with which Jafar was familiar.

And yet—his companion feared the Cats and he was *regretful*. As a Guardian, he'd had centuries to accustom himself to the wariness and fear that mortals inevitably felt in his company.

The stink of fear had permeated the public reception halls this morning and he knew that his fellow Guardians would carefully cull the truly fearful from the merely nervous. The women who were really frightened would be discreetly herded toward a separate section of the temple to scramble about until miraculously "discovering" the passageway that led to the surface and freedom. Each would be handsomely rewarded and leave thinking she had had a lucky escape from the harsh demands of the Cats.

Luck had nothing to do with it.

His Miu had chosen poorly when she'd challenged the Amun Ra. Instead of letting her leave with the other women who had no desire to become Guardian mates, he'd invited her to run deeper into the temple. Either a Guardian would catch her and mate her, or she'd reveal her true motive for joining the Hunt.

Already she'd made it all too clear to Jafar that her motive was theft, but what was she after? And who was this master she'd mentioned? The little *femi* had information he wanted.

And now he wanted *her* as well.

It was just sex, he told himself, the usual eroticism of the Hunt and knowing that, if he wanted to, he could chase this female and no one would stop him. She couldn't stop him. Hell, he'd make sure she didn't *want* to stop him. Hot fantasy bloomed in his mind: his feet pounding in a silent rhythm against the floor, mimicking the earthy pulse of his cock until he swung his larger frame against hers. Pinned her between his cock and the wall. All that sweet, creamy flesh for him to coax and touch.

If he wanted to.

Which he did.

Hell, had Amun Ra realized this was a possibility? Jafar wouldn't put it past that bastard to have thrown the two of them together just to test his Guardian's resolve. Jafar couldn't give in. Never mind that all he could think about was that luscious body of hers, and all the erotic possibilities of being alone in the dark with her. He was in control. Not her. Not Amun Ra.

Still, in the soft darkness of the room, he couldn't

help noticing the scent of feminine arousal that teased his senses. He realized with sensual satisfaction that his Miu was not only a thief—she was also a voyeur.

He was enough of a Cat to take advantage of that fact.

Deliberately, he pressed his body against hers, trapping her against the slim crack where the stone slab had failed to close completely. He smiled ruthlessly. His kind loved the dark, the almost tangible feeling of the lack of light as the still air caressed his body like a lover's touch. Without sight, the other senses were magnified. He could feel the smooth glide of Miu's silk robe against his own skin. Smell the faint, sweet scent of her skin and the warmer musk of her sex. She was still wet from their earlier embrace.

Graphic images flooded his mind at the thought. The sweet tease of her creaming sex. Yes, he wanted to chase her. Take her. Mate with her. He wanted to hunt her, mark her body as *his*.

With a groan, he shoved himself away from the delicious heat of her body. Outside, the Guardian disappeared down a side tunnel, still carrying his new mate in his arms. Lucky bastard.

When the heavy male body pinning hers to the door abruptly lifted, Miu didn't know whether to be grateful—or disappointed. Liquid heat pooled in her belly and lower, making her want to arch into his heavy touch like a cat in heat.

Primal.

Unfettered.

His next question cut through the sensual haze

fogging her mind. "Still not worried about the Guardians?"

"Should I be scared?" Rule number two: never admit your fear.

"Oh, I'd be worried," he said in that slow, honey-smooth drawl. "Did you take a *long* look at the male out there? Ever imagined a lover who could shift on you, so you don't know if the beast pinning you to the wall is man or Cat?"

His eyes bored down into hers. As if her answer mattered to him—which had to be a trick of the light. He couldn't care whether or not she'd be willing to romp with a Guardian in bed—could he? Besides, she didn't *have* an answer for him.

So she countered his question with one of her own. "Have you seen them before?"

"Many times."

Her brows shot up at his words. Was that possible? Had the man taken up residence in the catacombs?

They were wasting time. She had a necklace to steal, a sister to ransom. "Get a move on," she ordered. She needed to locate the necklace well before sunrise; otherwise she'd have to wait until darkness fell and the moons rose again to pick her way to the surface.

"Fine." He smiled over his shoulder. A slow, sexy smile. "Tell me which way you want to go."

His female smelled of cream. A sweet, honey musk that was going to light up the damn tunnels like a *mazhyk* beacon and call down the Guardians on them.

"Eyes on me, merck." His female paused in the doorway and then stalked toward him. He eyed the very feminine curves headed his way and didn't protest when she dug into her pack for a sheet of papyrus that she spread before him. "Here." Her finger stabbed downward on the map. "This is where we are. And here"—she dragged her finger several inches down and to the right—"is where I need to be. The catacombs. So we go this way." Her finger traced a tidy set of right angles over the surface of the parchment.

He silently ground his teeth.

This map of his temple was downright infuriating: now he not only had a thief to deal with, but a serious information leak on his hands as well. Not to mention what was fast becoming an overwhelming sexual attraction to the same thief. His feline senses told him she was just as attracted to him—and yet he'd have to take her to Amun Ra later on, after she'd led him to whatever object it was that she wanted from his catacombs.

Because that was his duty.

For the first time, he found himself disliking what he was going to have to do to protect the temple. Perhaps he could wait a little longer since he didn't know precisely what it was she'd come for—he needed that information, as well as the name of Miu's boss. Sure, he could put off her punishment for now.

But how long could he delay?

He rubbed an impatient hand over his bare cheekbones. He knew his brother Guardians. They'd have picked up the scent of his female and they'd follow. Some because they had a feline curiosity that only information could scratch. Others because she was a female—and it was the Hunt. There was nothing like the promise of hot sex and a new mate to motivate his pride brothers.

Somehow, Jafar needed to win her trust, so she would tell him what she was after and who'd sent her. Sure, he could shift now and have her pinned against the wall in seconds—his Cat growled with satisfaction at that mental image—but all that lovely, illicit knowledge she had tucked away in her head? Well, he'd bet she wouldn't be sharing that with him. He'd have the thief, but not the mastermind behind the theft.

"No more hanky-panky." She eyed him balefully, as delightfully pouty as a cat shut out of a room. "No touching. No kissing."

A feline smile curled his lips. "If you insist, my *femi*," he said. "It's entirely up to you."

"What's up to me?" She bent down and scooped up her battered leather holdall, dropping the strap over her head. The worn leather settled between her breasts like a lover's hand, separating the two mounds.

Great. He was jealous of a bag.

"Whether or not I touch you. I know you want me to. I can smell your desire," he said, deliberately ignoring her furious blush. "Sweet. Smoky."

"Too much information, merck," she muttered. She scrubbed at her cheeks, leaving a streak of dust behind. "I don't stink."

But she did smell sweetly of her arousal, a feminine perfume that he could never mistake. His cock throbbed, making demands.

"Think unsexy thoughts," he suggested cheerfully. "The Cats—they can smell feminine arousal from hundreds of yards away. All that delicate musk—I don't think you bothered with undergarments today, my *femi*." From the angry blush that crawled up her cheeks, he figured he was right.

She crossed her arms over her chest and stared at him.

"Let me get this straight. You're telling me that a bunch of tomb guards are going to be able to smell—" she hesitated, clearly unwilling to supply the word, so he supplied it for her.

"You."

"I don't think so," she ground out. "I had my bath today, merck. No worries on that score."

"Got excellent noses," he said cheerfully. And then, "Let's get going." He started off down the passage she'd indicated.

"No." She pushed past him in the passageway. "I lead."

Far above them, *levels* above them, he could sense the stirring of the Guardians and he knew he *was* in trouble.

Growly, surly, *stubborn* bastard. He certainly wasn't the Master's usual type. Had Lierr really sent him to protect her? The more she thought about it, the less likely it seemed. She needed—she tapped a finger thoughtfully against her chin as she shoved past the male and strode down the corridor—a test.

Some way to figure out just whose side he was *really* on.

His insistence that she needed protection was both frustrating and endearing. She could take care of herself, had been doing so for years, but the temple *was* a dangerous place and she wasn't stupid. Having a warrior like Jafar on her side could only help. The problem was, she just hadn't figured out what it was really going to cost her. Other than her peace of mind. Because when he was around, her nerve endings sizzled and he made her think about hot, hot sex. None of which was going to get her sister rescued. Yeah, you could say she was suspicious. He clearly wasn't telling her the whole truth—if he'd even bothered to tell her part of it.

With a growl, he caught up to her, his hand cupping her elbow possessively.

Possession. Now there was a litmus test she could apply. If he belonged to Lierr as she suspected, he should have a mark somewhere. All she had to do was find it—or not find it. Then she'd know for sure.

If he weren't a fellow thief, she'd lose him down below.

Naked, that was the key to sorting out her mysterious companion, once and for all. After all, how hard could it be to get him naked? She eyed his body, considering plans of attack. He stalked along beside her arrogantly, his eyes quartering the passageway as he searched the shadowed doorways for threats.

Yeah, all she had to do was get him naked.

Naked was good.

"No way." Miu stopped dead before the tunnel Jafar had indicated. "There are spiders in there."

Jafar was a madman.

Miu should have guessed there was a catch when he'd claimed to know a shortcut to the catacombs. If she hadn't been so desperate to get this job done, she would have heard other, more primal instincts shrieking their warning at her. *Warning: dangerous madman ahead.*

"Hell. No." She backed away from the tunnel. "Find another route."

The square, dark mouth stared back at her, a malevolent opening leading down to roomfuls of rotting, dead bodies. Lovely.

"This one's quickest."

"I. Don't. Care."

"You will." He turned those sleepy, dark eyes on her. How unfair was it that a merck had been given eyes like that? She shook herself. Focus. Business.

"I will? Why?"

"Because we have company coming," he said grimly. "No, you don't want to know," he added when she glanced over her shoulder.

Probably not. She'd been checking the tunnel compulsively for the last twenty minutes; it was good to know that her internal radar was still functioning. Particularly since it seemed to be broken where the merck was concerned—*he* was looking better and better with each step she took.

"My map says we take this tunnel." She indicated a nice, tall corridor that sloped downward on their right. A reasonably wide, at-least-we-can-both-stand-upright-in-it tunnel.

His option was distinctly less appealing.

Shaking his head, he indicated the low entrance again. "Your way takes too long."

Right. "What could be that bad?" She looked at the tunnel again, but the spiderwebs still formed a lacy drape over the entrance. No way was she going in there.

"We've got quite a crowd after us. A dark faerie and a daemon. Also a banshee. Way back but gaining fast, at least one Cat." He seemed unconcerned, but his body was tense. He really, really wanted her to get into the tunnel.

Time to use logic. "What stops them from following us in here?"

"Too small for the Cat. The others"—he shrugged—"shouldn't be tracking us with their noses. They won't expect us to go this way."

Which begged the question of how they were tracking her. If they were tracking her. Perhaps they, too, had paid a visit to the map man. Or perhaps her merck had reasons of his own for wanting to get her into a dark, narrow death trap. Like her map. And her treasure.

He swore under his breath. "Look, there's no time for this." His dark shadow detached itself from the wall and glided toward her. Moving sleekly like the large predator he was, he herded her toward his chosen tunnel. Before she could protest, he bent down and scooped her up.

"Front or back?" he asked pleasantly. "Give me your word you'll follow and I'll let you choose."

"Put me down." She wriggled determinedly, loosing a long string of very creative curses that she'd learned in the city markets.

He shook her gently. "Listen."

Taking a deep breath, she listened. Sure enough, she heard a faint scuffling sound. The thinnest whisper of a sound. Was that a cloak dragging on the ground—or a blade being drawn? "Back," she spat.

"I have your word you'll follow me to the end of the tunnel?"

"Yes."

He crouched and moved into the tunnel. "Coming?"

The tunnel was narrower, hotter, and . . . *webbier*

than she'd thought it would be. At least Jafar's large frame ran interference between her and the spiders. His broad shoulders brushed the walls as he maneuvered the flarestick before them. Each time the light moved, scurrying sounds whispered around them as the local residents angrily abandoned their webs, retreating to safer cracks or into the darkness.

Worse than the spiders, however, was the smothering weight of the darkness. She fought a feeling of panic as the stone weight of the ceiling pressed down on her. She must have made a sound. Jafar paused— and she ran straight into him. Every single hard, hot plane of him. Jafar's eyes were amused when he swung his head around—to check on her?

"All right?" His voice was a reassuring rumble. She wasn't alone.

"Yeah, peachy." Her sarcasm seemed to roll off of him. Apparently, crawling across a thick carpet of dust was just fine with him. The choking cloud of particles stirred by their movements didn't bother him. That, or he was just being stoic.

"Wait," she ordered. He didn't seem bothered by the dust, but one good cough would betray their position. While he paused impatiently, she tore strips of cloth from her once-white robe. Already, thick black bands of dirt marred the formerly pristine silk.

Tying the impromptu mask around her nose and mouth, she held out the second strip to him. "Here."

When he didn't take the material, she nudged him firmly in his ribs. Embarrassingly, her fingers left a dark streak on his smooth skin. So much for personal hygiene.

"Do it for me," he demanded in a low rumble.

"What? No hands of your own?" she grumbled.

"Just do it. I can drop all these cobwebs if you prefer." He gestured with his shoulders and she watched, fascinated, as the muscles of his back worked. Right. Yeah. His hands were full of sticky, gossamer strands. Some of the finer threads broke off and clung. Was that a skittering sound she heard? Looking up, she realized the ceiling was alive with insects.

The breath whooshed out of her, making the webs in his hand dance angrily. "Oh, Heqet."

"Squeamish?" he asked.

Absolutely. "No," she lied. Leaning forward, she tied the strip of silk around his nose and mouth. "Keep going."

With every foot she crawled, the moon's pull lessened. Somewhere, far above them, the moon was sailing proudly through the clouds, shedding her silver light over the Valley. Down here, though, she could barely feel its influence. No moonlight—she felt a wrenching sense of loss. She hated working underground, and the bastard who'd sent her here knew that. He'd sent her anyway.

"How much farther?" she asked, wondering forlornly how much more of this she could stand.

"You look sad," he observed. "Why?"

"Because we're a good mile underground, all right?"

He brushed a cobweb off her face. "Is it the depth that bothers you?"

She stared at him. Was he displaying a sensitive side? *Now?* He surprised her: Mr. Gruff-and-Tough alpha male could be *thoughtful.* Sweet in an awkward manner. Who knew that he had it in him? Or that it would attract her?

"Being underground does bother some people." His hand stroked her hair. "Don't like the sensation of all that dirt and stone pressing down on them."

Great. She aimed a look at the ceiling—a mere *six* inches above their heads—and shuddered. If she hadn't been claustrophobic before, she would be now as she contemplated the massive weight of the temple located right over their heads.

"Do I look like I'm scared?"

He considered her. "No. You look like you're in pain." And it almost seemed as if her pain bothered him. No, what he wanted was to pry. Get to know her inner secrets.

"I'll keep you safe," he promised and she shot him an incredulous look. Keep her safe? She could keep *herself* safe.

She knew better than to trust someone like him.

CHAPTER SIX

It took twenty minutes to slither through the narrow tunnel—nineteen minutes too long, as far as Miu was concerned. That tunnel had been sheer hell. Now she stood in a corridor that was distinctly *not* marked on her bootleg map, slapping spiderwebs—and spider bits—off of her damn partner while he returned the favor.

His hand landed on her ass with a sharp slap and she jumped. "Last one," he said innocently. "Spiders bite. Best to have them off."

Right. She shot him a look and he merely smiled that cat-in-the-cream smile she was starting to detest. That smile meant he thought *he'd* just won the latest round in their ongoing who's-top-dog contest. Sooner or later, she'd have to disillusion him.

At least he looked satisfyingly surprised when she landed a good swat of her own on his ass. "Spiders," she returned sweetly when he growled. Goody. He didn't believe her either.

A twisted maze of tunnels, corridors, and walkways snaked away from their spidery exit point. On the level just beneath them would be the burial chambers, room after room of the mummified dead laid out in their ceremonial best. Impossibly elegant tombs, decorated with fabulous gems. And around every corner, traps for the unwary. Apparently the Guardians relied on more than brute strength to do their policing. From her current vantage point, she could see several graphic examples of what happened to thieves here.

A skeleton still pinned to the wall by numerous blades.

A headless, handless skeleton.

A skeleton trapped in an impossibly small space.

"Did we lose them?" She could only hope.

He shook his head. "They're coming down your passageway and coming fast."

He held up the flarestick so she could examine the map. Unfortunately, as she'd already noticed, their current location was not marked on the papyrus. That made pinpointing their exact whereabouts difficult.

"We're here," he said, jabbing at the waxed parchment with his thumb. The tomb she was looking for was just below them. She had to hand it to him. He did know his shortcuts. He'd bought them valuable minutes.

"Thank me later," he said, looking amused.

"You didn't lose them completely," she pointed out.

"Got you here first," he countered. "Gives us the advantage. We can pick our ground. Stand or run, but we decide."

He had a point. And she liked the fact that he apparently knew his battle tactics and wasn't going to wade into a fight just because he could. In the distance—but still closer than she liked—she heard the soft whisper of rock on rock, as if their followers had grown careless or bored or overhasty and allowed one foot to drag too long, too low over the floor.

"Guardians?" she suggested, her mind sorting through possible defenses. Or, since she knew there was no standing against those hard-faced warriors she'd seen in the antechamber to the temple, possible hiding places and acts of misdirection. She wasn't going to be any male's *mate* and she certainly wasn't going to become a shish kebab either. Defense. Distraction. Disappearance. Those were her options.

"Not Guardians."

"How do you know?"

"Too loud. Too clumsy. They don't smell right, either."

As if he could smell them from here. Still, she inhaled deeply—and almost choked on the lungful of dead Valley men that she drew in. You could have reconstructed several bodies from the dusty particles floating almost invisibly through the stale air. An alcove must have caved in and dumped its load onto the unforgiving floor. Apparently, the Guardians were so busy ripping would-be thieves to shreds, they'd ignored basic structural upkeep.

Just peachy.

"I don't smell anything."

"I do," he said, and she shot him another sideways look. What *was* he? If he hadn't had that impossibly smooth face—completely free of the dark marks that branded the Guardians—she'd have been suspicious. He moved comfortably through the corridors, even in the semitwilight. Did his eyes glow golden? She hadn't paid attention.

No, she'd been too busy eyeing his magnificent ass. Her full-moon hormones were the devil.

Before them, the corridor branched, splitting into two equally dark passageways that dropped away to the left and the right. "Which one?"

She consulted the map. Making a mistake now could be fatal. "Left," she said.

He took the indicated tunnel. As they passed through the opening, she eyed the wooden braces with trepidation. All this stone and the temple's builders couldn't be bothered with more permanent supports?

"The catacombs outgrew themselves," Jafar explained.

"Too many dead people?" she asked lightly, to mask her unease.

"Something like that," he agreed. "The first levels were planned. After that, the Valley dwellers just kept bringing the dead and they had to go somewhere."

"So we've got the same three on our trail," she said.

He nodded tightly.

"Are we going to kill them?"

"They're thieves," Jafar said flatly. "How else would you deal with them?"

"News flash," she muttered. "Pot calls kettle black. What do you call yourself?"

"I'm not here to thieve, Miu," he said in that delicious rumble.

"Right. Pull the other one; it has bells."

"Not yet," he muttered.

There was no time for further chitchat.

Their new-found *company* burst from the main corridor as if they were being pursued by an army of death spirits or worse. None of them bothered to conceal their approach, although the dark faerie did pause. Wisely. The daemon simply barreled forward without hesitating. There was a sickening squelch as Jafar gutted the male. Withdrawing his blade from the body, he shoved the corpse to the ground.

Jafar certainly had the two survivors' attention now.

He had hers as well.

That move with the knife had been as cold-blooded as they came. Just a smooth, lethal jab that let the other fellow's momentum skewer him on the unforgiving metal.

"Fellow thieves?" he asked her.

Without answering, Miu rolled the body over with her foot and examined the daemon's face. It was possible. No one knew who else worked for the Master. Oh, there were the inevitable pairings and you certainly couldn't avoid spotting others coming and going from the Master's lair. But no one *knew* for certain. The daemon, however, was completely unfamiliar. She hadn't seen his face before.

"Call them treasure hunters," she snapped. "Sounds more professional that way. Because that's what we really are. Can't truly steal from the dead, can we? After all, they're dead. They don't need anything they've brought to the tomb with them. Those are unclaimed, ownerless artifacts, merck, and we're simply giving them a new owner. No harm, no foul. Dead aren't going to miss what we take, and we need it."

Her merck didn't look as if he agreed with her assessment.

"Ah. But do you? Need it, that is?" Casually, he bent

over and wiped his blade on the dead man's body. The blood left macabre black streaks on the moss green skin of the deceased.

The dark faerie perked up noticeably. That kind had a thing for blood, liked to use it in ritual *mazhyk*. If she'd had a choice, she wouldn't have spilled it in his presence.

"Master wants it, then Master gets it." Did she sound as bitter as she felt?

"What do *you* want?" Jafar's dark eyes examined her face thoughtfully. "Seems to me that's the more important bit of this discussion."

"No." The dark faerie spoke up at last. "No matter at all what she wants. None of us. We've come for a little bit of a necklace and that's what we'll be taking away with us."

"Nothing else?" Jafar sounded skeptical and she couldn't blame him. They were surrounded by a vast quantity of gold and jewels—and no one was going to make off with any of it?

The dark faerie shook his head. The banshee merely crouched on the ceiling, hissing with irritation.

"He must really want this necklace."

Jafar's gaze snapped to hers, his eyes suddenly intent. "Why?"

She didn't know and, judging by the look on the faerie's face, no revelation was going to be forthcoming from that quarter either.

Jafar shook his head. "No idea why he wants it—and yet you're going to haul a priceless *mazhykal* artifact back to him? No wonder he's the guy in charge. Sheep," he muttered in disgust.

The dark faerie barked a short, pithy curse that more than reflected how Miu felt about their current situation.

"It's not that simple, merck," she explained. "Look, you want a reason why we're all here? It's called leverage. The Master simply helps himself to whatever—or whoever—we care about. Then we have to toe the line. Ask them, if you don't believe me. I don't know what he has on them, but he has something."

"Is that true?" He angled toward the dark faerie, being careful to keep the banshee in his peripheral vision. He wasn't a fool.

The dark faerie shrugged. "True enough," he agreed in a gravelly voice. "Fetch back this necklace or pay the price."

"Which is?"

"Personal." The faerie's voice was hard. "A private matter between myself and the Master."

"And yours?" Jafar turned toward Miu.

"Same as his," she said bitterly. "Personal. And none of your business. All you need to know is these two are after the same necklace as us, they're equally desperate, and we all share the same rule: winner takes all."

Out of the corner of her eye, she saw the banshee move. Hell. She needed Jafar's attention and she needed it now.

One moment Jafar was listening with intense satisfaction as Miu's fellow thief revealed the object of their search, and the next minute he was trying not to gape as Miu grabbed his ass.

A hell of way to get his attention, admittedly. The

tangled scents and emotions swirling around him in the passageway were a distraction and worse was the rank despair shrouding the newcomers. They wanted the necklace badly, badly enough to confront Miu—and himself. Which all pointed to Miu's boss having a powerful hold over them. Jafar had to ask himself what that hold could be.

Miu's fingers flexed, squeezing the cheek cupped in her palm, and Jafar's thoughts scattered to the winds. Desire rose fierce and strong in him. His senses gathered, focusing on the exquisite feel of her bare fingers as they moved slowly, teasingly over the naked skin of his ass. He bit back a groan. Her warm palm cupped and squeezed.

Her free hand—the hand *not* palming his skin as if *he* belonged to *her*—shoved a plug of wax into his hands. She must have pulled it out of that pack of hers. He looked up—and spotted the female banshee inhaling.

Deeply.

"Oh, crap." Miu's hands fell away from him. "Quick. Into your ears. She's going to scream."

And scream she did. The blasted female threw back her head and loosed a powerful swell of sound into the narrow space, shaking the walls and making the floor buck and ripple beneath their feet.

With a loud crack, the supporting beam on which the banshee was perched split apart.

The world exploded around them in a seething whirlwind of dust and rock. From somewhere high above, the piercing scream of the banshee was abruptly cut off. The cave-in was first a slow-motion spill of rock and dirt, and then, with a tremendous roar, the wall nearest them collapsed.

Hell.

Tucking his female into his arms, he pulled her against his chest and dove for a storeroom. They made it inside in the nick of time.

Outside, wall stones and dirt rained down, sealing them in.

Their prison cell was twelve feet by twelve feet.

One hundred forty-four square feet of dust-filled space and a half dozen stone shelves lined with stone pots of various sizes.

"Damn banshee," Jafar said. That was an understatement. Miu had seen the banshee go flying from her perch with the first wave of rocks. Judging by the sheer volume of dirt and stone blocking their exit, she'd bet the banshee was even unhappier with the outcome than they were.

Jafar's eyes went to her forehead and he swore. "You're bleeding." Cursing, he ripped a strip from his loincloth and pressed it firmly to the cut.

Pain blossomed in her forehead. Great. Just what she needed. "Ouch." She swatted at his hands. "Quit that."

"Stops the bleeding," he said, ignoring her protest.

Carefully, he ran his hands over her body, checking for other injuries. It seemed to Miu he was taking his sweet time about the examination.

Discreetly, she tried to dislodge his hand from her breast. Was the caress intentional? The liquid spot between her thighs didn't particularly give a damn. Well, she reminded herself, there was still the question of just *who* had sent the merck. Get him naked and she could check for Lierr's mark—and indulge her own curiosity about the man trapped in the chamber with her.

His hand squeezed slowly, stroking the V of flesh revealed by the damn virgin's robe. Definitely intentional.

"Are you in pain anywhere?" His deep voice made her shiver—or was it the hypnotic stroking of his hand? Just small strokes of the upper slope of her breast. Only slightly wicked.

Should she let this seduction continue? Her body answered the question for her.

She raised her arms around his neck and pressed herself tightly against him.

"Tell me you want this," Jafar growled against her mouth.

Miu knew she should be grateful for his question, but she couldn't think straight. All she could do was sigh, "Yes."

Dimly, she realized this was out of character for her, and when she was more in control of her senses, she'd be mortified. Now, however, she simply let the pleasure wash over her. Each caress made the pain in her forehead subside further.

The clasp of the virgin's robe parting sounded unbearably loud in the room, grating on her oversensitized nerves. The silk fell to the floor in a smooth rush of fabric. His eyes heated and caught on her breasts.

"Clothes," she hissed, and he obliged her by slipping rapidly out of his. He might have used *mazhyk*; she no longer cared. Her sex tightened, all wet heat, as he exposed that smooth, golden skin to her. A wicked scar curled around his right side like a lover's caress gone terribly awry. Not a thief mark, but perhaps something worse.

She ran a questing finger over the skin. "Knife?"

He nodded curtly, his hands reaching for her, drawing her between his legs so she was cradled in the hot embrace of his arms and thighs.

Teasingly, she explored the flat male nipples, let her tongue lick delicately at the darker skin. A rumble of masculine approval made her smile. Her merck liked that. She did, too. His taste delighted her, an exotic mix of male and spice and something otherworldly.

"Do you want me?" Running an exploratory finger around his nipples, she let her fingers slide down along his ribs, over the taut, muscled expanse of skin. He was so large that he made her feel small. Protected. She'd never felt that way before; it was strangely seductive.

His answer was to lift her legs around his waist in a smooth, hot glide of skin. His thick erection rubbed mercilessly against the slick lips of her sex, his fingers curving around the cheeks of her ass as he lifted her effortlessly upward. She barely stopped herself from arching into his possessive touch, from sliding herself against his fingers.

With a growl, he backed her toward the wall, bracing her against the slick surface of the stone. "I've waited hours to do this," he said darkly. "Scenting your heat. Knowing you were wet for me. Waiting."

"Hold on," she protested—she had to see the back of him. There was no visible mark on his front.

"Do you want to wait more," he asked, "or do you want what I can give you now, *femi*?"

Her voice failed her. His fingers found her nipples,

stroking until bright pulses of pleasure built behind her half-closed eyes. He was taking charge. Taking control.

"I'm not *waiting*," he said, and his words made her sex cream more. He was going to give her pleasure, *make* her enjoy this whether she was ready or not. "I'm going to see to you now," he promised.

See to her. Even as her brain protested the arrogance of his words, her body tightened in welcome.

"Up." His hand stroked the hard shelf behind her, sweeping the small pots to one side. "I'm going to have you here. Make you wetter." His dark eyes explored her face. "I'm going to find out what your cream tastes like."

She couldn't let him take charge like this.

Desperately, she fought back with every erotic weapon in her arsenal, her fingers dancing up the thick length of him, nails scraping delicately over his slick head. The width of him, the uncontained power, took her breath away. The raw play of muscle and masculine power as he shifted in her embrace. His body flexed and stretched in a feline undulation that had her groaning with pleasure as the heated, hard length of him thrust against her drenched sex.

"You undo me," he said in a low voice. His whispered word extinguished the flarestick, plunging the room into darkness except for the faint glow of his eyes.

His eyes. She raised a hand to touch them, but his lids fluttered down, concealing the curious glow until she was aware of only the dark, powerful shadow surging deliciously below her. She touched his hair, her fingers moving over the long length, brushing it against his body, then exploring his shoulders, delighting in his smooth, warm skin. But when her hands found the chiseled planes of his abdomen and traveled downward, he groaned. "No. This is for you."

She didn't have a problem with that, she decided. How long had it been since someone had wanted to take care of her? She leaned backward into the large hands that ran down her spine, soothing and agitating the burn inside her. One hand kneaded her ass, while the other slipped between her thighs. The smooth, slick rub of her outer lips almost pushed her over into orgasm as they parted beneath his questing fingers.

"Open," he demanded, gently pushing her thighs farther apart. And then his fingers swept inward to find and rub the very core of her.

She bucked against the sweet probing of his fingers until she spasmed wildly.

"You liked that." His voice was a throaty hum against her skin.

She had. She'd never felt such intense pleasure. Her hands fisted in his hair, dragging his head down to her breasts. "More," she demanded. He'd said that this was for her; she hoped he meant it.

With a masculine chuckle that made her toes curl against the grimy silk of her once-white robe, he obliged, drawing a breast into the hot, greedy cave of his mouth. His tongue flicked mercilessly, flaying her nipple with pleasure and drawing the sweet nubbin into a tight, aching pucker that begged for more. More pleasure. More caresses.

"Yes," she whispered. "Just like that." He knew precisely where to touch, how to coax the flames of passion higher and higher still, until she thought she'd combust, her thighs clenching on either side of him.

She'd never been so greedy, but his eyes told her he found her hunger sexy and he was more than willing to do what she needed, using his finger with wicked skill. Almost mindless with the hot strokes of pleasure, she ran her hands down his back, over his buttocks. With the orgasm that roared through her came sweeping clarity.

There was no thief mark on him.

Who the hell was he?

He'd misled her. Lierr had not sent him. He had none of the Master's scars on his perfect body.

In the stifling darkness of their refuge, Jafar was a larger, blacker shadow against the rock-blocked entrance. Instead of retreating now that she'd found release, he pressed boldly, rubbing small, certain circles around her still-pulsing clit. Coaxing. Promising. Pressing firmly with his palm, he gently pinched the straining bud until new quivers built beneath his fingertips and shuddered into being in the dust-filled darkness of the alcove.

No. Not again.

"My *femi*," he whispered, and Miu knew he did not stay by her side because the doorway was blocked with tons of banshee-induced rock and rubble. No. He sounded as if he remained for other, more primitive reasons. Fear trickled through her. This was casual sex. Nothing important. Right? So why did he sound so *possessive*?

She recalled his finger, pushing its way deep inside

her body, her own mindless reaction. How long would it take for her memories of that thick finger spreading her, exploring her, to fade? How could she have let herself become so distracted from her real purpose here?

As if to remind her, the scrying bowl in her pack vibrated demandingly, shattering the sensual spell Jafar had cast on her.

"Off," she said, pushing frantically at his shoulders.

Jafar cursed low and long, lowering her until her feet touched the floor. Hastily, she donned the virgin's robe again.

Wet and clenched tight with fresh desire, her sex broadcast a determined message of its own. Fortunately, her mind now remembered what was at stake here.

She'd never had a partner like her merck. He was sweet and greedy and domineering—and she wanted to jump his bones and finish what they'd started. Even knowing that he'd lied to her didn't cool her heat. She hid her face in her hands and groaned.

"We're never going to get out of here this way." She was trying like hell to put a note of authority in her voice. "Why don't you start digging over there?" With a shaky hand, she indicated the blocked entranceway.

As soon as Jafar was occupied moving blocks of stone, Miu grabbed the scrying bowl from her bag. Sweat gleamed on his shoulders, beading in the enticing hollows and planes of his hard chest. Distracting. And enticing. The muscles in his arms corded as he turned his attention to shifting the debris that blocked the entrance to their refuge. Working single-mindedly to free them from their prison, he was even more attractive than before, but the Master was calling.

And in the scrying bowl was her chance to confirm that Jafar was not a fellow thief and to learn who had sent him after her. Chances were good, even if he didn't belong to the Master, the Master would know to whom he *did* belong.

Because the merck had her twisted in knots. There. She'd been honest with herself—and the truth scared her. How in the hell had he gotten to her so fast?

In her hands, the bowl warmed and she quickly shifted it behind a large funerary urn that had fallen on its side. She'd have to hope that the noise of the shifting rocks would mask a whispered conversation.

The Master's face swam into sight above the bowl. "Miu?" he snapped. Damn. His cold irritation almost froze her—and the temperature in their prison was sweltering. It was never wise to irritate the Master.

"I'm here," she said. "You rang. I answered."

"Report," he said. "Have you gotten the necklace?" Had his eyes softened? An illusion. She examined his face, looking for clues. Some emotion was flickering in his eyes, but for all she knew, that could have been the effects of last night's dinner come back to haunt him. She'd wondered before if he felt something for her besides pride in a student well trained, but there was just no telling. The Master showed nothing. Gave away nothing.

"Complications. I need more time." He'd originally given her only one week to reach the temple, steal the necklace, and bring it back to him. It would take three days just to make the return trip; there was no way she'd get back in time. And, since he had her sister, he would undoubtedly make an example of her. Panic surged and Miu fought it back.

"You did not expect complications?" His tone was mocking, but he was listening. Maybe she could convince him.

"Not this sort." She made sure she kept her eyes fixed firmly on his, showing no weakness. "You sent others in after me," she accused.

"Of course." He steepled his fingers beneath his chin and nodded for her to continue.

"One of them was a banshee. She screamed the place down around my ears." She didn't want to push her luck by pointing out that one of *his* flunkies had jeopardized the entire operation; she figured the Master would be able to connect those dots all by himself. He hadn't clawed his way to the head of a wide-flung network of thieves by being stupid.

"Did she?" He might have been discussing the weather. Across the room Jafar's head swung slowly toward her. For a moment, she thought his features took on a distinctly feline cast and then the impression was gone.

"She did. Took out one of your other thieves as well. Burst his eardrums. Stupid, really. The noise of the massive rockslide she started—well, let's just say that the Guardians would have to be really, really deaf not to have heard this one. And here we are—trapped and waiting for them."

This time, the Master winced. "Right," he said. "She shouldn't have done that."

"Give me an extension."

"I do have a policy," Lierr replied, casually inspecting his fingers, "of not granting extensions. You work with what you've got. Get back here in four days and"—he shrugged—"you'll still have a sister. I could let you choose." The smile didn't quite reach his eyes. "Pick the part of her you'd like to keep intact."

Panic threatened to choke her. "Hurt her," she threatened, "and I won't come back at all. No necklace." She smiled sweetly. "You can torture me to death from where you are, but you still won't have the necklace. How many of us did you send down here? The three on my heels are toast. And the Guardians are doubtless racing here right now. I'm your last shot."

This time, the Master's smile was overtly cruel. "You've still got just four days. Four days for your sister to live. Your choice."

"What about the merck?" Now was the time to find out for certain whether or not the Master had sent Jafar.

"The merck?" Something in the Master's voice made her pause. "You're not alone?" His dark eyes seemed to bore into her surroundings from the hazy aura above the bowl, even though she knew the *mazhyk* had its limits and he could no more see her prison than she could his elegant set of rooms.

"No. I've got company. One of yours?" His eyes sharpened. Next moment, it felt like she'd been hit by a speeding daemon. The bowl bounced, cracking on the stone floor as Jafar knocked it from her hands.

Miu smelled of despair, fear seeping from her body like some rank perfume. Her hands had cupped a small metal bowl, above which an image had formed.

Why had she been frightened of the person to whom she was speaking? Nothing—*no one*—scared his Miu.

He hadn't realized until now that he admired that quality in her. She'd go toe to toe with him even if she knew who he was.

What he was.

She had to be communicating with the master thief, the male she called the Master. Stalking across the room had been an easy call to make, as had been knocking the bowl onto the hard floor. Clearly spellbound, the bowl neither shattered nor spilled, a wavering image slowly reforming over the charmed water.

"What are you doing?" she screeched, grabbing for the bowl. Luckily for him, his arms were longer. Wrapping one hard arm around her waist to pin her in place, he easily grabbed the bowl first.

"Who's in the bowl?" The bespelled water remained firmly inside the bowl, even when he tipped the container upside down.

She scowled. "It's mine. Give it back."

Not likely. Not until he knew with whom she was trying to communicate and why. Every sense he had screamed this was an important clue in unraveling the puzzle that was his Miu—he was hardly going to hand it back over. For the first time, he felt like he was really getting somewhere.

"Manners," he said calmly, not betraying his sudden inner turmoil. She growled what sounded suspiciously like a curse. Hunkering down on the floor, he cupped the metal bowl between his hands. The metal warmed, its liquid surface stirring. As the aura sharpened again, cursing filled the room.

Male cursing.

Unfamiliar jealousy ate at him: she was supposed to turn to *him*. Instead, she was relying on some unseen stranger who was little more than a useless astral projection in a bowl of dirty water. Jafar was a Guardian; protecting was second nature to him. So why did he suddenly feel so unsure of himself? He didn't get the sense that she trusted this other male—but she didn't distrust him, either. Which made the unseen male a threat.

Competition.

"Miu? What the hell just happened?" The bowl vibrated with outrage.

Lifting the bowl, Jafar kept his face concealed. No point in tipping his hand—not yet. His companion's ignorance about who—and *what*—he was worked to his advantage.

"No," he said when Miu reached for the bowl. His low growl made it clear that he would not be crossed in this. Cursing, she backed against the far wall, rummaging in that damn bag of hers. Probably looking for one of that impressive collection of knives she'd been toting about.

He wasn't a fool. He'd lifted the lot and disposed of them before they'd entered the tunnel. She hadn't even noticed.

"Who is that?" snapped the man in the bowl.

"What are you to her?" The male in the bowl was handsome, Jafar decided, gritting his teeth. Women would like his looks. Pale skin. Dark hair clubbed back from fine cheekbones. The man looked like a bloody prince, but had the lethal intensity of a paid assassin.

"Give the bowl back to Miu," the male demanded.

Jafar shook his head slowly. "First, I want answers. I want a name. Yours."

A mocking smile crossed the man's lips. "She calls

me Master. You may do so as well." Jafar called *no one*, not even the Amun Ra, master. His pledge was to the Valley, to the task of guarding against incursions from the Qaf dwellers. That might mean acknowledging the Amun Ra as the titular head of his pride, loosely directing the actions of the Guardians and mediating between them and the outside world, but it did not mean blind obedience. Only a sort of casual deference. And a vow of honor.

"No?" The man's voice turned sharply cold. "I do not share my name with outsiders."

"Make an exception." Jafar examined the man's face for signs of weakness and found none. Unless Miu herself was a weakness—after all, he was fast discovering that she was *his* weakness.

"Who are you?" The male countered with a question of his own.

Across the room, Miu's head swiveled. Uh-oh, he thought. Now he was in trouble.

"Consider me an independent contractor," he suggested.

"Who the hell are you?" she demanded.

The male regarded him thoughtfully. No indication of what he was thinking crossed his impassive face. "You don't appear to be a Guardian," he said at last. "No bars. No marks. Although the build is right and I wasn't aware of any other—interested parties. I suppose you could be from Qaf," he offered, "although then, quite frankly, I'm surprised that you've left Miu alive. Still, there is something about your eyes. I wouldn't rule it out."

Jafar clenched his fists against an urge to destroy the bowl. Miu's eyes widened. *Qaf?* she mouthed silently.

"Does she even know why you really sent her here?" He had to ask, even if it condemned Miu. He had to find out as much as he could so he could stop the stream of uninvited intruders into the temple.

"Enough." The Master shrugged. "I told her just enough. As I did the others."

"Do we have a deal?" Miu came up beside him, leaning over his shoulder. This time, he let her.

"A deal?" The Master eyed her. "No. Nothing's changed. And I am going to suggest that you rethink your choice of companion. The banshee may have been a miscalculation on my part. This merck of yours is a similar misstep on yours. If he's not with me and he's not with the Guardians—then who is he with?"

"You said you were a merck."

The accusation hung in the air between them long after the bowl had gone silent and dark.

"You said you were here to *protect* me," Miu continued. They'd been shifting rocks for what seemed like hours. The bottom half of her ridiculous robe had been sacrificed to make more dust masks; motes of dust thickened the air, visible even in the dying glow of the flarestick. Pretty soon she'd be relying on her own eyes.

He didn't say anything.

The monotony of the work had given her ample time to contemplate his lie and to come up with a plan to ditch him. While she was stacking the smaller stones, she'd noticed an air shaft in one corner, a shaft that appeared to go straight down to the burial chambers below. But getting into it—without being followed by the merck—would take some planning.

Along with one of her disposable spells and a whole lot of luck. Carefully, she palmed the knockout spell.

Stun the merck and dive for the tunnel. Once in, she was home safe. With his broad shoulders, he'd never fit through the opening; even she would have to wiggle. Discreetly, she gave the elaborately carved grate covering the shaft a good tug. Loose enough. Presumably, the shaft was there to provide air for the stale confines of the catacombs.

She'd have to move the urns in front of the grate and slide it out of the grooves, get in, and then slide the whole lot back into place—with a good reinforcement spell—before her merck realized what she was up to.

He could find his own damn way out—she'd finish her job and save her sister. Alone. The way she should have worked from the beginning.

Before she could lose her nerve, she lobbed the spell at him.

And moved like hellhounds themselves were after her.

CHAPTER SEVEN

Miu immediately recognized the burial chamber from the Master's description. Sure enough, it was located right at the bottom of the air shaft. When she thought about it, the banshee had done her a favor, trapping her in that particular storage room. She still had the map to help her find her way out, and she no longer had to deal with her unreasonable attraction to the merck.

Now all she had to do was take the necklace.

She stepped gingerly into the burial chamber, scanning the room for hidden threats. For traps. Nothing. The room was blissfully quiet. But stepping onto the carnelian-colored granite floor blocks felt vaguely wrong, as if she were disturbing something.

Or someone.

Nerves. She'd let the merck turn her into a bundle of nerves with all his talk of danger and protection. She wasn't going to think about him. She had—finally—reached her destination. It didn't matter that she—almost—wished he were here to see the burial chamber. The merck could take care of himself. He was bigger, tougher, and savvier than most males she'd met; he'd be fine. She held her flarestick aloft as she peered around the chamber.

Fitting, that an alleged princess had been buried here. The room was every little girl's fantasy—if, of course, little girls daydreamed about possible funeral sites. In addition to the startlingly pink granite floor, the walls were an impossibly smooth pure white. Moreover, the walls were perfectly blank. No carvings. No friezes. No gold work. Just a pure white limestone that was blinding in its purity. Other than a handful of statues sprinkled in niches around the room, the only object was the coffin. Still, despite the beauty of the room, it felt half finished. Half empty. As if whatever had been buried here had been so terrible that no one had wanted to return, even when the other chambers on this level had filled up.

She scanned the room one more time, even setting off a small seeking spell that ricocheted merrily off the limestone walls. The spell left a small scorch mark that spoiled the perfect blankness but turned up no obvious *mazhykal* traps. Safe? Maybe. She'd still play it careful.

Get the necklace, she told herself. *Forget the merck.* Guilt was a luxury she couldn't afford. It didn't matter if the man had taken on that angry death spirit single-handedly. And had then carted her to safety when the banshee had wailed down the roof.

There *was* no reason for him to do these things— was there? He was just as self-serving as every other male she'd met. Because if she thought there was any chance that her hard-as-nails merck was harboring sweeter sentiments for her, she'd be rappelling back up the escape shaft—toward him—and that would never do.

She had to have the necklace. She wanted her sister back.

Decided, she strode across the chamber and threw open the lid of the coffin.

She'd double-crossed him.

She'd stunned him with a cheap witch spell.

And he hadn't seen it coming.

In a fit of rage, Jafar shifted, battering himself against the grille she'd used to block her escape route. Unfortunately, he was too large to fit through the opening to the air shaft. That impossibility made him grit his teeth; he'd bet the little witch had known the precise dimensions of the crawlspace she'd used as a personal, private staircase.

When he caught her, he'd wring her neck.

Wring her neck . . . When he caught her, she'd have stolen the necklace she'd come for and he would have to execute her. As one of the Guardians, he was honor bound to do so if he caught her stealing. While the actual method was up to him, the *yea* or *nay* was not. Thieves died. He'd never questioned that black-and-white pronouncement, had understood that the temple's dangerous proximity to the other realms required quick and summary justice. He slammed his hand against the stone wall of his prison, ignoring the fine rain of dust and gravel that showered down on him.

He was a killer. An enforcer. So why was he questioning the need to kill now?

He was growling when other Guardians appeared, shifting away the heavy rockfall with powerful forearms and even more powerful spells. How long had

Miu been gone now? Half an hour? More? When the Guardians finally neared the alcove, he overheard a pithy curse as they discovered the remnants of the daemon's corpse, crushed by a pair of falling girdle stones.

"Bloody hell," one Guardian muttered. "Hell of a way to go."

"No point in trying to resuscitate him for interrogation," another agreed. "Spirit's passed."

When the rocks fell away from the doorway, Jafar had his story ready. Leaning back against the wall, he deliberately kept his eyes away from the ventilation shaft where his companion had disappeared. If his nose had failed to scent the exit concealed behind the elaborate grillwork, these males should also be fooled.

Crossing his arms across his chest, he stared levelly at the males entering the alcove. The confined space meant there was no room for them all to shift, which significantly improved the odds in his favor. If he had to, he could hold them off with his longsword. Buy some time.

Buy some time? Was that what he'd decided to do? Perhaps if he could buy her time, she'd decide that she really could trust him. Strangely, he wanted her to do so. He wanted her to explain why she'd come for the necklace, why she wouldn't give it up.

For the first time, he wanted to know reasons.

"You okay, Jafar?" His pride members stood there, examining him cautiously. Three men, all well over six feet tall and dressed in black hunting leathers rather than the ritual white of the Hunt. Each had a longsword strapped to his back, as well as an arsenal of shortknives tucked into waistbands, boots, and arm sheaths. Three pairs of gold eyes examined him. Three noses scented the air, delicately.

"Seems fine," said Hebon flatly. His hand didn't leave his sword, however. Only a fool stood between Hebon and his target. Decades ago the male had channeled all his pent-up rage into his blades. He didn't draw until he was ready to kill. And he never, ever missed his target. His mood was as dark as his visage.

"Where is she?" Sanur teased. "You did have a female in here, didn't you?" He scented the air again. "I can smell her, my brother, and she smells good. Good enough to eat." A feral grin curved his lips as he stalked into the small room.

Brooding, Jafar fought back the unexpected impulse to rip Sanur apart. He'd seen his brother use that same charming smile on countless females. Jafar recognized the sensual prowl as the male strode unerringly toward the narrow passageway that had allowed his female to escape from him.

Sanur wasn't going to taste her.

Not today.

Not—if he were honest with himself—ever.

"Jafar doesn't take females." Hebon bit off his words, as if speaking were a waste of time, when he could be hunting down the intruder instead. His cold eyes examined the escape point. "He wouldn't take up with a thief and an intruder." The unspoken words *again* hung in the air between them.

Could Jafar really bring himself to turn Miu over to their untender mercies? He'd hunted thieves with these males for centuries. He knew their methods, and they were brutal.

"Where is whom?" Jafar asked innocently. Leaning back against the wall, he replayed his options.

"The female trapped in here with you." Sanur scowled playfully and nudged the still-silent Badru in the ribs. The other male grunted, but held his ground. "Damn it, Jafar, you know we can smell her, my brother. You had her here with you. Where did she go?"

"Are you hunting her?" Jafar knew *he* had to be the one to find her.

He was *going* to be the one to find her.

"Depends," answered Sanur, stepping through the wreckage. Picking up a small funeral pot, he examined the seal. "Not broken. Thank the gods. The alcove down the hall is filled with traumatized death spirits. You'd think they'd never left their bodies before."

That had to have been unpleasant. "Sealed them back in? Or sent them on their way?" Either way, he didn't give a damn, but conversation would give his *femi* a few more seconds of freedom. She hadn't admitted it—he suspected she'd traverse the spider-filled air shaft a dozen times first—but the stories of shapeshifting Guardians had scared her. And yet she'd seemed willing to trust him. To shove a plug of bespelled wax into his ears to prevent his eardrums from bursting with the banshee's wail.

Of course, in the end, she'd abandoned him inside the alcove and gone on her merry way.

"Is she a thief," Hebon bit out, "or is she your mate?"

"Did you bell her, my brother?" Sanur asked eagerly. Even Badru turned that eerie black gaze of his from his calm consideration of Miu's escape hatch and looked at Jafar. Badru never said much—hell, his brother never spoke at all if he could avoid it—but the Cat missed nothing. He knew precisely how Jafar's female had disappeared; he was just working himself up to the words.

There was only one option left, so Jafar took it.

He growled a warning. She was *his*. "Back off. She's not a thief."

"But is she your mate?" Sanur demanded.

"No." He had to admit the truth. She wasn't.

"Then what is she?" Hebon countered. His fingers caressed the black hilt of his sheathed blade. A blade that had killed more tomb robbers than any other in the temple; rumor claimed the shifter had struck a bargain with one of the more bloodthirsty gods. True or not, he wasn't getting Jafar's female.

"Mine," Jafar stated firmly. He shoved away from the wall, his hands going to his blades. One of his pride brothers groaned.

"Only if she's a mate," Hebon insisted.

"And not if she's nicking our stuff," Sanur put in. Jafar didn't underestimate the male, despite the lazy sensuality of his face. When Sanur decided to take his responsibilities seriously, he took them very, very seriously. "She shouldn't be down here. The other females remained on the upper levels." In the silence, three sets of eyes examined Jafar's face. "As expected. Yours did not."

"She's too close," Sanur added. Jafar knew that was true. As a Guardian, he worked the lowest levels of the temple, the first line of defense against the other realms bordering on theirs. Down in the catacombs, it was perfectly clear who the bad guys were. Come out of the tunnels and you were cut down. No exceptions. If you weren't a Guardian, you were assumed to be an Ifrit that had crossed over.

And no one hesitated to kill an Ifrit anymore.

"She won't go through the Doorways." Jafar didn't know how he knew, but he did. For some reason, his *femi* had a strong anchor in this realm. She wouldn't leave willingly. "She's not comfortable underground. She'll want to return to the surface."

"Not a mate." Hebon turned to the others. "We hunt her then."

Jafar's Cat didn't care for that idea either. The beast roared to life within him, suggesting that the men filling the room were a threat to his female. *Take them out.* He fought the urge, but something must have shown in his eyes.

Sanur threw up his hands in the universal gesture of surrender. "He's going to mate her," he said to the others. "He'll have the bells out before nightfall. Cat just doesn't know it yet."

That wasn't possible, was it? Dark heads swiveled toward him, their eyes crawling over his face.

"If she steals," Hebon said in the icy voice that made even other Guardians hesitate, "she's ours. Not his."

His brothers were skeptical and he couldn't blame them. He'd never taken the slightest interest in the bride Hunts.

"Why follow her, if she is not a thief?" Badru finally broke his silence, his voice hoarse with disuse. A good question and not one Jafar could answer. How could he explain that this small female fascinated him, that he wanted to see what she would do next? And if, he admitted to himself, she would indeed hang herself if he handed her the rope.

"He's hunting," Sanur argued, narrowing his eyes.

It was Hebon who asked the question they all were thinking. "But a thief—or a mate?"

Miu pushed aside the lid of the coffin, careful not to let the heavy wooden panel fall onto the floor. Carved with spells for navigating the afterlife, the lid's bright carnelian paint had faded considerably in the darkness. More to the point, someone had deliberately smashed the shabti statues for this woman. Someone had *not* wanted the dead woman to enjoy a pleasant afterlife.

That was a bad sign.

Forcing herself to take deep, even breaths despite the fetid stench that wafted up from the coffin, she examined her quarry. In the decades since her burial, the princess had lost most of her good looks. The ivory curve of ribs gleamed through the decaying remnants of a once-elegant dress. Time and a closer acquaintance with the dark, hot confines of the coffin had reduced the expensive fabric to tattered streamers of dull gray. But nothing could dim the glow of the jewel that hung about her neck.

The necklace was fascinating.

Miu had known it would be, from the moment she'd first felt the moonstone's pull when she entered the temple. Set in the middle of a stunningly simple necklace of silver, the jewel was a deep, unfamiliar blue that pulsated with color as if the necklace's creator had blended together sky, stars, and ocean to create this impossible mystery. Her eyes narrowed. The moonstone reeked of *mazhyk*. Was there more to this necklace than the Master was letting on?

Possibly.

Mazhyk or no *mazhyk*, Miu had to take the necklace.

Tentatively, she reached out her hand. Even though she was expecting something of the sort, Miu had to stifle a shriek when her fingers closed around the necklace—and long, pale talons wrapped themselves around her wrist. The nails bit into her skin, carving shallow crescents into her flesh. Blood welled beneath the pinprick wounds.

Heqet save her. A treasure daemon.

"Hey." The treasure daemon tugged insistently on her wrist. "Got you by the wrist here. Not letting go, bound till death does us part. You *are* familiar with that part?"

Miu was, but no point in letting the daemon know that. "Really?" She eyed the creature thoughtfully. "Nothing at *all* will make you release my wrist?"

"'Fraid not," the daemon said regretfully. His nails sank deeper. "Unless perhaps you're willing to leave the hand behind?" The note of hope in the daemon's voice made her shudder. Looking closer, she saw that the coffin already held a collection of hands. Unless the princess had had a rather unusual abnormality that everyone had failed to mention, the treasure daemon had already collected.

Multiple times.

How long had it been since the treasure daemon had moved in and set up housekeeping inside the dead woman's coffin? Fortunately, she'd come prepared. Always do your homework because you never knew when you were going to be tested.

"Perhaps we can negotiate," she suggested. The daemon looked bored, as if he had heard all possible suggestions before.

"Doubt it," he said. Just to punctuate his point, he took a good, long lick, the glass-sharp papillae of its tongue scraping over her skin. The skin broke, blood beading on the surface. "Oh, I doubt it. Too, too sweet."

Before the daemon could fasten onto her wrist—and either suck her slowly dry or force her to carve off her own wrist—she reached into her bag and whipped out a handful of herbs. The sweet-scented grass was the color of early limes, but far more potent than any citrus fruit. Usually, sweetgrass was difficult to obtain and cost more than your average treasure hunter earned in the best of years. She'd had the foresight, however, to insist that Lore learn both botany and herbalism. As a result, their kitchen gardens grew far more than squashes and lettuces. They provided a living, growing arsenal from which Miu culled the best, such as the sweetgrass she was now dumping into her palm.

A careful puff of breath sent the pollen floating across the dim air toward the daemon, who looked first surprised and then blissful as he inhaled. "Ah," he said in surprise, and then "Oh, you didn't." She'd seen smokeweed addicts take shallower drafts than the daemon's second.

"Got more of that stuff?" he asked, rubbing his crotch with lazy strokes. Her sister hadn't mentioned that the grass was addictive or—she eyed the daemon warily—that it apparently acted as an aphrodisiac. Great. She had one blissed-out daemon on her hands.

She countered, "Going to let me pass?"

A crafty look appeared in the daemon's eyes. "Hand it over," was all he said. And then, "I don't suppose you could help a guy out here?"

Disgusted, she shook her head. No way was she feeling up a daemon, not even to fetch the necklace. Shaking his head, the daemon grabbed the pouch from her hands and tottered out of the coffin. He curled up in a boneless heap in one corner of the chamber, slowly shifting forms as the weed took effect. "Enjoy," he slurred before closing his eyes.

Right. One obstacle removed. The daemon was vulnerable enough that she could have slid her blade through his neck, but she hated killing anything if it wasn't necessary.

Shaking the droplets of blood off her wrist, she reached farther inside the coffin. The hard wooden lip cut into her hips, forcing her to stretch off balance. The necklace was too formfitting to allow her to pull it over the dead woman's head; she'd have to undo it. There. Brushing aside the remainder of the rags, she twisted the necklace around until she spotted the clasp. Keeping half an eye on the daemon, who was now uttering small, wheezing snores, she tugged on the small lock.

The clasp didn't budge, but instead set up a high-pitched wail that would draw the attention of every Guardian for miles around.

CHAPTER EIGHT

The unearthly wail shattered the stillness, shooting up the escape shaft toward them. Jafar didn't blink, but he knew that scream. They all did. The privately wealthy could afford to bury their dead with elaborate grave goods. To keep away grave robbers, some purchased protective spells to guard the coffins. Judging by the strength of that scream, someone had just attempted to remove a very valuable object indeed.

Three dark heads swiveled unerringly toward the escape shaft.

Turning, he faced the males. Since he'd run with them in Cat form and fought by their sides in man form, he knew them. He knew how they fought—and what they were likely to do. Sanur had drawn his blades already, but the other two hesitated, Hebon because he hadn't decided if he wanted to strike a death blow, and Badru because, well, he'd never been completely normal. He *watched*, long after others had acted. Never mind that he usually came to the correct conclusion.

The Guardians would want to believe him. These were his *brothers*. Surely, he couldn't be forced to choose between them and the female.

Could he?

"Who is she?" Sanur's sympathetic face swam before him. "We can take her to the Amun Ra, Jafar. We can let him decide." His brother left the rest of his sentence unspoken: *We don't have to kill her now.* He was willing to bend the rules that much.

Hebon didn't say anything, but his arms tensed. Jafar knew he was ready to pull the blades and, if he had to, he'd throw them at Jafar. Duty first. Everyone knew that Hebon never wavered. Ever. Once he'd committed himself to a course, he stayed it.

"Not a thief," Jafar repeated through gritted teeth. He had no proof of that, even if he'd had his suspicions and even her own admissions to damn her. "Look around you," he invited. His brothers scanned the shelves of the small alcove, thick with canopic jars and the small ceramic figurines that the Valley dwellers loved to bury alongside their dead. "She took nothing," he continued. Hebon's eyes narrowed.

"From here," Hebon countered.

"From anywhere I've been with her. Those jars are worth a fortune. One jewel from them and she'd be a wealthy woman." If she made it out of the Valley and *if* she could find a gem man foolish enough to take the stones off her hands.

"So she's selective." Hebon shrugged. "Or stupid. Someone set off a warding spell down below and you know as well as I do that it's likely to be her. Who else is down here besides us?"

More creatures than he cared to consider, that was for certain. The Amun Ra needed to assess the security risks of their Hunts. Too many outsiders had used the Hunt to sneak into the temple this time. Tersely, Jafar sketched the list for his brothers. "Not the only one.

You found the daemon"—crushed and therefore unlikely to be the thief below, but he had a point to make here—"and he was not alone. Who do you think caused that cave-in? Banshee," he said grimly. "And she was traveling with a dark faerie as well." He'd seen three intruders, but that didn't mean more hadn't been lurking unseen in the shadows. He hadn't checked and now he cursed himself for his carelessness.

"Right." Sanur backed toward the entrance. "We have a breach. Did they come from above—or below?"

Jafar considered what he'd seen. None of the intruders was dark enough—or powerful enough—to have come from the underground realms. "Above. Definitely above."

"Any idea how they got in—or how they got this far?"

Jafar held up the square of papyrus he'd removed from Miu's person. "Maps," he said succinctly. "Someone is making maps."

Sanur swore. "Are they crazy?"

Probably just shortsighted—and greedy. Still, it was a leak that needed to be plugged and he knew that if Sanur and Badru didn't take care of it, Hebon would. The Cat's face was sterner than he'd ever seen it.

The screeching got even louder.

Unable to wait any longer, he shifted, letting the change shimmer over him. In the beat of a heart, his cells reshaped with a wrenching pleasure pain. He reformed, having called the werespirit from its resting place in the hard stone statue of the Cat.

The need to hunt, to feed, to fuck, poured through him, drowning logic. His werespirit had a very simple code—and very lethal talents. It protected. It ran. It hunted. Usually, the partnership between Guardian and Cat was a smooth one, a matter of deliberately blending the edges between his soul and the werespirit until there was just the one entity pulsing through the male body. But now his werespirit wanted the female, despite the man's reservations. The werespirit was ravenous with hunger for her. Had succumbed to the mating heat.

Before the other Guardians could move, he completed the shift, driving several hundred pounds of leonine force at the stone wall where his Miu had vanished. The stone cracked and gave, allowing him to batter his way through the narrow opening until he hovered on the brink of the chasm.

Off balance.

Rapidly, he shifted back, closing the opening behind him with a few well-placed boulders. Curses and the sounds of rock shifting followed him. The makeshift barrier wouldn't hold his brothers for long.

Pulling his blades, he dove down the air shaft, letting his body plunge hundreds of yards, banging against the stone walls as he plummeted.

The warding screams grew louder as the stone flashed before him.

Now.

At the last moment, he dug into the soft stone with his blades. With a wrenching sensation, his arms were almost ripped from their sockets, his entire weight hanging from the blades. He'd fallen several yards below the opening to the burial chamber.

Someone—Hebon—bellowed angrily far above

him. He'd deal with the pride later. Right now, he needed to collect his female.

He'd put his life on the line for her. Worse, he'd put his honor on the line.

And she *was* the thief.

Hand over hand, he began the upward climb.

The sword sliced through the neck bones of the dead woman, scattering vertebrae like pearls. No time for prayers or apologies—the alarm was no longer sounding, but Miu was sure it had done its job. Her fingers closed over the amulet, wrapping the silver in soft cloth and stowing it securely in her bag. She fingered the contents for the map. Damn and double-damn. No map after all. She'd left the map with the merck. *Well,* she thought prosaically, *couldn't be helped, could it?* She was hardly going to go back up *there* and ask him for it. Besides, he was probably ready to throttle her by this point. She spared him half a thought—she didn't want to know why the idea of him falling into the Guardians' hands made her stomach sink like that—and then darted for door.

A rasping cough from opening to the airshaft stopped her.

"Going somewhere, *femi*?"

Perched on the edge of the air shaft, Jafar regarded her with glowing golden eyes.

Heqet's shades, but the man had more lives than a cat.

She fought back the unexpected tide of relief.

"How did you get out?" Maybe reminding him that she'd left him behind had been a mistake. "I was coming back," she improvised, hoping he didn't possess anything remotely like a truth spell.

His eyes flickered over the desecrated coffin, the drunken treasure daemon, and the ivory confetti of the dead woman's bones, then stopped on the bag at her waist, where she'd slipped the necklace she'd just pocketed.

"We need to have a little chat, love. Talk about this propensity you have for darting off in unexplained directions. I thought we were working together."

"Hurt?" She could only hope.

"Confused," he replied coldly. "Put off my stride. Not sure what my employer wants from me here. The idea was to keep you safe, see, and letting you run around and pocket other daemons' treasures seems like a piss-poor way to go about it."

"Go away," she muttered. Could she make it to the door before he was on her? Her mapmaker had shown her the pattern of the floor tiles in front of the exit, had told her which ones she must avoid at all costs. She didn't *think* the merck knew the secret to crossing the floor, but he might figure he could handle whatever the chamber threw at him. He was large enough that a few knives might not stop him. She forced the breath to leave her mouth evenly. Panicking wasn't going to help here.

"Can't do that, love," he replied, jumping to the floor. Hands on hips, he strolled confidently over to the coffin and examined the mess she'd made of the dead woman. "No respect for the dead? I'm fairly certain she didn't look like that when you arrived."

"Prove it."

He just shook his head, stirring his finger through

the bones. "If that death spirit is still hanging around, she'll have a bone to pick with you about this."

He was probably right, but that was the least of her problems. She continued her slow, careful shuffle toward the main doorway.

"Stop," he ordered.

Ooh, she hated orders. Always had.

Miu kept sliding carefully toward the door. Her eyes never moved from the god-awful pink squares.

"Not wise," groaned the daemon, stirring slightly. His limbs flopped loosely as he held his head up, eyes glittering greedily.

Jafar fixed the daemon with a lethal stare. "*Your* job, daemon, is to guard treasure."

"True enough," the daemon admitted cheerfully. His pupils dilated as he ground a pinch of the grass between his webbed fingers and snorted it rapidly up his nose. "Ahhh. Good stuff, that. Fresh."

"He can be bribed," Miu explained. Twelve tiles between her and the door. Would she remember the pattern correctly? If not, the mapmaker had told her, a hundred knives would *mazhykally* fly through the air, making short work of any would-be thief. Her foot hovered in midair between two tiles of a particularly garish pink hue and then came down firmly. She held her breath, but no knives flew through the air.

"Bribed," the daemon chortled. "Bought. Had for a song. Although," he frowned with all the inebriated seriousness of a drunk, "not a song. Don't care much for music."

Jafar had apparently given up on making sense of the daemon's burbling. "You left me," he accused.

Miu paused. Ten tiles left. So much for hoping he'd

overlook the minor inconvenience of his incarceration.

"For your own good," she said breezily. "Didn't think you could fit through that little opening." Her eyes narrowed. "How *did* you get out?"

"Expecting me to be stuck a while longer, were you?"

She shrugged. "You're here now, aren't you?"

"But I'm not supposed to be."

"Going to hold it against me?" She leapt lightly across two more tiles.

"No more games," he snapped, crossing the room with rapid, ground-eating strides.

Eyes widening, she frantically dropped her gaze to the tiles, but he didn't make a single misstep.

"In fact, game over. Check and"—his arm shot out and shackled her to him with snakelike rapidity—"mate. It was a mistake," he growled, "to come to the temple with theft on your mind. The temple is too well guarded, my *femi*. Thieves are not tolerated. Put it back," he snapped. "Whatever it is that you took, return it. Now."

She stared at him incredulously. "Are you insane? After everything we've gone through, you want me to walk away empty-handed? No. I'll say it again, in case you weren't listening the first time. No. I've gotten what I came for and I'll keep it."

"It's not worth it."

"How do you know?" she snapped. "You're just along for the ride. The bodyguard. Sorry if this is turning out to be more than you bargained for. Oh, I know." She smacked a palm against her forehead. "Why don't you go your way and I'll go mine? Consider this ill-advised partnership dissolved. When whoever employed you asks the reasons why, I'll be happy to provide him with a list."

"*Femi*," he began, but the soft whuff of feet alerted him before she recognized the new danger.

"He's not one of yours, thief," said Hebon, moving to block the exit. "He's one of ours."

Heart pounding, she scanned their faces. The dark marks of the Guardians were all too clear from where she stood. As was the violent aggression directed toward her.

Well, hell, she thought, choking back the hysterical laughter that threatened to bubble up, that certainly explained his insistence that she return the necklace.

It was silly to feel hurt. Surely, she was used to betrayal by now and, if not, Jafar had just provided another valuable example. Of course, he wasn't really on her side. It had been foolish to believe he was.

"One of yours," she agreed.

In their male forms, the Guardians were beautiful. They had the same eerie sort of beauty that had attracted her to Jafar. Tall and muscular, they had the same golden skin and dark, flashing eyes. They were all hard planes and sculpted muscles, flowing with the same uncanny grace as if they glided across the stone floor rather than walking. The difference was in their eyes. Theirs were the eyes of predators. Cold, flat, assessing. These were not Jafar's eyes.

They stared first at her and then at Jafar.

"Jafar, stop," hissed the first. "This time, she truly has stolen from the temple."

The necklace burned in her bag. What could she say?

Jafar's hard gaze met those of his brothers, his body readying for battle.

"Turn her over for justice," urged another. "We will see to her punishment if you cannot. Or, yes, we can take her to the Amun Ra. Let him decide what should be done."

"The mating urge makes him weak," said another. "He sees only the bells and where he could place them; he does not see his duty clearly."

Was the possessive look on his face just lust? It didn't matter, she decided. He was the enemy, one way or the other.

"I do see my duty," Jafar said calmly. "Quite clearly."

"Good," said the first. "It has been years since we had so pretty a captive. I will enjoy punishing her."

Jafar shook his head. "No, Hebon."

"No?" The Guardian called Hebon advanced, flicking his blade lightly. "You have other plans for her?"

"We'll take her to the Amun Ra," Jafar said at last, eyeing that naked blade.

He turned to her. "*Femi.*" For a moment, it seemed as if he would say something else. Something *meaningful.* Of course, he didn't. Instead, shooting her a swift glance from beneath those impossibly dark lashes of his, he ordered, "Come with me." He reached out a hand to her.

Did he think she was simply going to give him her hand and let him pull her along, like a recalcitrant child, to the Amun Ra?

Apparently. He waggled his fingers impatiently. She tried to forget where those fingers had been. What they had stroked.

"No."

He sighed. "I don't have time for this."

Hebon glared at her. "He guards the Doorways between Qaf and this realm, female. Who do you think slips through while you distract him?"

None of this made any sense. Furthermore, she didn't care. This was about her—not some Qaf.

"You need to trust me, *femi*."

She'd sooner trust an Ifrit. When she told him so, the males lounging by the door laughed. "Take her to see an Ifrit, mate." The speaker smiled cruelly. "Maybe she'll sing a different song then. Good-looking males," he explained casually, "get lots of females following them. Problem is, they're a wee bit too brutal in their takings. And their leavings"—he shrugged—"well, personally I'm convinced that there's more than a bit of truth to the rumors about their cannibalism."

Miu was about to say something else, but Jafar shot her a dark look.

"Now," he said quietly, "would be a very good time to be silent. Shut up, love, and let me see what I can do here."

"No." He was a Cat. There was no way she could trust him, so she drew her blades.

"If you insist." With a sigh, Jafar stepped forward.

"Draw," she said, but he shook his head.

"Don't need to."

Carefully, she eyed his larger frame. He'd have a longer, more powerful reach than she, so her strikes needed to count. His head and neck would be most vulnerable, so she'd aim high.

He shifted so fast, she didn't even have time to scream. With a fierce roar, several hundred pounds of feline launched across the room at her, driving her to the floor. Hard. Black spots swam before her eyes as her head bounced against the tiles. The crushing weight on her ribs forced her down. Nothing broken, not yet, but she had to fight to drag a half breath into her burning lungs. Overwhelmed. Dwarfed. Familiar golden eyes glared down into hers. Then he shifted again, the fur receding and the teeth retracting. His hand jammed beneath her chin, pressing with deadly menace against her windpipe. Fingers found the nerve endings on the sides of her throat and pressed. Pain lashed through her, followed by a dull lassitude that froze her body. Dimly, she heard the soft chink of a blade falling onto the tiles.

Someone had dropped a weapon.

Was that her arm flopping like dying fish on the ground?

Closing her eyes, she let the darkness take her away.

CHAPTER NINE

Bleached bones of thieves' skeletons lined the corridor to the chamber as a reminder. Show no mercy. Spare none. Some thieves had died quickly, their throats slashed so their blood pumped out onto the thirsty limestone floors. Others had died more slowly, displayed in locked cages to terrify their companions. Either way, their pale, fleshless remains made for a ghoulish display. Jafar didn't need the reminder to know he was going to have just the one chance to make his case to the Amun Ra.

And even then, he wasn't going to be making a case to the Amun Ra for mercy.

Miu might consider death a more palatable choice than what he'd offer. But he wouldn't be taking no for an answer.

He'd never wanted a mate. Didn't want that responsibility.

And yet he didn't want to see Miu die.

Maybe he shouldn't have led such a monkish existence after Oni's death, but, hell, he hadn't thought he deserved any pleasure. Not when Hebon had been forced into a solitary existence.

He'd been unprepared for the bright sizzle of

attraction that had flared between him and Miu. He suspected that it would only get worse.

Until he had her.

So he'd take her, and he'd save her at the same time. She'd have her second chance and he'd have her. Punishment and pleasure, all bound together.

First, however, he had to convince the Amun Ra to release her into his custody.

The Amun Ra was sprawled on a large divan when Jafar entered the chamber. Jafar's eyes swept the shadowed corners of the room. None of his fellow Guardians was present.

Acknowledging the Amun Ra with a terse "My lord," he approached the male. His alpha. *He's giving me a chance.* No Guardians meant the Amun Ra had left them both negotiating room. Space to talk.

"Heard you wanted to talk." Lifting his female companion gently from his lap, Amun Ra set on her on her feet. "Run along now," he said quietly, not taking his eyes from Jafar.

The female pouted, but ran from the room, the slap of her bare feet mingling with the musical chime of the bells that dangled from her ears. Not a mate, but his lord had marked her. Cats were territorial, although willing to share with their pride members. Memories threatened to drown him and he fought them off. He'd brought another female here once, her cool hand clasped in his larger, warmer one. He'd thought the coolness had been due to nerves; he hadn't realized . . . No. He wasn't going to revisit those memories. Not now.

Amun Ra rose swiftly from the divan with serpentine grace.

"You've betrayed me, Cat."

With a grim shake of his head, Jafar responded, "Not yet." Reluctantly, he added, "my lord." No point in angering the Amun Ra. Not when the alpha could and would put a fast period to his life.

"Not yet?" The air crackled as Amun Ra drew *mazhyk* into himself and a glow of power surrounded him. "You stand there and tell me not *yet*? Unless you've got information I don't—which I doubt—no male in this building would deny me the right to send you straight back to the vortex. Better still, send you elsewhere and let your spirit disintegrate into a thousand bits and pieces. Bad enough being without a body, Jafar, but without consciousness either? Better off dead, but that you wouldn't be permitted. I can make you suffer for an eternity and we both know it."

True enough, he supposed. "Hear me out. You ordered me to apprehend her. I have done so."

Hard eyes stared at Jafar and the relaxed man with the elegant facade disappeared, an illusion. Yeah, the Amun Ra was a master of illusions. *Mazhyk* wavered in the air around him. Not a Guardian, but something else entirely, he'd been the one to summon the Guardians' spirits from the vortex, had given them these forms.

"You will bring her to me for execution," Amun Ra ordered. Razor-sharp silver tips appeared on the ends of the male's hands. He examined them casually.

A second, more powerful throb of *mazhyk* in the air had Jafar tensing. Stubbornly. "She's mine," he said harshly. "Mine. I protect her."

"Even if she breaks the laws that you swore you would uphold."

"I will not see her executed. Is there no other way?"

"Can't bend the rules for a bit of a female." Amun Ra's eyes held his, hard and unwavering. "Wouldn't do it even if I could. The law's the law," he said, instead of answering Jafar's questions. "Rules are there for reasons that maybe you and I don't know about. You guard the Doorways. I provide the guards." Knives appeared in his hand, materializing out of the air with a fine shimmer of *mazhyk*. "I'll send you back if I have to. Two hundred Cats out there, waiting to rip your little lady to bloody bits if you can't give me a reason to keep her alive. Convince me."

This was it. His one chance to sway the Amun Ra.

"Which do you *really* want?" he demanded. "Tell me, my lord," his voice mocked. "One thief, sent to do as she was told? Or the thief master himself?"

The blades stilled betrayingly. "She did not come in here alone," Amun Ra said.

No question there. "You know she didn't. Three followed her. One, I killed. The two others were probably crushed in the cave-in." He shrugged casually. "There could be more, but these penetrated my sector. And only one of them human—Miu. If I were you, I'd be asking myself why so many thieves? And why all of them seem to know precisely where to go and how. How the hell did they know where the entrance to the lower levels was and what to steal once they got there?"

The Amun Ra's eyes flickered. "They had a specific target?"

"Yeah." Interesting that Amun Ra hadn't known that. Or, perhaps he had and was merely bluffing. Only fools underestimated the male. "A necklace, one of the pieces from Pho's tomb. The 'princess' buried in the pink and white burial chamber. Of course, you and I know the truth of that story."

"We do, indeed." The Amun Ra tipped his head. "And I doubt either of us has forgotten your lapse of judgment."

"I took care of her." Jafar's voice was cold as ice.

"You did." Amun Ra nodded. "Although not before she'd done a great deal of damage. But, yes, you took care of her. We all did. And we tossed her into the first burial chamber we found and warded her body just in case any of her companions decided to come looking for her. Do you think it's an accident that so many of our recent guests have made a beeline for her final resting place?"

"You don't think it's a coincidence." Jafar studied the face of the Amun Ra. No expression flickered in the male's eyes, but some instinct warned Jafar that this opportunity was too important to dismiss. "Nor do I. And Miu may be able to lead us to the man behind these thieves."

"Interesting." The Amun Ra's face changed, melted. "I just might be in the market for a bargain then."

Dark satisfaction roared through Jafar. "Yes. I thought you might be."

"Terms." One long silver nail flickered through the air. "Tell me the terms you propose."

How the hell did you negotiate terms with an immortal who had the ability to yank your ass straight out of this realm and send it to another?

Carefully, Jafar decided. Very carefully.

He kept his eyes on the Amun Ra's face. All cold planes. No expression. He wouldn't have wanted to play cards with the male and he suspected that most of the Guardians felt the same way. The man was a cipher and none of them liked puzzles. His power was immense—and yet he refused to go belowground. He'd hosted orgies whose very memory made Jafar's skin flame, and yet he held to an esoteric code of honor that made a mockery of his licentiousness. Which was the real Amun Ra?

Either way, he couldn't imagine his Miu confronting this hard, cold figure. Her irreverent sass would get her killed before she'd finished her first sentence. Disrespecting the Amun Ra was a good way to die. If you were lucky, it was a quick death. Miu was like a living, breathing flame of life, all hot passion and delectable chaos. She'd brought his orderly existence down around his ears as effectively as the banshee had brought the tunnel crashing in.

Strangely, he wasn't sure he minded all that much.

Terms. Right. "You give Miu to me," he proposed.

Amun Ra smiled slowly. "And how do we explain such leniency to the others? She's a thief. The rules are explicit. Death."

Miu's death was not acceptable to him, although he hesitated to examine the reasons why. "No," he said.

Jafar marshaled his arguments. He'd made sure there was no concrete evidence of Miu's crime. Hell, the first thing he'd done was get rid of the damn necklace. While his brothers stormed about the chamber, posturing and bellowing, he'd popped the glittering stones back into the stone coffin, reaching behind him to stir the now-disassembled bones with a careful hand. While the destruction his *femi* had wrought would still be clear, it would simply look like a minor act of desecration. An insult to the not-so-dearly departed, sure, but not a killing offense.

As theft was.

No harm, no foul, or so he figured it. He'd bribed the treasure daemon to keep quiet; the stones were back where they belonged; and he would take his little thief in hand.

Where she belonged.

"Got no proof," he pointed out. "Hebon and Badru claim Miu came to remove the necklace from Pho's neck. Gaudy thing, set with a large moonstone in the center." His hands mimed an ostentatiously large jewel. "I'd argue that, even if she found it, she didn't take it. Stone's still there, though the grave is a wee bit disturbed. Wouldn't be right to punish her for a crime she didn't commit."

"A crime she didn't commit—or that *you* covered up?" Amun Ra's eyes bored into him. "You know the prey's name, Cat. Have you sided with her over us?"

He did know her name, but it hadn't occurred to him that naming her would be a weakness. He should have realized. Guardians didn't bother with names—only with deeds.

"There has to be a reason for all this sudden interest in Pho's necklace." He felt his way cautiously. "Miu came for it. The dark faerie we trapped mentioned it as well. And the male she calls Master wanted to know if she'd obtained it yet. He threatened her. He mentioned only that piece, so it would seem he has a very particular agenda."

"She's not your typical treasure hunter," Amun Ra agreed.

Jafar shrugged. "None of them are. That's what

makes me want to learn more about this necklace. Let me take Miu and I'll get the answers from her."

"She may not have them."

"Then she'll lead me to that Master of hers," he vowed. "I'll get my answers from him. This is more than just a simple ring of tomb robbers, and we both know it. There have been too many attempted break-ins. Too much of a pattern here, and I don't like it."

"I don't like it, either, but I need your word, Jafar." Amun Ra's eyes bored into him. "I need to know she'll not be running around my temple, unchecked. That she'll be at your side day and night. Tell me she's yours and I'll back off." He left the implicit threat unspoken. Refuse the bond and Miu died. "Swear to me, Jafar. Mate her and pry the information from her. One way or the other. Find this master thief and bring them both back here for us to deal with."

This was exactly what he'd been angling for. Mating would let him keep Miu safe—and, his body reminded him, would let him indulge his erotic fantasies about her.

Surely, she'd see the benefits of partnering with him. And he'd finally have her right where he wanted her: in his bed.

"Mates," he snapped, before he could get cold feet. "I'll do it." There was no other way to keep her safe. To find out the answers that he needed.

"Your word, Jafar." Amun Ra regarded him over steepled fingers. "Your word that you'll do it now." His heavy-lidded gaze dipped downward. "You appear to be up to the task. And, just in case you're thinking to get clever with your words, you vow to mate her by sunrise."

"Three hours."

"I'm feeling generous," the immortal mocked. "I should make you do the business out there in the gallery, so everyone can satisfy himself that the deed is done."

"Bastard," Jafar said, but the words held no heat.

"Quite," Amun Ra agreed. "After all, I'm only giving you what you want, Jafar, and we both know it."

Chapter Ten

Miu was lying on a pallet rather than in her grave.

Unless, of course, the Cats had simply skipped the killing and gone straight to burying the body. She tried to sit upright, but collapsed, wincing at the residual pain in her head.

When her nausea subsided, Miu levered herself into a sitting position, more slowly this time. The world tilted, whirled, and resolved itself into a small, four-sided room with no obvious door. A prison. Of course. It had been too much to hope that the Cats would settle for banishing her unwelcome person outside their walls.

Looking up, she realized that her prison had no ceiling. The Guardians had chucked her into a grilled cage set into the floor of the temple's antechamber. Dramatic. And it put her at an immediate disadvantage, forcing her to look up at her captors.

The grating above shuddered as something large and heavy strode over it. Not too far away, a Cat roared. A sitting duck, that's what she was. If this was what Jafar had had in mind when he'd said, "Trust me," well, she'd been right to fight him with everything she had.

Jafar. There was a name she was trying to forget.

Who would have guessed that he would turn out to be one of the damn shifters who guarded the temple and its treasures? "Enjoying your stay, my *femi*?" The familiar, raspy voice came from directly overhead. Looking up, she saw Jafar hunkered down over her prison.

Flipping up the grille that had sealed her into the cell, he reached down and extended one large hand.

She stared at it, considering. Stay here. Die.

Go with Jafar—and what?

Her merck-turned-Guardian hadn't made her any promises. He didn't need to. Right now he definitely had the upper hand in their battle of wills and they both knew it.

"Take my hand," he snapped.

She hesitated a moment longer and then slid her fingers into his. She was out of options.

Sliding his other hand along the smooth curve of her forearm, he cupped her elbow and then lifted. She rose effortlessly from the cell, the robe sliding back from her wrist. When she was steady on her feet, he strode toward the main gallery, pulling her along behind him.

"Where are you taking me?" she demanded.

"To the Amun Ra. To be sentenced."

Miu hated the bald starkness of his words. Was Jafar leading her to her execution? Her body felt oddly cold and the roar of the cats stalking the edges of the gallery retreated to a distant, metallic whine. Was that her breath coming in those frightened, shallow pants? She'd known that she could die in her line of work— she just hadn't really believed it would happen.

"Breathe," he instructed in clipped tones. "Don't fall apart on me now."

"You're not the one about to die. I think I'm entitled," she got out. The words opened up her throat and she sucked in oxygen gratefully.

He wrapped a large hand around her arm, halting her out of earshot of the cats in the gallery. "Listen to me," he said. "You're not going to die. I've made a bargain with the Amun Ra. But we've only got one chance to get this right. Are you listening?" He gave her a small shake.

"I'm going to be right here. Next to you. The Amun Ra has agreed to spare your life, but the Guardians don't know that. My pride brothers saw what you were up to in that burial chamber. Now we've got to convince them you're not guilty."

"I'm not guilty?"

His golden eyes bored into hers. "I'd say it's a matter of proof, love. Do you have anything stolen on you?"

The bag. Her hand patted her side out of habit, and she realized that, at some point, she'd lost her bag. Which meant she no longer had the necklace on her. And no one had actually seen her remove it from the princess's neck.

"Figured it out?" Jafar slanted her a look. "They may not believe you're innocent, but they can't prove you're guilty either. The Amun Ra knows the law must be upheld. It's the Guardians' duty."

"Right," she said sarcastically. "Your duty. Why do I get the feeling you Cats enjoy doing your duty a little too much?"

He dropped her hand. "We have a deal with the Valley. Made a promise, so we keep it. When the Guardians revealed themselves to the Valley elders generations ago, they met us with fear and loathing.

They didn't want us anywhere near their homes; they wanted us dead. Because we were different and that difference was a threat. But the Amun Ra showed the Valley men why they needed us. We've got a purpose here, and it's not just to thwart petty thieves like you."

She wasn't a *petty* thief. Not by a long shot.

"The Amun Ra ordered me to follow you yesterday," he continued. "We wanted to know what you were after, whether you would go down to the lower levels. There's a reason why we keep those off-limits. It's the same reason that the Valley elders are so glad to have us here. There are far more than thieves and dead men down there, *femi*. Some of those passages lead straight to Qaf. Trust me when I say that the Valley dwellers know very well they don't want *those* sorts of creatures coming through. Makes even the most bloody-minded of thieves seem tame. Have you ever faced an Ifrit?" he asked conversationally.

All she could do was shake her head. No. If she had, she'd have been dead.

"That's what I do, *femi*. Day in. Day out. I come up here to report on one of the latest Doorways to open between our world and theirs. Amun Ra wants to know when that happens, so he can dispatch more of us if necessary. See, the temple is more than just a place for sticking dead people and those shiny trinkets to which you're so partial. It's a battleground, love, and we're fighting a war here.

"And somehow," he continued, "you've gotten yourself mixed up in it. I think you know perfectly well that you're part of something much, much larger than you signed up for. You know what happens to the middleman," he said darkly.

"Woman," she corrected, licking suddenly dry lips.

"Woman." He nodded tersely and the hot gaze that moved down her body, lingering on her breasts for just a moment too long, told her he hadn't forgot she was a female. "I offered you my protection before. Heqet knows why, but I still want to stand between you and danger."

"This is your idea of protection?" She glanced at the Guardians descending from the gallery ahead.

He shot her an unfathomable look. "You're not dead yet," he pointed out. "And no one's touched a hair on your head. I've kept my end of the bargain."

"Some bargain," she groused.

He swung her around to face him. "I can offer you another bargain."

Hadn't she learned her lesson from the first bargain? "No, thanks," she said bitterly. "That first *bargain* of yours didn't work out too well for me, did it?"

"Doesn't matter now, does it?" He hauled her up against his body, turning her to face the Cats pacing toward them. Oh, gods. "You've got much larger problems on your hands now, love. Those Cats want you dead. Your only chance of staying alive is to do what I tell you to do, make some hard choices, and accept the consequences. Then you just might live another day."

"All right," she agreed. "Spell out the terms of this deal for me."

"You're going to agree to mate with me."

Miu stared at him speechlessly. She had to have heard him wrong.

He hadn't said *mate*.

Jafar knew damn well how she felt about the Cats

and this mating business. His hand tangled in her hair, pulling her head back so he could examine her face.

"I'm waiting for my answer," he said.

And apparently his blunt statement was all the proposal she was getting from him. Did he think she was desperate? She flinched at the ominous atmosphere in the gallery. Well, yeah, she was. She didn't need show-and-tell to make it clear that she wasn't going to enjoy whatever happened here. She just hadn't been expecting a mating.

Images flashed through her mind: Amun Ra, the nameless runner in the corridor, the *bells*. No way was she agreeing to any of that.

"Here's the deal," Jafar said. "You agree to mate with me. We go through all the little mating rituals that my people have—and I do mean *all*—and then you take me to your thief master."

"Lierr?"

"You take me to him, and I bring him back here. It's time he faced a little justice of his own."

She imagined Lierr out of her life for good. Her sister free. What choice did she really have?

"You've got a deal."

Just at that moment, the Guardians approaching them moved aside, letting through a commanding male. The Amun Ra. She blinked. Was this the same man she'd seen the night before, the man whose hands had parted, played with the hot, wet skin of his lover?

There was nothing soft or forgiving—or, Heqet help her, playful—about him now. He was all business as he strode through the circle of Cats.

"Well, well," he said. "Apparently, we didn't quite

clear the temple of yesterday's runners. I'm not sure we've ever had a participant who stretched her stay quite so long. You weren't interested in claiming a mate—nor, it would seem, the alternative prize? A dowry?"

She eyed Jafar but he seemed content to let her speak for herself. "No." To her irritation, her voice sounded thick. Nervous. Clearing her throat, she tried again. "I didn't come here for a dowry."

"What did you come here for?" The Amun Ra was not quite as large as the Guardians flanking him, but he gave the impression of lean, tensile strength. If he were a werebeast, she thought with a flash of realization, he would be serpentine. There was a look of cool cunning to his eyes that made her warier of him than of the large beasts encircling him. One misstep and he would skewer her himself.

"Nothing to say for yourself? That *is* too bad. I had convinced myself that you would spin us an elaborate tale. You're not the first, you know. There *have* been others who came here, all of you under false pretenses, wanting to help yourselves to something from the tombs or even—in one memorable instance—to cross over to Qaf itself. No one does succeed," he confided. "You all fail. I would be curious to know what brought you here. I'd pegged you as trouble—your eyes will always give you away, my dear—but not of that sort. I rather thought you more likely to gut one of my Guardians or even to be an assassin after one of the other competitors. A thief, though? That was disappointing news."

"Prove it," she said.

"Pardon me?" His eyes bored into her, giving away nothing.

"Prove it," she repeated. "Prove that I stole something—anything—from your temple."

"A challenge." He regarded her thoughtfully, playing his part in the drama perfectly. Miu was certain Jafar had told him what defense she would use. "Either you're bluffing, my dear, or you're quite certain I cannot. Which is it? I've the word of three Guardians that they found you in a burial chamber, the dearly departed grotesquely disturbed, and a spell-warded funeral necklace missing."

"But no one saw me take it. And I don't have it now, do I?"

"No." He regarded her intently. "Jafar argues that we should release you. He has agreed to take responsibility for you as his mate. I am content with that arrangement, but I must insist on one little variation to his terms."

The air in the chamber seemed to vanish.

Were those spots dancing in front of her eyes? Damn, she hated her weakness.

"First there must be punishment. We'll punish you and then he'll mate you." Dark eyes dismissed her. "Problem solved."

He smiled slyly at Jafar, who was scowling fiercely at him.

"You swore—" Jafar surged forward, but was restrained by several other Guardians.

"Your little *femi* will not be harmed, merely chastised," the Amun Ra said. "If you prefer, *you* may punish her, Jafar, while we watch."

Jafar shot him a look of pure hatred, then turned to Miu and swiftly grabbed her.

This wasn't part of their bargain! Struggling wildly, Miu tried to resist, but it was hopeless.

"Keep still, *femi*," he growled softly. "Better me than one of the others."

Jafar bent her ruthlessly over his arm so that her rear faced up. *Gods, what was he going to do to her?* The sharp crack of his palm sent heat blossoming across her cheeks—and heat flaring through her sex. She'd never imagined anything like the look on his face, either. Stern. Masterful. His eyes glowed with emotion, telegraphing a message straight to her sex. He was in charge here. Not her.

Plus, it felt so damn good.

Methodically, he paddled both sides of her ass until she wanted to rub the stinging cheeks—and then plunge her hand between her thighs and massage her engorged clit until she screamed. Each sharp jolt sent ribbons of liquid heat shooting through her sex until she couldn't keep back the moan that tore from her lips.

Without stopping, he murmured: "Not so bad, is it? I smell cream."

She creamed more. It was both embarrassing and arousing. If it had been one of the other males in the room, the casual possession in his voice would have angered her. But this was Jafar. The tough, reticent merck who'd vowed to keep her safe. She didn't want him to stop.

Particularly not when the orgasm of a lifetime hovered just out of reach.

His large hand shaped her ass almost casually, tracing the seam. Teasing her flesh. "Spread your legs more," he said. The harsh voice of a predator who'd spotted prey. "Show them how you cream for me."

Gathering the robe with one hand, he pulled it

ruthlessly over her head, dropping the fabric carelessly onto the floor. The silk slipped onto the floor like a lover's sigh, pooling over their feet. The heavy weight of his hand resting on the small of her back made her squirm, silently begging for more.

"Show them," he ordered again, and the heat built low and deep inside her. What *would* he do if she refused? He answered her unspoken question with a sharp stinging slap on her juicy sex.

She howled, arching up into his hand, dark crimson shards of pleasure shattering through her. Oh, this was a male who did indeed know how to punish—and to please. He expected her to obey, but had every intention of showing her pleasures she hadn't known existed. He landed three more stinging slaps and she could hear the graphic sounds of her own panting and the juicy sound of her sex, startlingly loud in the heated silence of the room.

Close. She was so close to orgasm. The white-hot pleasure built in harsh spasms, spilling from her very core. He could make her come like she had never come, with just one more stroke of his talented fingers.

Pleasure dazed her.

"Down here," he said, forcing her chin up until she met his eyes, "you will obey." His voice was a low growl.

"Yes," she hissed.

He nodded. "We are agreed then." What had she agreed to? He stroked his hand lightly over her sex. She was so wet and juicy that she almost came from the simple motion. She rubbed her thighs together. She no longer cared who was watching or where she was: she had to come, had to give in to the spasms.

She sensed the Amun Ra drawing closer. He grabbed her chin between his hands.

"You were a fool to enter my temple," the Amun Ra pronounced. "Do you know," he asked, "how long the Guardians go between females?" He did not wait for her to answer. She wasn't sure she could have strung two words together. Desire was humming through her, and his words washed over like the surf. "It is the summer season," he said. The heated press of male bodies around them moved closer. "The Guardians may have been set to guard this temple against the thievery of your kind, but they burn during these months. Even as the sun rises higher in the abovelands and bakes the sands to a glowing hotness, it heats them. It heats their blood, their bodies. They burn."

He slapped a hand around the thick, hard length that pushed upward from his loincloth. "Our flesh burns," he said in a low, dark voice, "and there is very little ease belowground. We wait until one of your kind is foolish enough to seek us out, to seek out our treasures and to pilfer. Then"—a slow, dark smile spread across his face—"then, we do find ease from the burning. We find it here." He turned to Jafar. "Finish it."

Jafar's thick fingers parted her soaked flesh. Oh, Heqet save her. With Amun Ra and the entire pride watching, he stroked and teased and penetrated her. Spreading her wide, he stabbed first one finger, then two, three, into her dripping sex.

With a scream, she finally came in great spasms, riding Jafar's fingers for all to see.

CHAPTER ELEVEN

Her Cat had gotten his point across.

Loud and clear.

Miu had never done anything like that before.
Heqet knew, she'd never contemplated making such a
public exhibition out of herself.

Such a public pleasure.

But before she could even plumb the true depths of
her humiliation, one of the Guardians stepped forward, breaking the silence. His eyes crawled over her,
dissecting and dismissing what he saw. She could smell
trouble brewing.

"I challenge your right to mate this female," he
growled.

"Don't do this, Hebon." Jafar's eyes were cold.
Clearly, he didn't care for the challenge.

"She ran with the Hunt yesterday." Hebon's gaze
was making her skin crawl. "No one caught her. She
wears no bells."

Jafar nodded shortly. "Not yet," he amended. "But
she will. Now that this misunderstanding about the
necklace is cleared up. You heard the Amun Ra."

The Amun Ra came closer.

"Gentlemen," he said. "I believe I hear fighting words."

The rest of the pride cleared a space as the two males squared off against each other. In the next moment, the tall Guardians were morphing into enormous, growling lions ready to tear each other's throats out.

Jafar could see Hebon's anger: the Guardian's aura was a rich crimson. Hebon wanted blood. Fine with Jafar. Lose this battle—and he lost Miu.

He knew why Hebon was so angry at Jafar's defense of the *femi*. Hebon remembered what had happened the last time Jafar had let a thief go. Eventually, that thief had died, but not before he'd killed Hebon's mate. No, Hebon had every right to question Jafar's decision.

Jafar couldn't afford to be wrong this time.

"Can't trust her, mate." The male's eyes met his fiercely, his voice thickening as he spoke through the Cat's mouth. "She's got you running in circles." Hebon didn't bother adding *like last time*, but Jafar heard the words anyhow.

"Not the same," he bit out. His paws found the familiar rhythm of the sparring circle, gliding smoothly over the marble as his eyes watched his opponent's body. Sooner or later, Hebon would betray his next move.

"What makes her different?"

Miu *hadn't* come through one of the Doorways between the realms, for one. She was no Qaf dweller. He'd bet his life on that. And he didn't think she'd plunge a dagger into a man—or his mate—just because she could. Oni had taken the knife in her throat, the smooth edge slicing open the white skin straight through to the ivory knobs of her spine. Even as Jafar had gutted her murderer, as he should have done when she'd first appeared, he'd known it was too late for Oni.

"Oni's dead," he said, but Hebon shook his head, striking out with lethal claws. Jafar rolled quickly to one side, sweeping a foreleg out as he did. His paw struck Hebon in the vulnerable skin behind the joint.

Hebon rolled, coming fluidly to his feet on the opposite side of the circle.

"Shift," Hebon demanded. "Meet me male to male."

Less safe that way, but it was the man's right. Challenges were usually conducted in Cat form because injuries were less likely to be fatal, but it was the challenger's right to choose. Jafar shifted.

"Maybe Oni is dead," Hebon spat. "And maybe not. She could be a death spirit. There might be some way to bring her back. And even if there's not"—his blade crashed into Jafar's with jarring force—"I'm not letting one of your 'finds' make history repeat itself. Your female needs to die, Jafar."

The blows landed with devastating force.

And yet Jafar knew they were both holding back. Had been friends for too long, despite the bitter words. Even now, he wanted to disable and not to cripple. It was an even match.

Around them, the Cats pressed closer. The air was still and tense with anticipation. Heat built until sweat dripped from the torsos of the circling fighters, making the floor a slippery death trap. One misstep could spell the end.

There.

Opportunity.

Jafar's blade tore through Hebon's chest, ripping into muscle and lodging against the bone. Blood poured from the wound.

"Change," Jafar growled. For a moment, he thought Hebon would refuse, would allow himself to bleed out onto the floor of the temple.

Then, with a snarl, Hebon changed, the man's wounds slowly closing as the lion slumped onto the floor.

Jafar brought his blades up to his chest in a gesture of respect. Inclining his head toward the Amun Ra, he stepped deliberately out of the circle.

"No kill?" The Amun Ra regarded him over steepled fingers.

Jafar grunted a negative, already striding toward his mate. He didn't need to compound his mistakes by killing a friend.

The Amun Ra reached out, laying a pale hand on Jafar's arm. "Wait a moment." Jafar's head swung around, lips peeling back in a grimace. Now that he'd won the right to bell her, he wanted his mate. Miu.

"If you have something to say, say it," Jafar snapped.

"Manners, Jafar." The Amun Ra smiled slightly. "She's all yours, but a piece of advice: Keep a close eye on her. We both know she's less innocent than she appears. Catch her with her fingers in the pie again and there'll be no rescuing her. Whatever she really came here for, she's leaving without it. Anyone who removes that necklace from the temple is under a death sentence." Power surged around him. "Got it?"

Oh, Jafar did. Very much so.

His little *femi* still looked stunned at all that had happened. No doubt she was also apprehensive of what was to come.

He felt a moment's regret at the punishment he'd been forced to mete out. But it had been the only way to save her life, he reminded himself. What the Amun Ra commanded had to be carried out.

In the aftermath of Miu's disciplining, the raw sexuality of the Cats was a shimmering haze of need rising from the gallery's occupants. It was critical that he claim her. Now. With the mating bells.

Just the thought of placing them on her body—in her body—made him bite back a groan. The few women in the gallery above wore bells around slender throats, or dangling from ears. Others wore them in less obvious places. Depended on the woman, Jafar knew—and her mate.

As he approached Miu, he considered each tempting spot where he might place the bells: the delicious curve of her ear; the sweet indentation of her belly button; the plump, inward curve of her sex. The bells should always brush the skin, a sensual tease and a mate's promise. Just as she would never escape the bells' presence and would come to crave the soft brush of the metal, so, too, would she come to crave her mate.

Bending his head, he took her lips in a hard kiss. The males around them raised their own blades in their right hands, pressing them over their hearts. When Sanur hesitated—perhaps his pride brother also worried about the wisdom of Jafar's decision—Jafar glared until Sanur pulled his own knife. He would have their acknowledgment—and he would have it now.

"I claim the female," Jafar repeated. "She is *my* mate."

Now she pulled against his grasp, but he had woven his fingers so deep into her hair that she had no choice but to keep still in his grasp. He lowered his head again. Half the males there would expect him to screw her in the sparring circle in a public display of possession, but he had no intention of taking matters quite that far.

Her teeth biting down on his tongue startled him. The copper taste of his own blood filled his mouth and he pulled back, swearing.

"I am not your mate," she hissed. Her eyes glittered with unfamiliar emotion, but it was her feet that he should have been watching. Her left knee swung smoothly upward, driving toward his chest in a powerful roundhouse kick. "But *you* can be *mine*."

He blocked her kick effortlessly. Amun Ra had been right: her eyes betrayed her. They were a seething pool of emotion.

"Not the deal we made, love," he whispered against her ear. "But feel free to try to persuade me otherwise when we are alone. Right now, it's time to pay the piper."

Chapter Twelve

"Run," Jafar growled into her ear.

His fingers rubbed the smooth skin of Miu's shoulders, kneading the tense muscles. Part of her wanted to lean into the caress, but that was the crazy part. The part that whispered she wanted more of this male.

"Why?" She shoved at his chest, demanding he give her space. He didn't budge.

"Because," he said after a long, hot silence, "I thought you'd prefer a head start. Having just fought a challenge with an old friend for your favors, I'm torn between paddling your delicious little ass for the second time tonight—and fucking the living daylights out of you. If you'd like an audience, by all means stay here. Otherwise, I suggest you head up that corridor." He indicated an unfamiliar corridor with a jerk of his thumb.

She fought a flush. Arrogant bastard. Who did she think he was? *Her mate*, a small voice whispered.

He pressed his lips against the back of her neck and she felt the wet flick of his tongue all the way down to her toes. A melting sensation unfurled inside her. She was furious with him, she reminded herself.

"Don't challenge me now, *femi*." His voice was a

sensual warning that she didn't know if she wanted to heed—or deliberately flout. "I'm going to take you now and you agreed."

He snarled—*snarled*—at her, a low, dark rumble at the back of his throat that should have scared the living daylights out of her. It shouldn't have excited her. Dimly, she recognized that her heart was pounding too loudly, her breath coming in small, hard pants.

And not due to fear.

"Mine," Jafar said. "Every inch of you is mine now. I've earned the privilege and I've probably lost a good friend over you. Convince me you're worth it." The spicy scent of his pheromones surrounded her. Made her sex weep for the pleasure he'd shown her earlier. "The only choice you've got now is where and, if you're very good"—his mouth curled—"how. One thing I can guarantee: I'm going to lick me a path from here"—his fingers swirled a teasing pattern against the tender skin at the base of her neck—"all the way down to the sweet bits." His finger traced a blunt path down the curve of her spine, pressing her into his hard, hot flesh.

He slowly thrust one blade into its sheath at his waist in a strangely sexual gesture. One large hand stroked gently over the sharp edge, drawing a bead of blood from his forefinger. He raised the injured digit to his mouth and licked the blood from it.

"So, run, my *femi*. But I'm going to be right behind you, every step of the way."

She ran. In a completely uncharacteristic response, Miu darted away from him and down the corridor he'd indicated, while his graphic description of what he

wanted to do—what he was going to do—replayed itself over and over in her head.

The corridors were dark. Empty. Even her moon
senses were of no use in the Stygian darkness that surrounded her. Finally, spotting what appeared to be a
room with a door, she darted inside, then held her
breath and waited, aware of the male following her
almost soundlessly.

Behind her, the door opened and closed with deliberate finality. Jafar made no attempt to hide his approach. The raw sensuality of the man striding toward
her made moisture slick her sex; she heard a satisfied
masculine chuckle from the darkness.

"Alone at last."

He knew what his hard voice did to her. That her
sex was swelling with anticipation, remembering the
masterful touch of his fingers, petting, stroking the
soft skin until she curled into his touch. She'd had
other lovers, but none who made her feel this achy des-
peration for his touch. None she would have allowed
to make her feel this way.

Her eyes adjusted to the blackness, the outlines of
the stone chamber coming slowly into focus. Somewhere far above them, a bit of the roof had fallen in,
allowing a little light to penetrate. This was no ordinary underground room, she saw. It was a kind of
cenote, a naturally occurring hollow where water collected. Most of the chamber was nothing but a deep
pool. Jafar stood by its edge. The hard planes of his
bare chest rippled as his hands went to the waistband
of his linen wrap and pulled the material down over
his lean hips. His scar gleamed, pale in the dim light of

their hideaway, but her gaze was pulled to the large erection he sported. The thick length grew more as she watched, the broad tip of him ripe with color and need. A clear drop of liquid escaped and she groaned. The knowledge that he wanted her as much as she did him aroused her more than she'd thought possible.

"Tossed virgin sacrifices in there, the Valley dwellers did, once upon a time."

"How very pagan." She licked her lips. He was glorious in his nudity, worthy of pagan worship himself. "Are you considering doing the same?"

"Do you qualify?"

He knew she didn't. His large hands skimmed lightly over the rocks around him, finding a natural depression that formed a sort of chair. He stroked the smooth rock indentation and her mouth went dry.

"Come here," he said. And then, "Place your leg here," as calmly as if he were offering her a cup of tea. "Hesitate," he added pleasantly, "and I will assume that our bargain is off. The Cats would be delighted."

Mastered. The sensation made her feel both vulnerable and aroused. He'd save her life and give her what she craved—but for a price. She'd answer to him. Sitting gingerly where he indicated, she swung her leg up and over the arm of the chair. The exposure was both overwhelming and titillating. In this position, her legs fell apart, but the worst part was that she wanted to show herself to him. He hadn't asked her to do anything she didn't secretly want. He examined her sex as he would an early-summer plum hanging from the branches of a fruit tree in a forcing house. It was as juicy now as any plum could be. Her lips parted with a slippery tingle as she placed her leg as Jafar directed.

He leaned forward from his perch beside her. "Very good," he praised. "You are wet. Put your fingers on your pussy," he directed, "and hold your lips apart for me."

Part of her still wanted to protest. "You might master me here," she gasped, letting her fingers fall to her waist. "But only here—"

His dark eyes held hers. "Lower," he demanded. "I want to see."

Shuddering, she let her fingers move lower. Jafar's eyes darkened. Whether he knew it or not, her Guardian wasn't as in control as he thought he was. He *wanted* her. She loved his reactions, the blazing light in his eyes, the almost imperceptible tightening of his muscles as he held himself back from pouncing on her. Her flesh swelled more, growing damper and wetter and slicker. In another minute, the cream would slip from her pussy and onto the unforgiving stone. Deliberately, she eased herself open, watching his face.

"Have you displayed yourself like this before?" Polite curiosity colored his voice, but his eyes were that hot, molten gold she loved so much. Blazing with heat.

He slipped the tip of one finger inside her and her sex gaped greedily around the digit.

His thumb gently stroking the side of her pussy drove all thought from her head. A bolt of pleasure streaked through her. Knowing fingers. An urge to push down on the invading finger almost overwhelmed her. "Imagine how those Cats in the gallery would have taken you if you had not agreed to our bargain. They toy with their prey before killing, you know." He looked down, examining her slick flesh with a heated gaze, and pleasure shot through her. "I'll be large, more than you can take, but they would have had you, one after another. They would have crammed all that cock into your pussy until you howled."

Holding her gaze, he slid two fingers into her clenching pussy. "Would you howl," he asked her, "from the pleasure or the pain of their possession?"

The fingers stroked gently but firmly. "Put your fingers on your clit," he ordered. "Obedience. That was our bargain."

Greedily, she did as he ordered. Her fingers pulled and teased the turgid bit of flesh. The orgasm was boiling up inside her and then the spasms seized her flesh, milking her Cat's fingers.

He stared down at her wet, clenching sex and smiled slowly. "Every day," he promised. "I'm going to make you come every single day."

In the semidark, she did not see where he'd been keeping the bells. All she knew was that the feel of the metal moving over her was a cool shock, the bells warming rapidly as they slid over her skin, along the curve of her throat and down to circle both breasts and her nipples.

"Sweet," he said, pausing to explore the soft indent of her belly button. His hands skimmed lightly down her thighs with a soft chime. His hands fastened something—the chain—around her waist and the cool hard-sweet touch of the metal followed as fingers delved with shocking bluntness between her thighs, stroking the stiff clit and pushing the bells inside her.

"Where," she panted, "do you Cats usually place them?" The male in the catacombs had left too quickly.

She'd seen nothing there. Now, she felt Jafar's hard mouth stretch in a smile against the taut skin of her belly.

"Wherever brings our partners the greatest pleasure. Some like to wear the bells for all to see; those choose the curve of an ear, the throat, or wrist. Others are naughtier."

She could believe that.

"We can find out where you like them best." He tugged gently and pleasure exploded inside her, a liquid burning rushing through her where he'd placed the bells. As if every nerve ending in her body were now intimately, directly connected to Jafar. She could feel his heart pounding and the loud rush of his blood. Then there was an incredible pulling sensation toward him. Sound roared in her ears, her entire body thrumming with tension. Desire. Unbearable heat.

Dark words, poetic and brutal, poured from Jafar's lips. "To you, my Huntress, I offer my soul. In you I trust and in your keeping place my soul. Your enemies are my enemies. Your lair is my lair. I defend you at all costs and none shall reach you but through me. You are the pride of my heart, hidden in the shadow of my arms from those who hunt us. You are my Huntress, the light of my life and always by my side. Call on me and I come eternally."

With each word, his fingers rubbed wickedly against the bells he had placed inside her. Fiery darts of pleasure rippling through her, she *felt* the mating bond snap into place between them. She could *hear* the blood rushing through his veins and the frantic pounding of his heart. When he reached out a hand toward her, she *felt* the smooth glide of muscles and—his Cat. She knew Jafar's werebeast was close to breaking free, that he was fighting not to change in her arms.

Miu was liquid fire in his arms, deliciously sensitive to his touch. As the chain of bells locked into place and the words of the mating ritual poured from him, pulled out of him by an unseen force, the mating bond activated. Bound them together with shooting tendrils of sensation that connected her body to his and his to hers in ways he couldn't have imagined. Every luscious stroke of his fingers against her sex plucked at his own sensitized nerve endings. Sent the pleasure he gave her straight back to him. He fought to control himself, to keep the werebeast locked away. Away from her.

If he felt what she felt, would he feel her pain as well?

It was almost as if this new connection between them would not end when he slipped himself free of her body. That they were truly bound together, forever. Just mating with Miu had made him more vulnerable than he'd ever dreamed possible.

Her hot, wet sex clenched around him in a sensuous demand. "More," she ordered. "Give me more, Jafar." Just who had mastered whom?

"Yes." Oh, he'd give her more. He had to give her more. "Open up," he growled into her ear. Placing his hands on her thighs, he moved them firmly apart. She hesitated, gasping as her sex slowly parted again, the lips parting like well-oiled petals in a smooth rush that he felt in every inch of his own cock.

Oh, gods above. Pink and glistening, she was spread open before him like the hauraru flower that bloomed in the abovelands. He caught the same rich, exotic scent as he inhaled deeply. Moisture ran from her sex, the small opening already fluttering in tiny spasms. He stroked a finger around her hole, rubbing the bells against a particularly sensitive spot, and she moaned, her flesh clinging to his.

His cock twitched wildly, alive with the pleasure of the same stroke. Mirroring hers. Each touch he gave her came back to him a hundredfold through the mating bond, his cock swelling to the same rhythm as her clenching pussy.

Leaving the tip of his finger hooked in her hot sex, he bent his lips to the stiff clit that begged for his attention. Moaning softly, she pressed her legs wider—no reluctance, no fear of the Guardian between her thighs. Satisfaction and something stronger throbbed through him.

"Pleasure now," he promised, need making his voice harsh.

She panted beneath him and, for the first time since he had been ruthlessly inducted into the ranks of the Guardians, he felt something new.

"Pleasure for my *femi*." His voice was a harsh whisper of need. Pinioning her hands behind her back with one of his, he used his shoulders to spread her thighs and her sex wider, and then he ate her. His tongue licked roughly, demandingly at the hard kernel of her clit. He suckled her without mercy, withdrawing each time she neared the edge, withholding the orgasm from her.

"You will not come," he promised. "Not until I am inside you."

"Wanna bet?" She stared up at him, dazed with her

arousal. Oh, gods, he loved the sight of her. But her words? He laughed darkly. Oh, that was a challenge she would lose. He had spent a lifetime learning sexual restraint, sexual discipline. It was time he taught her, too.

Moving his lips slowly back up her body, he finally claimed her mouth. He stood her up in the water then, ignoring her protest as he turned her around, bent her over the large stone where she'd been sitting. He grabbed both her hands, anchoring them on the rock with one of his. He was in control. She would not come until he allowed it.

Jafar nudged her legs wide with his thighs and she could feel his cock at her entrance. This time, when he held her swollen, wet lips apart, he removed the bells, placing himself inside her instead.

She shuddered with the pleasure. His mouth had teased and tormented her, denying her the relief that hovered so near.

This was better.

Thicker, fuller, sliding in and out with a sensuous rhythm that made her want to squirm beneath the heavy weight of the male body that pressed her down.

And yet he held her still, prevented her from grinding back against him to take for herself the orgasm that she needed so badly. In. Out.

The water of the cenote was warm, lapping teasingly at her pussy as he forced her legs wider still.

She didn't care. All she wanted was that orgasm he held so tantalizingly out of her reach—and that he was strong enough to give her. This partner, she thought with delight before pleasure rendered her incoherent, this partner could make her come for hours.

His lower body thrust in a faster, deeper rhythm, surging inside her with powerful strokes that claimed her, marked her as his.

"Now," he promised darkly, sliding the hot, thick length of cock deep inside her aching sex. "Now you will come. With me."

He rode her with deep, fast, rough strokes. One bronzed male hand slipped around her body to find her aching clit.

She could only keen with pleasure in response. His fingers stroked and tugged at her clit, massaging in deep circles around the pulsing point.

The orgasm, when it came, ripped through them both.

Chapter Thirteen

What could she say to him?

Thanks for the most erotic night of my life? True, but the sentiment tipped her hand a wee bit.

Do it again?

Yeah, she liked that one.

Let me go?

Fortunately, she didn't have to choose.

She woke up alone.

Jafar had apparently carried her off to his private chambers and left her there, mistakenly believing sex had resolved matters between them once and for all. A small smile curved her lips. Poor kitty. He was in for a shock if he thought she'd settle in to being a compliant little mate after one night of sex, no matter how mind-blowingly satisfying.

Snap out of it. No time for mooning after the male. So what if he were the hottest thing she'd ever run across? The mark on her forearm twinged, reminding her that she had precisely one week to retrieve the necklace and take it to Lierr. Her hired guard Ebo was patiently waiting just outside the Valley. Just the travel from here to Shympolsk would take a week. Time was running out.

She couldn't afford to be sidetracked by the bargain she'd made with Jafar. So what if last night had been the best, most intense sex of her life? Just recalling Jafar's feral intensity made her sex cream. Licking and biting. The sexy growl that erupted from his throat as he thrust deep inside her. He'd had her clenching and moaning and seeing red when she closed her eyes. He was that good. All right, so she'd fallen in with one sexy kitty—but she still had her priorities straight. Get the necklace. Leave the Valley. Exchange the necklace for her sister.

Except she had acquired a different piece of jewelry altogether: Jafar's bells. She could *feel* the damn things whenever she thought about it: first the soft press of the chain, and then the luscious slickness where the bells stroked her pussy. The slide of the metal against her labia as arousal built in a slow burn. Before she could stop herself, she stretched luxuriously beneath the thin fabric of the sheet, drawing the teasing metal caress up and down sensitive skin.

Stop, she scolded herself. There was no time for self-indulgence. No more time to think about the Cat who'd tried to master her.

She'd kept her end of the bargain. She'd mated with Jafar. Now she needed to be on her way.

A god-awful racket coming from outside the room had her wrapping the sheet around herself and striding to the wide arch of a window. The opening looked out onto an interior courtyard currently being used for weapons practice.

Tracing the noise to its source, she was reminded of just why it was wise to fear the Guardians. The warriors were sparring. Hard bodies collided, filling the air with male grunts and a musky, alluring scent. Counting quickly, she spotted more than thirty males down there. How was she to get past that many shifters to go looking for the necklace again? They dominated the open space, prowling about with lazy, lethal grace.

Amun Ra had himself an army.

Behind her, the door opened. Closed. The cinnamon-rich smell of bread filled the air. Good. Apparently, kitty wasn't planning on starving her. When her stomach rumbled, he laughed.

"Catch."

A cloth-wrapped bundle flew toward her and she plucked it unerringly out of the air. Breakfast. Unwrapping a flaky pastry and sinking her teeth into its sugary glaze, she perched on the windowsill and stared out.

"I'm curious," he said, watching her lick sugar off her lips. "How'd you get involved?"

"With what?" She rooted around in the basket for a fresh pastry; there was no point in letting perfectly good food go to waste.

"With Lierr."

"You've been to Shympolsk?"

"Once or twice." When she raised an eyebrow, he smiled. "We don't *have* to remain in the Valley, love. We have been known to travel a bit."

"Well, there weren't that many options in Shympolsk for my sort of girl. I was the mixed sort," she explained, watching his face. Some people found her daemon blood offensive. She'd assumed a shifter would be all right with that sort of a birthright, but you never knew. "Human mother. Daemon father. Most of the city residents dislike the daemonkind." And that was an understatement. She'd seen daemons plucked limb from limb when a crowd got angry. "So I was fortunate to get a job at the tea gardens." When she was small, she'd fetched and carried, made herself useful in a dozen small ways. When she'd started developing, the garden's proprietor had been less sure what to do with her. Most of his girls danced and poured tea, some of them doing a lucrative sideline in whoring, but she was a hands-off kind of girl.

"It's a long step from tea-garden girl to thief," he pointed out calmly. "Maybe you'd care to explain how you made that leap."

"Leverage."

He raised an eyebrow, but she shook her head. "He came to the gardens one day."

"Lierr?"

"Yes. Of course, none of us knew who he was. He was just getting his start then; his first apprentices were only beginning to make names for themselves. The thefts had got some notice, but he hadn't pulled off anything spectacular. Not yet."

"He was recruiting?" Jafar's hands tightened.

Why should he care? It happened every day in Shympolsk.

"I don't think he ever stops." It was one of the reasons why she was so desperate to get her sister out of his grasp. Eventually, he'd figure out another use for Lore besides leverage. "He watched us for quite some time, ordering tea, sampling the gardens' pleasures." He'd had a dancer on each knee, but even as a six year-old, she'd known he wasn't paying those girls any attention. No, his real focus had been fixed elsewhere. He'd sat there, still and watchful, the dark folds of his robe pooling around him in a graceful circle that had fascinated her younger self.

"He recruits children?"

"Children learn better. Faster. And neither of us had any sort of future to look forward to. I would have ended up dancing in the gardens, entertaining customers on the side. What Lierr had to offer was better."

"Why you?"

"I was quick. Observant." And very, very vulnerable. He'd seen her for what she was. One of the many orphans who struggled to survive on the streets, but with one critical difference: she had a sister. He'd recognized the potential at once. He'd bought the two girls from the tea garden, used Lore to coerce Miu into joining his thieves.

"And he's the one who told you to come for the necklace."

"I had to."

"Why?"

"Because I'm desperate," she admitted. Was that her voice that sounded so tired? "He has my sister, Jafar, and since he's not overly endowed in the scruples department, he'll hurt her or worse if I don't return, necklace in hand. When I signed on with him, I agreed to perform one hundred thefts. I've successfully completed ninety-nine. I only owed him one more. This was the last one, if I succeeded. After that, I'm a free agent.

"Yesterday, you said that if I led you to Lierr, you'd bring him back here to face justice. I don't know if you meant that, but with you or without you, I've got to get the necklace and take it to Shympolsk. And I've got less than a week to do it."

Lierr was capable of anything. In the twenty years she'd learned from him and worked for him, she'd never found anything remotely resembling a scrap of conscience in the thief master. He was cold to the bone. If it took hurting Lore to make Miu come back, Lierr would do it in a heartbeat. And he wouldn't care what obstacles Miu faced on her return journey—Lierr simply didn't accept excuses. Ever. That trait had guaranteed him success as a thief master.

"Right." Jafar eyed her. "So you need to get out of the Valley. With the necklace. Fast."

She nodded her head. "Will you help me?"

"I will. That was part of our bargain last night. There's just one problem."

She didn't like the direction in which this conversation was headed. "Are you telling me you're changing the terms of our deal?" Over her dead body.

He shook his head. "Not me. Amun Ra. He will allow you to leave this temple, to return to Lierr. But—"

"Here it comes," she added bitterly.

"But he will not permit you to take the necklace with you. The necklace stays here because it is too dangerous to be allowed out into the world."

"And you agree with him? You made me a promise!"

"I do agree with him that the necklace is dangerous and taking it out of the temple is fraught with danger. But," he shrugged, "I see no other way to coax your Lierr out of his hidey-hole so quickly. You said yourself that he will give you no more time to bring the necklace to him, that he may even now be hurting your sister. No," he pressed a finger against her lips, "I don't think he will kill her. Not yet. Not until he sees for himself whether or not you can bring him the necklace."

"He'll see when I show up and can't flash him the jewels."

"Yes, he will. And that is why I believe we will need to take matters into our own hands."

She stared at him. "Into our own hands?"

He answered her question by casually dropping the necklace into her lap in a smooth rush of metal. "While you were sleeping, I went back to the burial chamber and retrieved this little bauble. A lot easier for me to pull off than for you. I will take both you and the necklace out of the temple and to Lierr. We will let him lay his hands on this necklace that he wants so badly."

"You want me to be bait."

"It's what we agreed on last night. I believe I can still take down Lierr for you—and rescue your sister. But we're going to be up against both the thieves and the Guardians, so you must decide whether you want to take these odds—or not."

"With you."

"Yes, with me. I never fail," he said stiffly. "Guardians do not fail. It is unacceptable."

"Never?"

"No. Guardians who fail are tossed back into the vortex from which we were called." His eyes darkened. "It is most unpleasant and quite fatal. No Guardian goes willingly into the vortex, nor do we cross that border unless we are forced to do so."

"Like being fired."

"No," he said. "Not precisely like being fired."

* * *

Being sent to the vortex was far worse than merely being fired.

The vortex was an endless swirling, empty space. It pulled a Guardian's essence in so many directions that he was literally shredded. Although those shreds could then be reknit into new beings, the Guardian himself was gone. The agonizing pain of stretching and pulling was unforgettable, even if life before the vortex was no longer recalled. The Amun Ra had discovered the secret of knitting Guardians together out of the vortex and had put their knowledge to work when he required guards for his temple. Invincible, otherworldly guards.

Jafar had no distinct memories, of course, of those moments before his body had been pulled together from the darkness swirling in the vortex, but he did remember the sharp pain that cut like a knife. He had no desire to relive it.

Ever.

And yet if he left the temple with the necklace, if he were caught by the Amun Ra, then that was where he would go. But for Miu, he would take the risk. She was his mate now; she wore his bells. He would do whatever was necessary to protect her.

He seated himself on the low bed beside her, and began laying out an arsenal of weapons and leather travel wear for both of them. She looked at the blades and bows as though she half expected his brother Guardians to come bursting through the chamber door at any moment.

"So how do we get the necklace out of here?" she asked.

"This is no ordinary temple, *femi*."

"Believe me, I've noticed," she muttered.

"When we take the necklace out of the temple, we will trigger alarms, *femi*. Wards."

"I've heard stories about snakes. Nasty reptilians aiming for all of my soft, warm spots. Any truth to that?"

He arched an eyebrow. She had warm spots he would like to explore himself; he thought of licking that pink sex and was pleased to see that she squirmed.

"Not just snakes," he admitted.

She cringed. "There are more traps?"

"The Guardians themselves will be our biggest problem. Once they sense which way we are heading, they will move to cut us off at the exit point I choose." His eyes held hers calmly. "This time, there will be no trial. This time, my brothers will consider you to have been warned by your previous encounter with our kind."

"And?" Her voice sounded a little anxious.

He pulled her up against his hard chest. One large hand stroked the curve of her throat.

"We Guardians have strong appetites and spend much of our time alone. And the summer heat drives all of our kind strongly. Since their orders will be to kill you and since their blood will have been heated by the recent Hunt," he shrugged, "I imagine the un-mated pride members would toy with you before they finish you off."

"Even though I'm your mate?" she shot back. "No paws-off policy with you Cats?"

"But are you really my mate?" he demanded. "Yes, you wear my bells, but I'd be willing to bet that you've been lying here all morning, scheming how you can get out of the temple on your own. I saw yesterday just how little you want a partner."

"You got the necklace for me." She smiled sweetly at him, but he didn't trust her sudden docility. "Of course you're my partner."

"Convince me," he said, leaning back. "Convince me that you *want* to be my mate."

"What," she asked, her voice sinking to a low rasp, "would I have to do to convince you?"

Miu's eyes flicked to the enormous bulge in his black loincloth. Jafar wore only the small loincloth, which wrapped snuggly around his hips and left little to the imagination. The heavy crest of his cock strained above the fabric; the dark plum-colored tip with its small drop of clear liquid fascinated her. He wanted her again, she thought, dazed. The heat of his body and his eyes threatened to overwhelm her.

His eyes challenged her. "Everything. You would have to do everything. Would you have sex with a shifter again, my Miu?"

His hand stroked down her arm, massaging the muscles and tugging gently on her fingertips, releasing a small sting of pleasure. Relaxing and arousing her. She wanted him to repeat that same stroke until he buried his fingers in her sex, petting and pinching until she exploded around him.

"You can ask me to take you." He stared at her, noting her interest. "And I will give you pleasure. You are my chosen mate. It is my duty. My pleasure."

Yes, he would.

He had.

"Or you can go through that door alone, try to find your own way out of the temple," he said. His hand shaped her breast, parting the silk clasps of her robe until it fell back around her waist. Teasing the nipple, building the heat in her. "I can pleasure you. Or," he pinched her nipple gently, creating a sweet sting of pain, "you can take your chances with the other Guardians. You must choose. Make the right choice, my Miu, and I will protect you from their less-than-tender mercies."

She placed her hands deliberately on his chest, feeling the hot burning muscles leap beneath her touch. "Are you so merciless to your mates? Show me," she purred. "Why don't you show me what they will do to me?"

"They will savage these," he promised. He took her nipple into his hot mouth. She could feel the heat transferring from him. Building.

She pushed the robe off, feeling the teasing trickle of beads of sweat rolling down her exposed flesh. The heat was incredible. "Doesn't the heat end?"

He shook his head. "Never."

"How can you stand it?" She wanted to scream from the sensations.

He shook his head. "No more questions. No demands. Show me you wish to be my mate."

His hand stroked down her back, delving between the curve of her cheeks. The fingers of his other hand rested on her pussy.

"Open yourself for me," he ordered.

She pulled the lips of her sex apart and shuddered at the agonizing rush of sensation as they parted. The swollen, damp feel of her own flesh met her. She was slippery with her own juices. His fingers did not hesitate, driving deep inside her flesh, probing, finding a hidden sweet spot that made her arch her back and whimper with the pleasure.

"You could take many men this way," he promised. "One cock." He shoved and his own slowly slipped inside her. "Maybe two. They would try."

His fingers pushed inexorably inside. Full. So full. Stretched. Aroused and vulnerable. And yet there was a thread of gentleness beneath the dark promise of his words. His fingers moved in counterpoint to his cock until the pleasure threatened to tear her apart.

"There would be a half dozen at the least," he continued. "More waiting. One or two to take your mouth. As many again for your pussy. And then," his other hand stroked down her back, "another for your ass." Dark pleasure unfolded in her. His finger stroked the smooth, hidden skin between the opening to her pussy and her asshole, tapping lightly so that pleasure strummed through her.

"Have you been taken here, Miu?" he demanded. "Have your lovers stood you up against the wall, made you hold apart your own cheeks while they reamed your pretty pink ass?" Gods, she couldn't think. Could only feel as he filled her and filled her.

He pulled free from her body with a wet sound. "Tell me," he demanded. She couldn't think, couldn't respond to his erotic authority as dark, forbidden images flooded her mind. A fantasy male parting her cheeks with a darker promise, the blunt fingertip tracing the seam of her ass and then forcing its way into her asshole, twisting until a dark pleasure spiraled through her. Only his finger, moving ruthlessly in and out of the enveloping darkness while she moaned helplessly, trapped by that single digit, connected to him by an unspeakable pleasure that followed the dark pleasure-burn of each invasion.

Jafar could do this for her.

Would do it for her. If she could convince him she really wanted to be his mate. But the words of submission would not leave her lips.

"And why shouldn't I take my chances with them, Jafar?" Pulling free, she twisted slowly away from him. "Why not?"

"Because," he said fiercely, "for them it will not be a mating game. They will not stop and they will not care if you find pleasure. For them, it will be a death sentence that they carry out, and you will find, my *femi*, that you do not care for sadism even if you might enjoy it when"—his eyes darkened—"I paddle your ass for you again."

Truth, she acknowledged. She'd seen sex slaves before, slaves who were expendable and whose owners were both harsh and brutal. "Why else?"

"Because," he said with a groan, "even if I am one of the temple's Guardians, I cannot bear to hand you over to them. I would keep you, my mate."

He gently pulled her toward him again, and she did not protest as he parted the robe once more and plunged his cock deep inside her. She screamed with the pleasure of it, as he drove into her again and again, seeking and finding their peak together.

He gave her the pleasure he'd promised, and more. Even though she had not spoken the words he'd wanted to hear.

CHAPTER FOURTEEN

Miu discovered Jafar had not been exaggerating when he'd said the Guardians would sense which way they were heading. They heard the sounds of pursuit almost as soon as they entered the obscure tunnel exit he had chosen for their escape.

"You must listen to me," he warned. "They're already after us. I will do what I can to stop them—but you must promise you will do precisely as I ask." He laid a warning finger across her lips. "There is no time to dispute this. You know what we're up against now. Are we in this together? You must decide. Trust me. Don't trust me. If you would prefer to take your own chances, I can send you out the escape shaft. I can stay behind. It will buy you twenty minutes, maybe more, depending on whether Amun Ra sends all his Guardians or merely the best after us."

She let herself imagine that sort of power unleashed on them and had to wonder: what would happen to Jafar if she left him there to hold the tunnel behind her?

"They will kill me." He shrugged, answering her unasked question. "But you will have your head start. You will be free of the temple and the rest of it will be in your hands and up to your ingenuity. The Guardians will not stop hunting you just because you step outside the temple."

Her emotions were a welter of conflicting desires. She'd never worked with a partner before. Did she dare trust Jafar? He radiated strength, both inside and out. She'd known him for such a short while and yet she wanted to know more. He would be as strong emotionally as he was physically—he could truly match her.

She made her decision.

"Tell me what I need to do."

Hanging from a rope in pitch darkness, Miu couldn't believe she'd followed Jafar into this predicament. She'd balked when he'd led her to the vertical air shaft, but he'd given her no chance to turn back.

"It's our best chance of getting out," he'd explained. "The Guardians will have to climb after us one at a time. I can pick them off one by one if I need to."

It took half an hour to reach the top; climbing up had been an agonizing matter of placing the grappling hook in the stone over and over and then forcing her arms to move along the rope, ignoring the painful burn in her oxygen-deprived muscles and concentrating on each movement. Mind over matter. So far, they had heard no further sound of anyone following.

"Don't stop, *femi*," Jafar growled from below her.

Right. Easy for him to say.

"You failed to mention that someone's capped the shaft." When she gestured at the stone grille that blocked the exit, the rope swayed nauseatingly. She had no idea how far up they'd climbed, but she knew falling would mean instant death.

"Hold still," Jafar said, and that was all the warning he gave. His large body moved swiftly, smoothly up the rope, surrounding her in the hot cage of his arms. His body pressed skin to skin with hers.

She eyed the rope hook—had the hook shifted? Or was she imagining things? "Too much weight," she protested.

"The rope will hold." He dismissed her concerns as if he'd done this before. Perhaps he had. How did she know what he had or hadn't done? *Note to self: ask for details of escape plan before agreeing to engage.*

One hard arm wrapped around her waist, drawing her securely back against his chest. With his other arm, he reached out and pushed at the capstone. The heavy stone slid easily to one side. The temple's builders had placed the heavy stone on grooves so that it slid smoothly at the slightest touch. Outside, a cliff awaited her. The air shaft came out at the back of the temple, between its massive stone wall and the steep incline of one of the hills ringing the Valley. Her rappelling wasn't finished for the day. He pressed a quick kiss against the top of her head.

"*Femi,*" he began.

They were going to make it! Welcome daylight spilled down over her face, the light so blinding after the temple's perpetual dusk that at first she didn't notice the eyes. When the grille had moved, it had revealed a deep, low trench cut around the shaft. Shadows shifted. *Slithered.* Dozens of black eyes stared back at her. And none of them blinked.

Snakes.

Miu froze. Oh Heqet. Dozens of slim black bodies filled the trench, a boiling sea of writhing, reptilian bodies. Flat black eyes met her panicked gaze.

"I did tell you," he said apologetically. "The minute we crossed the threshold of the temple with the necklace, we triggered wards set to prevent thieves from ever making it out of here alive."

"Draw your blades," she cried. "*Do* something." The snakes were surrounding the exit, making it impossible for either of them to crawl out the opening.

"Damn it, Jafar," she protested, "you said you knew how to get out. To *trust* you."

"And I do," he roared. He hooked her by the collar of her tunic, swinging her upward. "Pull your flarestick. Now!"

She slid the flarestick from her belt. The snakes paused at the blinding light, leaving a small space where she landed. Jafar scrambled out of the shaft after her. Their only choice now was to either stand their ground or allow the snakes to drive them back down the dark shaft. All the way down.

The first snake uncoiled and launched itself at her. She fried it with the flarestick before it crossed the line she had mentally scratched in the air. One down—she gave up counting how many more were left.

After all, the number of snakes probably exceeded the number of minutes that she had left to live.

As the snakes launched themselves in full-scale attack against her, harsh, sibilant words poured from the lips of the male behind her. There was the strange sensation of air pushing out around them in a determined flow of *mazhyk* and hardening into a sphere.

She looked at him appreciatively as the snakes suddenly stopped their advance, sliding off the orb of air and light that he had woven.

"Nice trick." She stared at the orb. "Care to teach me that one?"

He shook his head. "You don't need it. I would never allow you to face such danger alone."

"Right." Secretly, she reveled in the warmth his words imparted: he'd chosen her. No one had ever chosen her before. Just maybe she meant more to him than sex. More than mating.

He was doing that trick with his eyes again, the golden glow. She could feel the heat pouring off his skin.

"They cannot penetrate," he said, completely unconcerned that the snakes were writhing over the orb, seeking a way in.

"I will always keep you safe," he repeated. She no longer gave a damn about the snakes. She had a feeling that Jafar would be more than a match for them. Indeed, as the orb began to glow with stronger energy, the snakes slithered away, apparently repelled by whatever Jafar was doing.

"Will you really?" She wanted to say something, explain to him what that meant to her.

The orb winked out, but his eyes continued to glow hotly. "*Femi*—" he began.

Before he could say anything, the first group of Cats burst onto the cliff top. No wonder there had been no further signs of pursuit. The Guardians had gone around the outside of the temple to intercept them.

CHAPTER FIFTEEN

They were trapped.

Jafar hated making mistakes. Hell, he never made them. So picking this time to start, when it was his mate on the line, didn't sit well with him.

Before he could second-guess himself, he fastened the necklace around her neck.

"Keep this safe, *femi*. There's going to be a fight." He put both hands on his longswords and it didn't escape him that none of the other Guardians backed down either. This wasn't a friendly encounter. They were here to stop him. Regretfully, he drew the first blade in a smooth rush of metal, letting the familiar weight of the weapon settle into his palm as he assessed the threat.

Amun Ra hadn't held anything back on this one. He'd gone full out.

Hebon moved to the front of the group blocking their way. Jafar checked, but the male's blades were still safely stowed. Maybe he wanted to do a little parley before he got down to business, but there was no mistaking the look on Hebon's face.

Payback was going to be a bitch.

"Move out of the way," Jafar growled.

"Not a chance." Hebon pushed off the wall and strode toward them, stopping only when Jafar pulled his other blade and met the male's advance with four feet of cold steel.

"No closer," he warned. "We're leaving. I'd rather no one got hurt in the process." He'd prefer to leave without bloodshed, but if they forced him to choose, well, he'd already made the choice, hadn't he? And he'd chosen the female at his back.

Not his brothers.

Miu wasn't expecting the attack. One minute she was crouched on the edge of the too-narrow ledge, watching Jafar fight off the Guardians one by one with those lethal swords of his, and the next she was tumbling over the edge, sharp claws digging into her ankle.

There was a sickening sensation of falling, abruptly cut short. She'd landed on another ledge maybe fifteen feet below the first one. Above her, she heard Jafar's roar of outrage.

The Cat crouched over her shifted back to male form, like night washing over the hills. Hebon. The hot press of his body made her want to scream. This close, she could smell the pheromones, the palpable anger that seemed to consume him. When she shoved him away, however, Hebon's lean arm shot out with snakelike rapidity. One arm twisted hers behind her back, while the other dragged her up against an undeniably hard—and male—body.

"It was a mistake," his raspy voice growled into her ear, "to come here for Amun Ra's treasures. The temple is well guarded, little one. We do not tolerate thieves."

She didn't know what Hebon's deal was, but it was

pretty obvious that he had a very personal bone to pick with temple thieves. Tilting her head back against his chest, she looked up into his face. Why were they all so damned good-looking? Hebon smiled slowly and his smile disturbed her more than his threats. "Yes," he said, "you will get what you deserve here."

"I don't deserve this," she protested.

"Not nice to steal," Hebon remarked casually, halting her awkward scramble toward the edge with a pair of hard arms. With his short hair, he looked, if possible, even colder and more focused than the other Guardians. "Not nice at all."

A wicked blade materialized out of his leather boot. Oh, hell.

"Why kill me now?" she panted. "Your Amun Ra made a deal. He wants what I can bring him."

"Which would be what? The male who orders you to thieve, who sent you here to collect this necklace for him?" His fingers flicked the edge of the silver necklace.

"Yes." She fought to keep her voice even. Why did she find Jafar so attractive when this Guardian merely scared the hell out of her? "I'm going to give him Lierr."

"Right." His dark eyes examined her face. "Unfortunately, you are not supposed to give Lierr that necklace. Jafar knows that—why else would he have chosen such an inconspicuous route out of the temple? He knows very well that Amun Ra promised a death sentence for anyone who went after this necklace again. No questions asked. Just instant death. You're still breathing," he said, looking down at her and answering her unspoken question, "because Amun Ra told me that he wants you. Rather," he chuckled darkly, "he wants the pleasure of killing you. Made an interesting friend there, female. I'm not sure if I should congratulate you—or commiserate with you. He has some dark tastes. Ones he does not indulge with his lovers. Apparently, he's decided that you'd make an excellent appetizer. I haven't decided whether I'll grant him that request, or if I'll exercise my right and take your life right here. Right now. First, however, I'll have the necklace."

"The necklace?" She gaped at him stupidly, her hands flying up to cover the piece.

"Take it off," he ordered. "The necklace doesn't leave the temple. Neither do either of you now."

Without the necklace, she had nothing to bargain with. No ransom for Lore. "No," she protested, but her words were choked off as one dark hand wrapped itself around her neck. Pressure slowly cut off her air until blackness buzzed angrily in her ears. Then he released his grasp and brought his shortknife up against her throat. The blade scraped against her tender skin, leaving a sharp sting and a crimson necklace of tiny pinpricks in its wake.

"Don't. Say. No. To. Me. Shall we play, you and I?" He vibrated with anger and her stomach roiled with unexpected nausea. He was going to kill her. His fingers were prying hers off the cold metal and there was nothing she could do to stop him. His greater weight held her pinned to the unyielding ledge, slowly crushing from her lungs what breath remained in her.

Spots danced in front of her eyes and she felt the clasp of the necklace part, scratching across her skin. "I'm owed this," he growled. "More than you could ever imagine. No one—*no one*—is taking this necklace out of here. Not when people have died for it."

Whoever had died for it had mattered a great deal to Hebon.

His arm wrapped around her throat and her hands pried at his golden skin. "Don't fight me." His sigh ruffled her hair. "There's only one way for this to end, female, and you won't enjoy it."

The hands around her throat tightened and the breath rushed from her body.

She knew with heart-stopping certainty that she wouldn't be rescuing anyone from Lierr.

She was dying.

Rage consumed Jafar.

The mating bond was taking over. Consuming him. Miu was *his*.

He was methodically running through the pride of Guardians standing against him. Although killing them was still not his intention, Jafar nevertheless knew he'd left more than one set of injuries behind him and felt a feral sense of satisfaction about the damage he'd inflicted. They would *not* prevent him from taking his mate out of the temple.

Still, his brothers had inflicted damage of their own. Some fought him in wereform, while others came at him with blades. He saw regret in some eyes, caution in others. The raw tide of emotion kept him going, emotion that connected him to Miu. He knew Hebon had pulled her over the side. Only his thready awareness of her through their bond kept him from shifting and destroying the pride.

She was in danger.

He had to finish this. He could hear the breath tearing from his chest in harsh pants. Sweat slicked his forehead and trickled down the thick muscles of his abdomen. "Come on," he taunted the Guardian nearest him, inviting him to join the deadly dance of blades and fists. When the male advanced, Jafar swept his leg up, clipping his opponent under the chin and knocking the male backward. Another warrior promptly took his place.

The blade rose and fell in a starkly disciplined sweep. A fine dance between life and death until his awareness of Miu flickered like a light being put out. The bond between them stretched, thinning.

Hell.

She was dying.

With a roar, he forced his way over the side.

The temple was merely a fuzzy outline dancing in front of her eyes. There was the vague sensation of hands being wrenched away from her throat and then Miu was abruptly pulled behind something large, solid. Sucking in air through her raw throat, she heard the brutal sound of flesh meeting flesh. A blade flashed and flew through the air in a dizzying arc. Hebon fell away.

"Hold on, *femi*," a voice growled in her ear. "We're going down."

Right. Breathing was an agony, as she sucked desperately for breath through her swollen throat. "Can we strangle him first?" she rasped, only half joking.

"No need," Jafar replied cryptically.

"Did you kill him?" she asked.

Without answering, her Guardian tossed her over one broad shoulder and began rapidly climbing down the hill.

"Won't the Cats follow us?"

"I killed some; the rest are in no shape to give chase."

"But the Amun Ra will send more," she guessed.

"Don't pass out on me," Jafar warned. "I'm going to need to put you on your own feet in a minute."

"Fine with me," she retorted. "I do best on my own feet."

CHAPTER SIXTEEN

With Jafar directing them, they broke into a lurching run down the far side of the Valley. Fine. *She* lurched. Hell, she'd just been mostly strangled, so she figured she had an excuse. Jafar, however, ran as smoothly as the damn Cat he was. His eyes moved possessively over her, one large hand cupping her ass and scooting her in a new direction.

"Hey," she glared. "No backseat driving there." Unfortunately, her serious lack of breath ruined the effect.

Low, scrubby bushes slapped at her legs as they ran pell-mell down the steep slope. How soon would the rest of the Guardians be after them? Time to call in the cavalry.

Skidding to a stop, she caught herself on a conveniently placed boulder.

"Why are you stopping?" Jafar growled. Clearly, he was all too aware that he'd left behind a really pissed-off group of warriors a half mile back. She couldn't blame him.

"Reinforcements." She shoved her hand into her bag and groped. There. The smooth round curve of the scrying bowl fit itself into her hand. "This." She pulled out the bowl and waved it at him.

"A bowl. Right. Very helpful." Didn't he recall what she was holding in her hand? Didn't he realize it was a means of calling for help? Perhaps he thought there *was* no one who would help her.

"This," she said, just so they were clear, "is going to save our asses. You can thank me later." She figured his thanks were going to involve some serious groveling.

"Bowl's going to sprout wings and fly us out of here? Erase the scent trail we've just plastered down the side of this hill like a great big come-and-get-me sign?"

"No." Under other circumstances, she'd have countered his sarcasm with a few quips of her own. Now, however, she was operating under a serious time crunch. "None of the above. It's the scrying bowl."

Apparently, he thought he'd cracked the bowl into oblivion during their friendly little cave-in encounter. Well, she'd slipped the bowl back into her bag, and now? It was going to come in handy. Very handy.

Stirring the bespelled surface of the water, Miu chanted in a rapid slur of words that would have made a drunk sound lucid.

"You're working *mazhyk*?"

"Bingo." Small tendrils of *mazhyk* stirred the hair on her neck. Ick. It was like being dipped upside down into a vat of particularly unpleasant oil. She rubbed her arms nervously.

"Thought you didn't like *mazhyk*."

"Exceptions," she replied sweetly. "Being chased by a pack of revenge-minded Guardians? Makes a girl rethink her priorities." And how.

An image wavered, forming over the surface. Surely

her Cat hadn't just mouthed, "About time," had he? She didn't wait for the image to form fully. She didn't have that kind of time. The bowl vibrated in her hands.

"Ebo." There was a pause that seemed far too long. Damn it, why wasn't the guard answering? She gave up on the social niceties—Ebo knew better than to expect those from her anyhow—and got straight to the point.

"Get me out of here. Now." This wasn't the time for her hired helpers to sit around with their thumbs up their proverbial asses. She had Guardians on her tail and she needed to move, move, move.

Jafar pulled her to her feet. "Walk and talk," he mouthed.

Good idea.

The water in the bowl sloshed as she tripped over one of the many damn stones that littered the lower slope of the Valley. The image floating above the bowl flickered again and finally resolved itself into the familiar hard-featured glare of Ebo.

"Look, we're a little busy here," he bit out. She caught the flicker of color beyond him. The camp's perimeter warnings. Only something large—and sporting powerful *mazhyk*—would have set off those flares.

"Company?" she asked. Damn.

Jafar caught her before she could trip over another invisible root. He didn't say anything. Merely picked her up and cradled her against his chest. "Safer," he said.

"Did you get it?" Ebo asked.

She nodded and then realized he couldn't see her. Because he wasn't watching her.

What was happening at her campsite that was so bad Ebo wouldn't make eye contact with her?

"I did," she said instead. "But I'm not going to hang on to it, Ebo, if you don't haul your ass up here and get me out."

Damn, but she hated admitting that part. That she wasn't going to be able to do it all by herself.

Jafar's arms tightened around her. "Not alone," he whispered into her hair.

"You got that, Ebo?" she added, when he didn't say anything.

Ebo seemed to have frozen, staring to his left as if the apocalypse had just crashed his backyard barbecue and scared off all his guests.

"Yeah," he said, "but it's still going to have to wait." She heard the soft snick of steel as he drew his blade. There was a bellow and the sound of crashing in the underbrush. "This isn't good, Miu."

"*This* isn't good," she hissed. "I've got Guardians chasing me, Ebo. They're going to catch me. And I've. Got. Their. Damn. Necklace."

"Right," he muttered, clearly not listening to her anymore. "Good. Good job. Congratulations."

"Ebo," she demanded, swallowing a shriek of frustration. "Who's in charge here?"

"You are." He still didn't look as if he cared. Somewhere behind him, a man screamed. Oh, Heqet.

Jafar picked up his pace. "How far down the hill is he?" he asked. She didn't know. Heqet, she just didn't know.

"Do you know what they do to thieves here?" she asked Ebo. Maybe a little pressure would help?

Concern flickered in his eyes. "Yeah, but we've got bigger problems here, Miu. Real big problems."

Ebo opened his mouth to say something and then he dropped his bowl. As the water rose upward, the last thing she saw was a dark crimson tide and then the thirsty ground swallowed the liquid, severing the link.

Behind her, Jafar cursed and put her back on her feet. "Very helpful," he said. "Now run."

She didn't need a second invitation.

CHAPTER SEVENTEEN

"That must be your meeting place, just up ahead." Jafar jerked his head toward a narrow slit of darkness that split the stony cliff face to their left. Clearly, he'd recognized the possibilities of the site and figured she or her men had as well.

"Recognize it?"

She did. She trudged up to the narrow opening in the cliff side, peered inside, and realized the day was not about to get any better.

Not only were there no horses waiting at the rendezvous point; there were no guides. From the gory bits left splattered about the cave, Miu correctly deduced that someone had eaten her hired help.

At her side, she heard Jafar swear. She could almost sense the protective urges rolling off him as he fought the need to shove her behind him. Unfortunately for him, neither of them knew where the danger really lay. Move, and they could be stepping straight into it.

"You're not leaving me behind," she said, just so there could be no misunderstanding. Taking her hand, Jafar stepped into the cave, pausing to scent the air. Still, he didn't turn toward her and she was grateful. She wasn't sure she'd gotten her face under control yet. Her foot nudged something warm and soft and she stifled a shriek. A booted foot. Without its owner.

"Reconsidering?" he asked without turning around.

"No. Give it up, kitty."

He grunted and reached out a hand, pulling her up against his side. Although she wouldn't have admitted it, she was grateful for the warmth. The cave felt unbearably cold, as if the rocks were bearing silent witness to whatever terrible fight had taken place here.

"Frightened?"

"No."

He looked down at her, cocking an eyebrow. "Right," he said. "And your skin is clammy because you're enjoying yourself here?"

These were—had been—*her* men. If things had gone according to plan, she would have been here with them and she couldn't tell if she was horrified or, worse, grateful that she hadn't been. She was still alive. They, on the other hand, were dead.

Extremely, thoroughly dead.

"Predator?" She was thankful her voice didn't shake. She'd seen violence before, but nothing like this. Little unidentifiable bits of *flesh* were stuck to the rough stone cave walls.

"No." He sounded more contemplative than regretful as he examined the evidence. Rolling over a body, he crouched down and examined the wounds. At least, she thought it was a body. From where she was standing, it looked like a gnawed-on hunk of raw meat. What had once been a man with two arms, two legs, and a head was now just a dismembered, bleeding torso.

"Not the work of other thieves," she said quietly.

"No," he agreed.

"You're sure it's not a predator?" she pushed. "Some really large, ravenous animal?" If it wasn't an animal—well, she didn't want to know what kind of living, breathing being could do this to a man.

"Not a predator," he repeated. "I've seen this kind of damage before," he admitted reluctantly. "Only never outside the Valley."

"How would you know?" she argued. "How often have you been out of that damn Valley anyhow?"

"Often enough." He stood up, brushing dirt from his hands. "I've traveled. Not recently, mind you, but quite enough to know what I've seen. And not seen. Those aren't the marks of any teeth you'll find in a four-legged creature."

"Not even one of your Cat friends?"

"No. Although," he added as an afterthought, "you're quite welcome to check, particularly if you're worried that the Guardians got here before us and took care of a little business, seeing as how your companions were clearly not the most upstanding of citizens." He bared his teeth in a parody of a grimace, his canines shimmering and elongating for a second.

"No games." Heqet knew, she was too shocked now to play with him. He actually looked concerned when she failed to take his bait.

"We kill cleanly, *femi*. Go for the throat. One good bite and a man's as dead as he needs to be. This"—his hands indicated the gore on the walls—"this was done for show. To leave you a message. What I'm wondering is whether you understand what's being said."

She could guess. Her hand went to her throat, wrapping around the chill surface of the moonstone. No matter how long the damn stone sat against her skin, it never warmed up. She supposed that should have been her first clue that the necklace was trouble. That and Lierr's painful insistence on obtaining it. She'd just thought he wasn't ready to dispense with her company yet, picking a task that was nigh on impossible for her to complete.

"You've seen marks like this before?" She wasn't sure whether she wanted him to agree or deny it. Just the thought of him facing some being that could wreak that sort of havoc made her throat choke up. And that made her mad. She wasn't going all soft on her Guardian, was she?

Because that would be stupid. Even she knew there would have to be a little parting of the ways, despite all this mating business, once she'd led Jafar to Lierr. She wasn't about to trade the chains of obligation to one male for the mating bond of another.

"It's not too late to go back," she told him. It had to be said, because some previously unknown part of her kept imagining Jafar lying there torn to pieces. "I'll keep going, you head back to your temple, and we'll call it an amicable parting of ways."

He glowered at her, but his tone was firm. "You wish. You're my mate, *femi*. You promise obedience and docility and I provide protection."

"Docility wasn't part of the bargain," she muttered. Male wanted his pound of flesh.

He eyed her ruthlessly. "Obedience was," he pressed. "You agreed to mate with me in exchange for some very important concessions. Starting with permission to continue your chaotic, rule-breaking, anarchic little existence."

"Mighty benevolent of you," she snapped. "Next time, check the terms of the agreement before you sign on. I don't recall promising docility. Or," she considered, "even obedience."

He loomed over her, six-plus feet of domineering male. "You promised to be my mate," he said in a tight voice. "In every way."

"And that gives you the right to order me around? Think again, kitty. I don't blindly obey anyone."

"Except Lierr," he bit out.

"Not even him," she disagreed. "Not blindly, anyhow. I only follow his orders because he's got my sister."

"You're my mate," he said firmly. "That means I protect you. If there are Ifrits running around loose—and I think that's what we're looking at here—I damn well have a lot to say about where you go and what you do. An Ifrit will as soon tear you limb from limb as look at you."

Limb from limb certainly covered the carnage inside the cave. She remembered what Jafar had told her about the Doorway he guarded. "I thought the opening from Qaf was down in the temple."

He shot her a look and grunted. "Ifrits shouldn't be this far from a Doorway. Prefer their world to ours, they do, and generally stick to it other than popping over here for a bit of shopping."

"Shopping?" Somehow, she didn't think the Ifrits were in the market for a cloak.

"Shopping," he repeated. "And items one and two on their list are attractive females and *mazhykal* artifacts."

And wasn't that a bad bit of news? She supposed she

should be flattered by the roundabout compliment, but it was hard to overlook the price of the Ifrits' so-called shopping.

"Problem is," he said thoughtfully, rubbing his hand over his chin, "neither of those two items were here, now were they? Just a couple of hirelings and their horses. I suppose they might have had some *mazhyk* on them, but whatever they had couldn't have been terribly powerful or there wouldn't be such a mess in here. You tell me what kind of fighters you hired, but I'm betting you put your money on men who fight with conventional weapons. Swords. Knives. A little hand-to-hand." He continued when she nodded, "Right. And I'm betting they weren't fresh from the farm either. So whoever took them out was either extremely fast or just came in here wielding so much power that your mercks never stood a chance. Ifrits could do that, but the real question is why?"

"Why?" She felt like a stupid echo, but she was starting to see—and there was nothing like firsthand knowledge—that these Ifrits had to be stopped. She couldn't imagine letting this horror run unchecked.

"Yeah. There shouldn't have been anything to attract them here. And, if an Ifrit actually made it out of the Valley—which is where the nearest Doorway is—I should have known about it. Might still have got away from me"—he sounded doubtful on that point, though—"but I'd have known they were out here. I'd have been tracking them."

"Are there other—Doorways?"

He smiled approvingly. "Right you are. Of course there are, but the Valley's is the closest. And none of the known Doorways are unguarded. Possible that a new Doorway has opened up somewhere, but there's usually a good bit of disturbance when that happens, not to mention a sudden surge in the number of murders and rapes. News like that tends to get around, and we hear of it fast enough."

"Perhaps they learned a bit of discretion?" She didn't know how bright these Ifrits of Jafar's were, but it was clear that they were brutal and quick. Having wits thrown into the mix just seemed cruelly unfair.

"It's possible." He eyed the carnage around them and sighed. "But unlikely. They're the stab-and-grab sort. Not colonizers by any stretch of the imagination."

"Right."

"So now what?" He folded his arms across his chest and looked at her.

"Excuse me?"

"I got you out of the temple. Down the hill." He checked the items off on his fingers. "And to your meeting place, which, I might mention, is not particularly hidden if that was what you were going for."

No. Clearly not, given what had happened to her mercks.

He looked around the clearing, but then there was a faint whistling sound. As if someone had tried to moan, but had so little throat left that the cry was the merest whisper of sound.

"Over here," Jafar snapped. Striding to the farthest side of the cave, he crouched down beside a pile of mutilated flesh. One hand reached for his blade, slicing strips of cloth from his robe. "Got a live one here." More dubiously, he added, "Sort of."

Dear gods. Had one of her males managed to survive the carnage?

She wasn't sure how she made it from one side of the cave to the other, only that when she crouched down next to Jafar, she understood the reason for his hesitation when he'd described the state of the male lying on the ground. Sure, the merck still clung to life, but the coppery scent of blood was almost overpowering. Something—or someone—had pulled Ebo apart at the seams. She swallowed hard, fighting back nausea as she stared at his armless, legless torso.

His eyes blinked.

Dear Heqet above, the man was indeed still alive. His mouth opened and sound wheezed out.

Squatting, she knelt by his side. She was no healer, but even she could tell that the Moirae were about to cut this man's lifeline. She half expected to see the three sisters circling above the body. Gray streams leaked from his aura, the spirit bleeding away as he forced himself to remain chained to this world. Waiting for her?

Ebo had been more than seven feet tall, a prime merck not only because of his height, but also because of his strength. Some masters would have admired his looks as well; there were lords who believed in hiring the best-looking help available, no matter what the job description entailed and even if it would never involve bedwork. Her merck's ebony-colored skin had given him his name and she'd never dared ask him if he resented being named for his parts rather than his whole; given the cold rage that burned in the male, she figured she knew the answer to that question.

"Yours?"

How did she answer that? Sure, she'd bought the male lying there in front of them, but not with the intent of keeping him. It was one more rule to break, right? Since Lierr expected her to keep a coterie of fighters for those unfortunate thefts that required more brute force than mental acuity, she had—but on her own terms. All her mercks were freed men, even if none of them bandied that fact around. All of them got that the joke was on Lierr. Her Ebo had been silent, sure, but appreciative of his liberation from the slave pens, even if what she'd offered had been a harum-scarum life as bodyguard for a thief. He'd known the risks they'd taken—and he'd wanted the rewards, same as the rest of them. Being a slave, he hadn't had a family.

A loner.

Just like her.

"Necklace," he wheezed.

She nodded, smoothed a hand over his forehead. "Who?"

"Don't know. Tall. Came out of nowhere. Like—" His eyes flickered closed and he forced them open. She couldn't imagine the strength of will it had taken to survive this long. "Like living flames," he said finally. "Column of smoke and fire. Upper torso looked human, bottom half"—his mangled body shuddered—"nothing but smoke and wind. Moved fast."

His eyes drifted shut again.

"Not Cats?" she asked quietly. Beside her, Jafar tensed, but she had to know. Trusting him was naive, and she had every intention of making it back to Shympolsk alive and in one piece, unlike her poor Ebo.

"No," he breathed. "Wanted the necklace. Knew we'd come for it and were looking for you."

Were Ebo's attackers still here?

"Gone," he groaned. "Told them nothing. Sun rose and they left." He'd been lying here like this for hours? His remaining hand shot up and wrapped around her throat. "Don't," he said, "take the necklace off. Whatever you do. Means something. Find out before you hand it over to Lierr. Don't trust that bastard."

"No," she agreed.

"Tried to fight back," he whispered. "Tried."

"Lierr's got a lot to answer for." And she planned on making him sing like a caged bird.

"Hush," she said, and stroked a hand over Ebo's forehead. He grunted and closed his eyes, clearly feeling that he'd completed his job and was entitled to a little shut-eye. She couldn't argue; she was more surprised that the tattered bits of his spirit still hovered over his body. Watching them slip away from his body was almost easier than realizing what the Ifrits had done to him. He was at peace now. Moving on to the next adventure, the next stage of his journey.

Unfortunately, that meant she was now guardless in a world where there were daemons and Ifrits and monsters that could rip a seven-foot-tall man to shreds and escape without a scratch. Heqet help her. She'd stolen plenty of *mazhykal* artifacts—but they'd belonged to *this* world and her competition had been other thieves. Humans.

She stroked a hand over Ebo's forehead as she considered what she'd just learned. The return trip to Shympolsk had just grown infinitely more complicated.

Chapter Eighteen

Watching Miu pace back and forth in the mouth of the cave, Jafar wished he could have spared her this sight. Hell, he wished he'd never taken her out of his chambers back at the temple.

Double hell. He had it bad.

He could feel his emotional toughness slipping away, like shadows fleeing before the moon. It was more than just erotic attraction he felt for her, he admitted silently: he'd started to have emotions about her—and not just protective ones. How could he do what must be done if he had *feelings* for her? He should have excised those feelings as ruthlessly as the Ifrits had slaughtered Miu's men, made this just about sex and power—instead of about the woman he'd held in his arms.

He felt compelled to keep her safe. Hell, he hated this vulnerability. Was this what Hebon had felt for his mate? The incessant need to protect, to touch. He wanted to *cherish* her, as if she were some priceless treasure. When he knew damn well she was a living, breathing, stubborn female who insisted on giving as good as she got—and who'd managed to steal not only a necklace but a piece of his heart as well.

The musky notes of his *femi* teased his senses. Sweeter, spicier than the large white blooms of the night jasz that crawled up the thick trunk of a tree just outside the cave. He should leave her to mourn her fallen companions while he combed the clearing for more clues. The Ifrits' scent trail disappeared into the shadows that surrounded them; it might be possible to track them, follow them to the next scene of butchery.

And there would be a next scene. It was why the Guardians were sworn to root out the Ifrits mercilessly. Since Jafar was the only Guardian on the scene, it fell to him to stop them. Never mind that he was now rogue, with a death sentence undoubtedly imposed on his head; he was still sworn to protect this world. If he'd been sure how the Ifrits had made it into this realm, his job would have been easier. Unfortunately, he only had his suspicions and, to confirm them, he needed his *femi*'s help.

"Hey, kitty." She snapped her fingers in front of his face, trying to regain that tough facade she always hid behind. "What now?" Her teary eyes glowed silver as the moon snuck up into the sky from behind the stand of trees where it had been lurking. Hours had passed while they buried her men, while she grieved for them.

She'd never admit to the tears, but they were still there, breaking his heart.

"Don't," he said, capturing her fingers in his hand. Rubbing the slender digits, he tugged at the pads, smiling at her involuntary intake of breath. For a thief with a seemingly insatiable lust for jewels, her fingers were surprisingly bare.

Her fingers curled into his palm. "What was that for?" As always, she eyed him suspiciously. He stroked another long, luxurious caress over her skin, enjoying the way her muscles flowed and relaxed beneath his touch. Her body was learning to trust him even if her mind resisted.

"Mates touch."

She eyed him and then said, "It's a strategic alliance, kitty. Purely business and you know it."

What would it take to get her to admit to the truth of their relationship? He took a step closer. She glowered up at him, uncowed. "I had your promise otherwise."

"Promises made under duress?" She shrugged. "Don't count, in my book."

"I gave you a choice when we were making our escape. You agreed to trust me. We're partners now."

Deliberately, he crowded her, dominated her. He wasn't going to let her ignore him.

"Did I?" She peeked up through her lashes at him. "And you believed me? I don't want to be anyone's mate. If I had needed a male, I would have brought one with me."

"From the pleasure gardens of Shympolsk?" He ignored the small throb of jealousy. It wasn't *him*. It was all males that she distrusted, and given her history, it was no wonder. Surely, if he kept that fact in mind, it would make her rejection less painful.

"Sure. Wherever." She eyed him.

"And would you sleep with your thief master, too?"

"News flash, kitty." She smiled benevolently at him. "We're not precisely *sleeping* together, are we?"

No, they were only having the hottest sex of his life in either realm. From the self-satisfied little smirk on her face, she knew it, too. His eyes narrowed. Admitting as much would be like handing her the reins of their relationship. And, knowing his mate, she'd drive away from him just as fast as her hot little body could take her. There had to be a way to make her stay.

"What do we do now?" she asked, cutting into his thoughts. "I've got no guards, no horses, and just one week to get the necklace back to Lierr."

"We stick to our original plan. You've still got me."

Swinging her up into his arms, Jafar carried her toward the darkest side of the clearing.

"Why, Jafar," she said, in a tone he couldn't quite interpret, "Don't tell me you're a closet romantic?"

Just because he could—just because he clearly *shouldn't*, since there were things going on here that they needed to figure out—he wanted to kiss her. What could be more romantic than a full moon and a darkened clearing? Hell, he could even hear the faint, melodic sounds of water. Undoubtedly, in daylight, the water would turn out to be a brackish, muddy trickle issuing from some equally grubby rocks where a merchant caravan had stopped to water the camels, but at night . . . Well, in the dark hours, Jafar was smart enough to realize that the same miserly trickle of water was a *mazhykal* thing. And he knew enough to keep their boots out of the dung patties the clearing's previous occupants had left behind.

There was a second, smaller clearing tucked away on the other side of a stand of trees. His *femi* paused, a tense, prickly little armful, but the stiff line of her spine relaxed ever so slightly when he put her down in the open, moon-bathed space. She turned her face up so she was washed in the clear, cool light.

Moonlight.

"You're a moon daemon," he remembered.

"Half daemon," she corrected. "On my father's side."

"The moon calls to you, draws you."

She nodded. "It always has."

"I wonder if that was why Lierr sent you."

He looked at the silver necklace glowing in the light of the moon, and knew it was time to let Miu in on some of its secrets. If the necklace could do what he suspected it could, this wasn't just about her sister anymore. Heqet, it wasn't just about the two of them anymore either.

"What did Lierr tell you about the moonstone necklace?" he asked. "Why do you think he's so fired up about getting his hands on it?"

Touching the heavy piece of jewelry around her neck, she traced the silver in her hands. Even after almost dying for this hunk of metal and stone, she still couldn't figure out what the attraction was. "He didn't share his reasons, just the consequences if I failed to bring it back." She held the piece up to the moonlight, where it seemed to take on an unearthly glow. "He's targeted particular pieces before, but he's always been willing to pull back if it looked like we weren't going to be able to acquire them."

"And he's not the only one after the necklace," Jafar added. "There has been a dramatic increase in intruders to the temple lately."

"And all of them were human thieves?" She arched a brow at him.

"No," he replied thoughtfully. "Not all of them were *thieves*. Some were Ifrits."

"I thought you had Ifrits crossing over all the time."

"But not all in one section of the temple."

"Which section is that?" She had a sinking sensation that she knew. Jafar wasn't just making conversation. He was making a point.

"The points closest to Pho's coffin. The princess you exhumed." He dragged a hand through his hair.

"You're on a first-name basis with the dead?"

"This one, yeah. I killed her."

He cut her off before she could ask questions. "She had the necklace on at the time." He reached out to finger the glowing moonstone.

His little *femi* was no fool. She could see the regret that must be visible on his face. "What's your interest in all this?" she demanded. "Talk."

"I made a mistake, a mistake I can't fix. Doesn't matter that I want to, that if I could go back and do it all over again, I'd do what I was supposed to do, no matter what."

"What were you supposed to do?"

"Down there in the catacombs, standing watch on the Doorways, it was all just routine to a young Cat. I was bored, Miu. I didn't find it particularly exciting to stand guard where I'd been told to stand guard, and I thought I knew better than older, wiser members of my pride. Why couldn't they see that nothing was going to happen where I was assigned? That's what I told myself and I was convinced I was right. When the first Ifrit came charging through the narrow crack, I was *elated, femi*. I thought I was finally going to see a battle worthy of the name. Of *my* name. I cut the Ifrit down and never stopped to ask myself why he went down so easily."

"He didn't put up a fight?"

"He did. Enough to lull my initial suspicions, enough so that I felt strong. Powerful. Lethal. When the female followed, the first death had dulled my killing edge just that little, necessary bit. I didn't swing automatically when she slipped through the Doorway. I stopped. I took a good look." His gorgeous golden eyes turned dull, flat, tracking the memories only he could see.

She wanted to strangle the woman who had done this to him—and that confused her. Heqet's balls. She was starting to think of him as *hers*. She wanted to keep him.

"She was a female. She was young. I dismissed her as absolutely no threat at all and let her come through."

Threading her hand through his tawny mane, she rubbed gently at his scalp. Keeping him was impossible. She was a thief. He was a Guardian. Right?

"But she wasn't harmless." It had to be said and she had to keep him talking.

"No," he agreed heavily, pressing a kiss against her exploring palm. "Pho did a world of damage. I brought her up to the surface. Let her run free for a bit, thinking to gain her trust. She had spun me a tale of being abducted by the Ifrits, forced to serve them in Qaf. It wasn't unheard of." He lifted a shoulder. "It had happened. Sure, we'd never got one of those females back alive, but sometimes the Qaf dwellers would push the brutalized bodies back through the Doorways. A sort of taunt that they'd won that particular battle. I figured she'd been lucky enough to tag along behind a warrior headed for the Doorways. She had the bruises—the scars—to back up her story. Whenever one of us got too close, she'd tremble like a leaf."

Once again, Miu fought an urge to rip the long-dead woman to shreds.

"Of course, I was just about as wrong as they come. She wasn't harmless and she wasn't scared. Just clever enough to play on our delight in having rescued a female from the hands of the Ifrits. We let her wander around the temple and congratulated ourselves every time she looked a little less frightened."

"So you were nice to her. She took advantage." There had to be more to the story than a male feeling foolish over a female.

He pressed a hard kiss against her throat.

Just for once, she decided, she wanted to be wrong. This was not going to be a happy story.

"You could say that. She slipped into a guard room and slit the throats of a half dozen Cats before I caught her. And Hebon's mate Oni was there, one of the first victims of Pho's bloodlust. Maybe if she hadn't been there, the Guardians would have reacted faster, but Pho's turning on us was unbelievable. Straight out of a nightmare. Just standing there, laughing, blood dripping from her blade. She just stood there and waited for me to see what she had done, and then she used the blasted necklace to open up a Doorway between the temple and Qaf."

Miu stared. "She didn't get away?"

"No," he said grimly. "She overlooked the possibility of my becoming sufficiently angry to forget the gentlemanly traits that had protected her so far. I stuck a blade in her as she stood there, laughing, with one foot in each realm. Portal closed and I'm pleased to say that only her foot made it back to Qaf. The rest of her we threw into the first empty chamber we could find."

Miu thought of the dead skeleton from whom she'd plucked the necklace. Had all the bones been there?

"I won't make that mistake again. Haven't made it. Whatever comes through the Doorways, I kill."

Miu realized it was a miracle she herself was still alive. And no wonder Jafar was so determined to learn why Lierr was after the necklace. His story explained so much.

"I have a pretty strong feeling that moonstone around your neck opens Doorways. What I need to know now," he continued, "is why Lierr sent *you* for the necklace."

"Because I'm his best?" She tried using her usual sarcasm.

"How much do you want to bet that it takes a being with some pretty powerful moon *mazhyk* to make the damn thing work?"

Automatically, she shoved at his hand and he let her go. She didn't go far, stepping away from him to look up into the darkening night sky. The first silver points of starlight pricked the blackness around the rising moon.

"You're saying Lierr wanted me to go after the necklace because he needed a moon daemon to make the stone do whatever it does."

"That's what I think." He reached out and put his hands on either side of her face, forcing her to meet his gaze. "Unless he's got a mage or someone equally powerful in his keeping, you're Lierr's best hope of making that necklace work. I don't know why your thief master wants this particular ability, but the man can't possibly have a good reason."

"There's only one hole in that theory," Miu replied, scuffing her foot on the ground. "Lierr may know that I'm a moon daemon, but he also knows I'm not a very good one." She pulled her shoulders back and looked up to face him. "He knows I'm a weak, weak halfling. If I had any real power, don't you think I would have used it by now to get my sister away from him?"

"How do you know you have no power?" he asked intently.

Miu stared at him impatiently. "I think I'd know if I had any awesome moon daemon *mazhyk*, don't you? In the last two decades, I can assure you I've done squat as far as moon *mazhyk* is concerned."

"There's one sure way to test my theory." He smiled slightly. "If you're not afraid?"

"Be my guest." She gestured with her hand. "If you want to stand out here, testing ridiculous theories, while we wait for the Ifrits to track us down, you go right ahead. I'll even give you five minutes of my time," she added graciously.

"You need to bleed."

Miu had just known that satisfying the tall, arrogant, hulking male looming over her was going to take more than parading around in the moonlight like a fool. She'd honestly tried to get in touch with her daemon *mazhyk*, but no luck. Daddy dearest hadn't left her with an instruction manual. She'd wrapped both hands around the stone and flapped it in the pool of silvery light. Nothing. She wasn't surprised. No spooky *mazhyk* in her.

"I'm no expert on how the Ifrits travel between realms, but I know there was plenty of blood around when Pho opened that Doorway." He cursed and took a step closer to her. Right. As if she were letting him anywhere near her after that statement. She glared at him.

Smart male. He stopped walking, but his fingers were clearly itching to draw a blade. She kept one eye on them and hefted the necklace again. "See? No moon *mazhyk*. Nada. Nothing. Got any more ideas, or can we get on with returning to Shympolsk sometime before Lierr decides to make shish kebab out of my sister?"

"Got to activate it." He frowned and she suddenly found herself staring at the endearing little crinkle of skin between his eyebrows. *Snap out of it, girl*, she reminded herself. *The man wants to stick you like a pig and you're admiring his facial features?* She had it bad.

Behind them, the moon inched higher. In minutes, the silver circle would be directly above them. With the moonstone around her neck, she could *feel* the hot prickle of the light crawling over her skin. Awakening her. She had to fight to remain still. Heat unfurled low in her belly.

What would sex with a Guardian be like on *this* evening?

He smiled grimly and she realized that *that* was precisely what he intended to discover.

"Oh, no." She shook her head. "No way. I'm not helping you out here."

"It's for a good cause, *femi*," he said in that low, chocolate voice that she was coming to dread. It made her *do* things no self-respecting female would ever dream of doing.

"You can feel it." Jafar's head dipped toward hers. When she bared her teeth at him, he smiled, low and dark. "Heat. *Mazhyk*."

"No." She denied it.

"You're. Not. In. Control. Here." His words were a dark promise, full of liquid heat. His eyes watched her.

"I am," she challenged him. She couldn't afford to lose this battle. Her sister was at stake. There was no time for sex.

"The moon, Miu," he coaxed. "Look at the moon. Feel all that power? Imagine how it would feel running through that necklace of yours." Her hands sought and found the heavy weight of the necklace clasped around her neck. She should take it off. Should throw it away.

He pulled her roughly against his body. Pressed against the hard, hot, masculine heat of his thighs, she could feel the leashed power.

"One finger," he promised darkly, his eyes never leaving hers. His body demanded, pressing against hers. "I'll put one finger into your pussy. No more. Imagine that, *femi*. I can feel how wet you are. How long would it take for you to come?"

He pushed her up against a tree in a smooth rush of muscled strength, lifting her thighs around his waist. Her breath caught at the feeling of being dominated, pinned open. He held her there, pressed against the smooth bark by his lower body. One hand slapped the trunk beside her head, creating a hot cage of male sinew and skin. Heqet, that skin. She wanted to taste it with her tongue until he hollered.

"Yes," he coaxed. "One finger? All you have to do is ask."

Right. She wouldn't beg. Instead, she turned her head away, neither refusing nor permitting the caress.

His eyes gleamed darkly. One thick finger traced a wet path from the top of her pudenda down to the greedy opening to her body that fluttered in wicked anticipation. His finger found the front of her trousers and opened it, plunging boldly through the soft slit.

Pleasure howled in her veins. "Wicked," she accused, wrapping her arms around his neck. "Naughty kitty shouldn't do that."

Of course he shouldn't, but he did.

"No polite request? I'm disappointed, *femi*," he said, and then he pierced her with his finger, boldly pushing through her cream-slicked lips and deep inside. The hot flesh gave readily, her imagination fired by his bold words.

He whispered rough compliments against her neck, his heated breath raising its own army of goose bumps on the graceful curve of her throat. His dark form dominated her smaller, paler body.

She wiggled experimentally, sinking further onto his finger until her hard little bud slid teasingly along that spearing digit.

"Let me fuck you, Miu," he demanded in a quiet, fierce voice.

He did something with his finger and his thumb, a rubbing motion that made her mewl into his mouth. With each new stab of pleasure, she gasped.

His kiss was the kiss of a desperate man. No finesse

and all hot, wet caress. His tongue stroked along the seam of her mouth, demanding entry, so she opened and he swept inside, conquering. Warning signals flashed in the distant part of her brain that was still functioning. The rest of her, though, drank in the lush taste of the male who held her, just as her body had drunk in the moonlight.

"Feel it, too," he groaned, lifting his mouth from hers. Pressing that wicked mouth against the curve of her jaw and lapping at the sensitive spot beneath her ear. "You feel the moon?" Her entire body was trembling, awakening as if the biggest orgasm of her life were about to crash over her. He shook his head, his mouth taking hers again. He pulled her body against his, arching into her flesh like the feline he was.

"*Mazhyk*," he growled.

"Yes," she breathed. He was *mazhyk*, his touch setting fire to her blood.

"Sex *mazhyk*." Was that regret she heard in his voice? Her eyes flew open.

"Sex *mazhyk* and blood," he repeated. "Always worked for the Ifrits." With a quick movement, he slashed his blade down the inside of her arm, reaching for the moonstone.

CHAPTER NINETEEN

"You bastard!" Miu's hands locked around the necklace, pulling at the silver links.

Burying his face against her neck, he muttered words of apology in the old language of the Guardians, the tongue they'd used before they'd mastered human speech and language. *Dasht menya paz. Forgive me, lover.* He'd had to do it. There was no other choice.

He hadn't been sure he'd be able to do it. Stab another lover. Of course, he'd only pinked Miu's arm. He hadn't jammed the blade deep into her devious little heart as he'd done with his Ifrit. He wondered if the Amun Ra had known that he'd mourned his Ifrit, even if she had betrayed him and maddened him and stripped him of his honor. He'd thought he loved her.

Perhaps he had—but it was nothing compared to what he felt now for the female in his arms.

Raising his hand, he smeared the sticky crimson liquid over the glowing surface of the moonstone. Blood dripped along his arm as her fingers twined around his, whether to stop him or aid him, he could not tell. He felt his Cat stir and forced the shift down. Not now.

He took a deliberate step forward, out from under the tree, into the silvered patch of moonlight. As she tightened her legs around his waist, he waited for the *mazhyk* to begin. Nothing happened. Moon rays traced dark shadows over their enmeshed bodies. In the half twilight where the moonlight penetrated the nighttime darkness, the necklace glowed faintly, as if it pulled the moonbeams through the pale, surf blue stone set in the dead center of the silver circlet.

"It glows," she said. "And burns." The circlet branded her skin. A soft pink flush radiated out beneath the heating metal. He swallowed back his bile. It wasn't hurting her, he told himself. She would be fine. She had to be.

And yet no portal opened. He fought to remember what he knew of these portals. Had there been other keys between the realms? He'd heard of a few, but had never seen one.

"It's not working," he growled, without taking his eyes from the slow trickle of blood. Something was not right.

Above them, the moon sailed majestically across the sky. A peaceful, calm look spread across Miu's face. The look of a woman who had been well satisfied in bed.

"Ummm," she breathed, raising her arms.

Moments ago, she'd been writhing on his finger, looking to *him* to bring her satisfaction. He would be the only one to make her face assume that blissed-out expression. Not some damn moon goddess. He wrapped his hand around her wrist, bringing her back to the present.

"What's that for?" She glared at him. Deciding silence was definitely the better part of valor this go-round, Jafar settled for a grunt. Heqet, was he jealous of a goddess?

Moonlight suddenly jerked downward. Soft, swimming bands of light violently rerouted, pulled down and through the necklace's stone, impaling her. Miu shrieked with pain, clawing at the band.

The necklace didn't budge. Didn't come off. "Get it off," she pleaded with him.

Screw the portal. Screw getting the Amun Ra the information he'd demanded. Jafar couldn't stand there and watch his mate burn. Frantically, his hands pulled at the clasp. His Cat roared inside, demanding he let the beast loose. He fought down the change, his fingers moving frantically over the metal. Miu's skin flushed and darkened, pale blisters forming beneath the edge of the necklace.

"Damn the Ifrits and damn Qaf." His own fingers blistering, he shoved the material of her cloak beneath the metal, buying them seconds. Vibrant light played over, around them and he could *hear* voices hissing in the light stream. Ifrit voices. Miu screamed once more, her entire body exploding with the channeled light, light pouring from her fingertips and eyes.

A violent blast of light tore away the clearing—and then the door was there.

With Miu's legs still wrapped firmly around his waist, he stepped through.

"Where the hell did we just go?" Miu wouldn't have believed it was possible if she hadn't seen it with her own eyes. One eensy step through the shimmering Doorway and she was in another world.

Her first impression was of heat. Air shimmered

and danced before her eyes. It was dark here, too, but with a bloodred moon high in the sky. The unfamiliar sphere was a violent spot of color in the inky darkness that gave landscape a harsh, otherworldly glow. As if this place needed that. Bad enough that coming here was like stepping into a furnace.

Carefully, Jafar set her on her feet. The sand was so hot, she could feel its heat through her shoes. Miu would have fallen if he hadn't thrust out a hand to cup her elbow.

"What is this place?" She'd never seen such a hard world. Huge cliffs towered above them, holding the darker shadows of entranceways. The sands, littered with the fossilized remnants of another time, fell away at their feet.

Jafar drew a pair of blades. "This is Qaf."

That didn't bode well. Qaf was where Ifrits came from.

"How'd we end up here?" Something howled on the other side of the hill and it was definitely not happy.

Jafar swore. "The necklace," he whispered. "I was right—it does open up a portal. And you activated it."

She looked around again. This was the most threatening place she'd ever been. It made the temple look like a pleasure garden. "I didn't sign up for this, Jafar. Why did you have to go through that Doorway?"

"I had to find out if I was right. If the necklace would really do what I thought."

"And what about me? Don't I get a vote? Maybe I didn't feel like making a social call on these Ifrits of yours."

"If I'd given you a choice, would you have come with me?"

Her silence spoke volumes.

"I thought not. You don't get high marks for obedience, little *femi*."

"You could have at least given me some warning, Jafar," she said. "You can't expect me to jump without knowing the reason why."

He withdrew another blade, handed it to her. "There may not always be time for discussion, *femi*," he warned.

"Fine. If we're in mortal peril, I vow to obey you first and ask questions later."

He nodded. "Good. We're in agreement then. And, for your information, I consider this entire trek to fall under the rubric of 'mortal peril.'"

"So this is Qaf. I thought it was a city." She squinted into the darkness. No walls. No buildings. No recognizable signs of life. Except—something was moving on the face of the cliff. Black shadows slipping in and out. "Where do the Ifrits live?"

"Caves, *femi*, carved out by ancient lava flows."

"Why do all the bad guys live inside rock?"

He ignored her implication that the Guardians were bad guys, too. "Almost impregnable, that particular fortress is. No one sneaks in there."

"What are the shadows?"

"Ifrits."

She didn't like the sound of that.

"Let's get the hell out of here." She certainly didn't see anything worth sticking around for. Her feet were already burning through the thin leather of her boots.

"Yeah, now that we know what the necklace does, I'm curious to find out why Lierr wants it so badly.

What is he planning to do with a *mazhykal* artifact that opens Doorways between realms?"

"Why do we care?" she grumbled.

"Because if he wants to travel to Qaf"—Jafar's face tightened—"then I would be very interested in knowing why."

"Perhaps he's an Ifrit." She watched Jafar for a reaction.

"I hope not."

"Why?"

"Because the Guardians thought we would know if there were Ifrits roaming about our world."

"How would you know? Maybe you missed one."

"*Femi*, we've tracked and destroyed every Ifrit that made it through the Doorways. But what if we missed one? What if some of them have found a way to open new portals? Ones that aren't guarded. What if this Lierr *is* an Ifrit?"

"Then we'd have a very large problem on our hands."

"Exactly." Jafar scanned the sky. "But there's an even larger one headed our way."

Dark shadows filled the air above them, diving with a low roar from the sky.

"Ifrits," he said grimly. "Thank Heqet I've got a bow."

Cursing, he began pulling arrows from the quiver and notching his weapon.

Was it her imagination or was the moon lower than it had been? Miu marked its passage during the space of time it took for two Ifrits to sail across the lower end of the range and empty their bows on her position. Shit. Not only was the moon setting, but it was setting faster than she'd ever believed possible.

Arrows flew steadily over her head, picking off their attackers one at a time. Slow going but, she had to hand it to her Cat, they were, surprisingly, still alive.

"Got to go," she hissed.

"Not yet." Jafar reached for another of those flaming arrows. Bully for him that he had *mazhyk* at his fingertips and could set those things on fire, but she wasn't joking.

"No," she said. "We really, really need to go now." How to tell him that she could *feel* the *mazhyk* draining from her with each inch the red moon sank below Qaf's horizon? Would serve him right if she just opened the Doorway and left him here.

Beside her, Jafar took aim. Again. His arrow sank deep into a wing, sending feathers scattering over the smoking-hot sands. One of the larger Ifrits, too, who was forced to break off from the attack formation and circle back toward the cliff dwellings.

"Got him." Coolly, he selected his next target, lining up his shot.

Lovely. She'd congratulate him on his superb marksmanship while she explained that they would soon be stuck here. For good. Unfortunately, she didn't get the impression that Qaf was open to immigrants. Definitely a closed-border policy operating here.

An Ifrit landed a short distance away in a whirl of air. Coughing on sand the guy had kicked up, she eyed the newcomer uneasily. Jafar took aim.

The Ifrit carelessly fended off the arrow, raising a

longsword with casual precision to block the *mazhyk-*enhanced point. "No warm welcome?"

No, she wasn't going to like him.

"Get away from him," Jafar snapped. He didn't take his eyes from the newcomer. "Get behind me."

"I don't think she cares for your brand of protection, Cat." The Ifrit strolled casually forward. Miu could see the dark swirls of *mazhyk* moving with him; the Ifrit had warded himself heavily. "Perhaps she would like a swap?"

Miu seriously considered kicking the Ifrit in the balls. Or trying to. She doubted those wards were going to just part and let her in. Think. She needed options.

Miu had never seen such a beautiful male before—or one who left her so bone-cold. There was something chilling about the Ifrit's eyes, about his methodical assessment of her body, as if he were weighing her capacity as a breeding machine for baby Ifrits. His eyes examined hips, breasts, and ass, but never rose above her throat.

"Procreate with me, female." What a positive waste of gorgeous masculine skin. Stalking toward her, the creature was all smoldering sensuality—except for the eyes. The eyes were cold and hard.

She ignored the Ifrit and turned to Jafar. "We've got to go." Jafar looked as if he were ready to pull his blades and take on the Ifrit hand to hand—and that would hardly be a quick piece of business.

As Miu watched the two males face off, she wondered what it would be like to really, truly be partners with Jafar. To stand by his side and have him stand by hers. *Forever.*

Looking up, she realized this was no time to indulge in fantasies. The moon was almost down. Taking a step closer to Jafar, she reached out and grabbed his arm. They'd been touching when they had gone though the portal the first time. She needed to keep physical contact with him now, too. No way she was leaving her Cat behind in this awful place.

Dragging Jafar's blade down her palm, she forced open the Doorway. They'd discovered why so many coveted the necklace: it could open powerful portals across realms—now they needed to find out why Lierr had demanded she steal a fast-track pass to Qaf. Why would he want to go there?

The sooner she got back to Shympolsk, the better.

CHAPTER TWENTY

Miu walked through the Doorway to find the lights of Shympolsk winking out as the night waned and a bleary-eyed sun crept over the horizon.

"What the—" Jafar looked around at the city's crowded buildings as if he had no idea where he'd landed. He probably didn't. One minute he'd been about to launch himself at a rabid Ifrit; the next he was standing in a garbage-strewn alley.

"I opened a Doorway," she explained. "I was thinking of Shympolsk—guess that's how it works."

"I thought you agreed I was calling the shots while we were in mortal peril." Jafar gave her a fierce look, ignoring the curious glances of some nearby beggars.

"Fine, you wanted to stay on Qaf permanently?" she asked sweetly. "You did notice that the moon was going down? It was open the Doorway right then, or kiss our asses good-bye. I don't think that Ifrit was part of any welcoming committee." She set off toward a seedy little inn where she'd stayed from time to time. "Let's get off the street," she called back over her shoulder, leaving Jafar no choice but to follow her.

Miu decided Jafar was unshockable when he walked into the questionable little hostelry as if he owned the place. He ordered the best room in the house and slapped down a pouch of stones she hadn't even known he possessed.

"We need to talk," he said, taking the steps two at a time. The hallway was particularly unclean. It appeared that they'd gutted the last guest—and hadn't bothered to clean up. Dark, rust-colored stains disfigured the walls and made climbing the stairs an unsavory endeavor.

"Really? You mean we're actually going to discuss our plan this time? Agree on it beforehand?"

He shot her an unrepentant look as they entered their room. It boasted a bed barely large enough for the two of them. Nothing more. "I suppose you think you're just going to waltz up to Lierr and hand over the necklace?"

"Something like that." She sank down on the bed, exhausted. How long had it been since she'd slept, had anything to eat?

"I told you, I'll get your sister out, but we can't let Lierr keep the necklace. Surely you can see how dangerous that would be."

"But we don't even know where he's holding Lore," she argued. "He'll have a dozen safeguards in place. You don't think you're the first person to think of stealing from him, do you? If I could just waltz in there and carry her off, he wouldn't have much leverage over me."

"Other than your word to serve him."

"Right." Her word. She'd discarded honor years ago. That commodity was just too expensive for her to afford.

"I'm a hunter," he said, when she didn't elaborate. "I'll find Lore."

"You're familiar with the city? Spent loads of time there?" He shook his head. She'd figured that would be the answer, so she continued, "Hard place to find someone, particularly if someone else doesn't want her found."

"Trust me, okay?" She didn't, they both knew it, and they both knew that was a problem.

"Find my sister first," she said.

"Just trust me, damn it!" he bellowed. "Have I ever given you any reason to distrust me?"

"Didn't tell me you were a Guardian when we met, did you?"

"You didn't ask," he gritted out.

She shrugged. "I'm sure that must make it all better. Oh, wait." She pretended to consider. "No, not really. Kinda the opposite, kitty. Makes me wonder what else I didn't ask that you neglected to tell me."

He shoved his hands through his hair. "Trust me now," he growled. "Marching straight up to Lierr and handing over the necklace is a piece of monumental stupidity."

"Really." She tapped one nail against her lips while she considered his words. "No, really, I'm still not convinced. You see, I came up with my plan and I trust me. We're back to the not-trusting-you business."

"How can I convince you to trust me?"

"You want a homework assignment? We don't have time for that."

"You don't have time for that. You have a deadline for getting back to Lierr with your stolen goods. I have all the time in the world. More." He smiled wolfishly. "There are advantages to being darn near immortal."

She could see that.

Would it really hurt if she trusted her Cat this one last time?

Stupid. She shook her head. That was as stupid as he claimed taking the necklace to Lierr was.

"Look. You need to make Lierr come to you. Draw him out of his city stronghold to neutral ground. Go straight in there to him, waving the necklace around, and he's just going to pluck it right out of your fingers. No questions. No answers. You need leverage."

Cat had a point, she reflected. "Safer bringing him out," she mused, "than going in to him."

"Right," he agreed cautiously. "Spin him a tale. Convince him you've got me on your tail and that he needs to come out and fetch the piece so you don't lead the Guardians straight to his doorstep. You can use that scrying bowl to contact him."

The master thief looked as cool and implacable as ever when he appeared in the bespelled water of the scrying bowl.

"Have you brought the necklace?" were the first words out of his mouth.

"I've got it," she answered, noting the greedy look that appeared in his eyes. "What, no thank-you? It was damn hard to steal."

"Where are you?" he demanded, ignoring her attempt at levity.

"In Shympolsk."

"What are you waiting for, then? Bring it to me, or you know what will happen to your sister."

She knew, all right. Lierr didn't bluff. He wouldn't hesitate to hurt Lore. "You'll get your necklace."

A hot presence pressed against her back and she just managed to force herself not to lean against Jafar's hard body. Into the reassuring warmth. "The merck," Lierr said. "He's still with you?"

"Yeah, Lierr, he is." No choice but to brazen it out, convince Lierr that Jafar was in her employ, her control. "That first banshee you sent after me was a tad on the murderous side. And then there were all those Ifrits. Ate my men, Lierr. Chewed them up and left me a few thank-you bits. What was I supposed to do?"

"Ifrits." If she hadn't known that nothing shocked Lierr, she'd have thought he looked vaguely surprised. And somewhat green, to boot.

"Yeah, don't tell me they're news to you." Or maybe they were. Had Lierr truly *not* known the bloodbath into which he was dropping her? No, she decided. He'd known. He just didn't have the balls to admit it to her.

"Ifrits, Lierr. You didn't tell me the Ifrits would be after your pretty piece." She raised her eyes to his. "They fight *dirty*."

He shrugged, his image rippling and distorting in the hazy mist above the bowl. "You've survived."

Barely. "At a cost, Lierr. Here I am, paying for what *you* want."

"No," he contradicted her gently. "*You're* paying for what *you* want." He shifted, and Lore's face appeared in the scry circle, Lierr's hands cupping the soft curve of her cheeks.

"Sunk to a new low?" she asked him.

Her sister grunted and Miu swung her attention to

the familiar, pale face. "Has he hurt you?" He had, she knew, but there was hurt and then there was *hurt*. Some things could be glossed over with time. Others couldn't.

"Lore." She fought the urge to close her eyes and bang her head against the wall.

"The baby sister." He smiled, and it was an expression of pure evil.

Lore opened her mouth and he pressed a finger against it. "No, darling. I think your contribution at this point is rather superfluous. You've sent a charming message to your sister."

"Lierr—"

Lore stared at her from the scry circle, a tear streaking down her cheek, looking for all the world like the naive baby she was.

"Let her go, Lierr."

"Bring me the necklace, Miu." Lierr pressed a small, hard kiss against the corner of Lore's beautiful mouth. "Don't make me mad."

"Right, there's just one problem. I've got Guardians tracking me. You ready to have them trail me right to your hidey-hole?"

"Cats?" he asked, looking doubtful for the first time. "I don't think much of the friends you've picked up, Miu. Meet me in the tea garden where you used to work. Midnight."

The connection broke and the surface of the bowl slowly flowed back to perfectly ordinary water.

Jafar took the bowl from her hands and gently set it back in its pouch.

The small crinkle of skin between her eyebrows

made something in the region of his belly ache. He frowned. No one had told him that this mating business meant *hurt*.

"No worries, love," he said. "He touches her, I'll kill him."

"Do you think he'll really bring Lore to the tea garden?" She chewed on her lower lip, mangling the tender flesh. Inside him, the Cat shifted, scenting blood.

"I'll find out at midnight, won't I?"

"*You'll* find out?"

"Yeah, you'll be waiting here, safe and sound."

"No." She didn't even bother looking at him. "My sister. My job. I go with you."

"Why can't you let me help you?" Flesh smacked flesh and he looked down in some surprise at the bright sting of pain blossoming in his hand. He'd just slammed one fist into his other palm.

"I'm just not used to having help." She stood and paced across the room.

"You don't trust me." It was as plain as the nose on his face and he didn't need the senses of his Cat to pick out the distrust emanating from her.

"Sure I do." And wasn't that about as unconvincing an answer as he'd ever heard?

"You do?"

"Sure." She paced back to the bed. Flopping down on it, she drew up her knees and wrapped her arms protectively around them.

"We're mates." He kept his voice calm. "Mates look out for one another." And he looked forward to the day *she'd* look out for *him*, although he wasn't holding his breath. "Why won't you trust me? Is it because of Lierr? Because he's the one who convinced you that all males are untrustworthy pricks who you should kick around and belittle?"

She looked up, met his eyes.

"No," she said.

He was sick and tired of one-word answers. "No," he agreed. "So who did teach you that little life lesson? Or did you just make it up on your own?" He didn't wait for her to answer. If he did, the Cat was going to burst free and show her *precisely* how mates treated one another.

"No," she burst out. "*Lierr* didn't teach me that lesson. He didn't have to. I'd already learned it a dozen times by the time he plucked me from the tea gardens and informed me that, in all his benevolent goodness, he'd decided to make a *project* of me. I knew what he was and what he'd want from me—and I went with him anyway. No surprises there."

He brushed a strand of cinnamon hair back from her face. "You knew."

"Yeah, I knew."

"And you decided to let him use you so you could use him."

"Yeah. So you don't have to pity me or feed me this I-understand-your-pain crap. It was a business arrangement. I don't trust anyone."

"Other than your sister?" He watched her carefully.

"Not even her." She shrugged. "Not really. Love her, yes, but she'll do what she needs to do to survive and I can respect that."

"I need you to trust me," he growled. "That's part of being a mate. Our females have to trust us, have to know that even if we change, we will not harm them."

He reached out and took her face between his hands. "You've seen my Cat. Are you afraid of it?"

Miu sat silently on the bed, gazing up at him. Holding her breath.

Was she frightened? He scented the air, pulling the warm, delicious tendrils of scent deep inside him. Female musk. Soap. Just a whiff of anger.

But no fear. The Cat growled with satisfaction. She could hold her own.

The mattress whispered pleasantly as she shifted toward him slightly.

"Touch me," he demanded, feeling the change beginning.

Would she do it? Did she dare?

Coming up on her knees, she laid a small hand on his shoulder, where the skin flickered between its familiar golden color and the thick, furred pelt of the Cat.

"Like this?" she asked, her voice breathy.

He remembered her fear of the Cat in the tunnel. And also her excitement. Eyes narrowing, he swung his gaze to meet hers. "Will you lie down with my Cat, Miu?" His voice was a low, deep rasp. He didn't want to disgust her, make her fear him, but he couldn't hide who—or what—he was any longer. If she stayed with him now, she accepted the male and she accepted the Cat.

Both of them.

The Cat chuffed, a low, feral hiss of sound. His nails curved, lengthened—and the fabric of the bedclothes parted.

Protect. Pounce. The conflicting urges threatened to pull him apart.

Her eyes examined his face, watched as his Guardian form was subsumed by the Cat. "Yes," she whispered.

Yes. He was afraid to admit the satisfaction that one word gave him. The visceral jolt of liquid pleasure made his cock thicken and strain toward his mate.

Her eyes dropped to his cock and flew back to his face. "We're in this together. I trust you, and you let me go along to meet Lierr. You up for that, Cat?"

He was. He used the raw heat of his huge Cat's body to back her against the headboard.

What sent him over the edge was the faint, unmistakable sound of bells as she slowly stripped off her clothes.

"Here, kitty, kitty," she said.

The wet heat of his rough tongue stroked her neck. The hard press of his body made her glad that she was already on the bed. Less distance to fall, because the damned Cat turned her knees to jelly. When his tongue slid over her breast, exploring, she choked on a moan. He was tasting her and she wondered what he tasted. She craved his touch on some fundamental, primitive level of her being. His urgency beckoned to her. No matter what form he took, he wanted *her*, and that was an aphrodisiac unlike any sold in the city.

"Kitty," she breathed, surrendering to his ministrations. With erotic efficiency he licked her, bringing her to the edge of orgasm again and again. Between her thighs, she could feel his thick golden fur, rubbing her most sensitive spots with delicious friction.

And then he was changing back, taking on his Guardian form with liquid rapidity. Thick fur shifted and became skin, vanishing as he pressed his face against her throat, inhaling.

She wanted this, she realized. Wanted him. Only him.

"Mine." Grasping his hair in both hands, she swung his face up until his eyes were level with hers. He growled. She smiled. "Mine," she said again. "You keep saying we're mates. Fine. I'm good with it. But it works both ways, kitty. *You're* mine. Got it?"

He nodded curtly.

"Yeah," he rasped. One hard hand threaded through her hair, holding her in place for his kiss. The other hand—she shuddered—stroked down her shoulder with authoritative firmness, over the rounded curve of her belly. No finesse and she wanted none. Just primitive possession. "Mine," he growled, his fingers tangling in the fine threads of the gold chain he'd locked around her waist, plucking at the links until they tugged at the bells that stabbed the very core of her.

The bells were a lush fullness, sliding slickly through the swollen, wet folds of her sex. A teasing weight. Smooth and heated by her own skin. A caress she was aware of every moment of the day. Heqet, he might as well have branded her. She couldn't escape from the memories of his arms, his lips, his touch. Now he plucked at the very core of her.

Worse yet, she didn't want to escape.

She loved him, the bastard.

A sharp tug of the chain sent bells jolting upward, blazing an electric path of sensation through her sex. The bells stabbed at her clitoris and she gasped. Flashes of electric light exploded behind her closed lids. "Mine," he said again.

Yeah, she got that.

This worked both ways. If he had taken her, well, *she* had taken *him*. Clearly, he needed a reminder. She wrapped both hands around his heavy sex. "And this is mine. We're perfectly clear. So get on with it."

Much to her satisfaction, he did. And as he stroked her to shuddering orgasm, she wasn't entirely sure whether it was man or Cat who claimed her.

Had he hurt her? Locked deep inside him, the Cat protested. The Cat certainly hadn't intended to hurt the female Jafar was cradling in his arms. No. The Cat adored that female. Only wanted to be close, close, close.

It didn't matter. He had no right to do this to her.

He knew better than to take any female when the transformation threatened him. Pulling out of her soft body, he examined her face for signs of distress.

Her eyelids fluttered and she stared up at him.

"Your Cat came out," she said quietly.

He stilled, waiting for the anger. The disgust.

"He's as playful as you," she said, to his surprise. Then she smiled and he thought he would fall over from the shock of it. "And I think he likes me."

He knew his Cat did.

"Let me go to Shympolsk for you, lover," he said, settling back into their old argument. At least that argument was familiar ground. He knew what her objections were *there*. "Let me look after this one thing for you."

She was shaking her head before he'd finished. And then she stood his world on its head with one simple question.

"Are you crazy?" She swatted away the warm hand that feathered erotic patterns over her shoulders and the upward slope of her breasts. "No. We're partners. We settled that."

Jafar lay spooned behind her, his large body curled around hers.

"Let me be close to you," he whispered, and she was lost.

The moment was ineffably sweet, a bright blossom in the very dark air of the room, a softening of the edge of bright fear that she kept carefully tucked away. The fear that she would not escape from Lierr. Wrapped in a cocoon of night dark and Guardian *mazhyk*, she heard only the soft slide of fabric and the shifting of their bodies.

He lay on his side behind her, lifting her to her side and wrapping himself around her. His thick erection stroked gently at the tight seam of her thighs for long minutes. Just the velvety soft tip of his penis stroked deliciously, as the lazy excitement built. Cream slipped from her body.

He parted her thighs with his knee. The broad head of his erection separated the lips of her sex, sliding into her body slowly. Filling and stretching her.

"You feel so good," she whispered. "Move now."

And he did. Long, slow, luscious strokes that seemed to suggest they had all the time in the world. "Like this?" He stroked deeply into her, pulling back with a delicious friction that made her want to grab his body and pull it back to hers. Hard.

Instead of answering, she reached down to cup the heavy weight of his testicles, savoring the heat of them. The position was awkward but rewarding. She stroked the tender skin stretched between his balls and his perineum. He was taut with excitement. He was beautiful.

He reached around to pet her clitoris, tugging gently. They came together in long, slow shudders. This time, he was silent and the sex was slow and sweet and close. It was as if she were becoming one being with this Cat lover, she realized, and she could only hope that her instincts had not been misguided.

CHAPTER TWENTY-ONE

Miu settled herself at a table in the tea garden just before midnight. Jafar had objected strenuously to the idea that she was to be the distraction that would keep Lierr from noticing his own presence, but, as she'd pointed out, there really wasn't much choice. The thief master was unlikely to hand over her sister unless he saw both Miu and the necklace.

The seconds seemed to tick by with agonizing slowness as she waited. And then, across the garden, she spotted him. Dark, ageless, and uncannily good-looking, Lierr stepped closer, moving into the circle of light cast by the candle on her table.

"Why, Miu," he said softly, "I almost think you're not pleased to see me."

"Your damn necklace just about got me killed," she complained. Not to mention mated. For life. With a Guardian.

"I never promised easy," he said lightly, and she gave in to the urge to look up. She hated speaking to Lierr's chest. She'd forgotten just how large he really was.

"This makes us quits," she warned. She wasn't handing anything over until he agreed—again—to the terms of their contract. As far as she knew, she was the first thief in a decade to complete the terms of her contract. She wasn't letting him suck her into another hundred thefts because she was too stupid to close all the loopholes before she handed over the goods. It would be just like Lierr to figure out some clever way of binding her to him right after he released her.

She narrowed her eyes.

Lierr had controlled her through the markings on her forearm. Somehow, he'd been able to send unimaginable pain—as well as just discomfort, so nice to know he had a sliding scale—to whatever portion of her anatomy he'd decided to assault. That particular hold he had over her was going to break. Now.

"Remove the mark," she ordered, knowing he would expect that to be her first demand, "and then I'll hand over your necklace and be on my way. You can play dress-up with it on your own time."

He smiled softly and she really, really disliked the sympathetic look he shot her. "I do need you to hand over the necklace, Miu, but that's not all I'm going to need."

"Take off the mark," she repeated. "And then let me see my sister."

"You opened a Doorway." He shrugged lazily. "Yes, I know about your mysterious arrival in Shympolsk. I have eyes everywhere in the city. And besides, how else could you have traveled here from the Valley in so little time?"

"So you know I can control the necklace." Jafar had been right all along. She examined the thick shadows behind Lierr, knowing Jafar was hidden somewhere among them. She had to pull off her part in their scheme. Get Lierr to hand over Lore before actually giving him the necklace.

He'd moved silently closer to her. "Let's complete our deal, love. You give me the necklace." He held out his hand, palm up. "I release your delightful sister."

He nodded his head toward one of the rooms where girls entertained customers. His bodyguards surged forward, dragging a reluctant Lore with them. Miu eyeballed her. Lore was minimally clad—Miu would have expected no less from Lierr. He'd had her hands tied, leaving all of her glorious curves on display. Even from where she stood, Miu could see Lore's eyes, and it was obvious her sister was spitting mad. The bodyguards holding her were doing their damnedest not to look down at all the lush flesh on display. "I'm not sure you're returning her in one piece, Lierr."

"She'll be fine." At his signal, the guards forced her sister into a carriage that had pulled up just outside the garden.

"And they're taking her to—?" she asked delicately.

"To wherever she wants to be taken." He smiled coldly down at her. "That's my end of the bargain kept, love. Now yours."

She hesitated. Could she pull this off?

"Miu," Lierr said warningly. She didn't have to look down to know that the dark markings on her forearm were glowing a warning red. Bloodred. "We can do this simply." He didn't voice the other half of his threat. He didn't have to. Delicate ripples of pain pierced her forearm.

A warning.

A reminder.

She knew she had no choice but to carry out her end of the scheme she and Jafar had worked out. Lierr was planning to use the necklace for some nefarious purpose of his own, and she'd long since come to agree with her Cat that the necklace was better off—safer—deep in the catacombs where it could be well guarded.

She reached up and removed the circlet, slapping the still-cool metal down on the table before her.

"Take it," she said.

"My thanks." His fingers closed around hers. Heat roared up her arm.

He spoke the ritual spell, a set of unbinding words in an unfamiliar tongue. Miu fought not to stagger at the power rushing along her arm, through her body from where they were connected. The tea garden wavered and she would have fallen if Lierr hadn't pulled her up against his hard body. Funny, she thought dimly. She hadn't really been convinced that Lierr had those urges.

The power shifted and she looked up. Something was *happening* to Lierr. Something grotesque. As the power rippled outward from the necklace, Lierr's face looked as if it were cracking, melting before her eyes. The features rearranged themselves and the handsome face grew harder.

"Surprise," he said softly. "Although I did think you'd figured it out earlier."

Dumbly she stared up at him. Lierr's new face was harsher, starker, and unabashedly saturnine. He still had the same liquid eyes, though now they blazed with an unfamiliar violet light.

"Contract's complete," she said.

"Not quite." Regret flashed in his eyes.

"One hundred thefts," she countered. "Done. Delivered."

"Well, yes," he said. That *was* regret she heard coloring his voice. "But now I need something else from you. Something that has nothing to do with our oh-so-convenient contract."

Lierr put his arm around her shoulders, immobilizing her against his much larger body. He stroked her hair away from her throat, fastening the necklace around her. Familiar weight settled on her skin.

"No." She put up a show of objecting. Lierr knew her well, knew she would not go along with his demand willingly. Act convincingly, and he wouldn't guess that she and Jafar had planned this. Once the Doorway opened, Jafar would leap out of hiding. There would be no time for Lierr's guards to react. She, Lierr, and Jafar would step through the Doorway, right into the temple. At least, that was what they hoped.

"Yes, love." He bent his head to her ear. "Unfortunately, I'm afraid I need a moon daemon to make the necklace work for me. You see, when I still had my poor Pho, she never had any problem whatsoever with the damn thing. Opened Doorways like a dream. She and I could move anywhere we wanted."

He'd been partners with Jafar's Ifrit?

"Pho insisted, of course, that she wear the necklace, and I was perfectly willing to let her. The necklace was crafted for female power and, though I could force it to do my bidding, I would have run the danger of shattering the stone. So I let Pho wear it and I just made sure I kept close tabs on her. Very close tabs." A small, dark smile curled his lips. "Call the moon, Miu. Open the Doorway. It's time I went home."

* * *

Lierr had spent the last four decades suppressing his natural appetites, making do with backstreet whores and tea-garden girls. When he pulled Miu's soft, curved body against his own, he had to remind himself that sex really wasn't important.

Not in the grand scheme of things.

And if he'd waited this long, he could wait just a little bit longer. Once Miu transported him back to Qaf, he'd be able to satisfy every urge. Including the desire for revenge that had eaten away at him every second since Pho had died. He might not have loved the beautiful little bitch, but he'd been fond of her in his own way. And they'd been partners—so letting an Ifrit lord get away with her death was unacceptable. The lord had to pay, even if it took everything Lierr had and then some.

Gasping, as he tightened his arm inexorably around her throat, Miu called down the moon as if she were opening a tap. At first just a small thread of light and then more, rushing faster as the bright strands poured from the sky. Knowing his unwilling assistant too well for comfort, Lierr tightened his grasp around her. Miu would leave him behind if she could. He'd always admired her stubbornness; it was a quality that had made her an excellent thief. Too bad he'd have to break her now. He almost thought he would have finally given her the independence she'd coveted for so long; they really were kindred spirits.

But revenge was—when you got right down to it—well, revenge. He couldn't release Miu and have his revenge, so he was going to have revenge. And then he'd take whatever was left of Miu. It would have to be enough.

Again, he spoke in the language of Qaf, reciting the spell that would direct the opening of the Doorway to form a portal between this world and his own.

A glow lit up about Miu and, just like that, a Doorway shimmered into existence. Through the hazy surface, he could make out the familiar outlines of Qaf. Home. Even if his fellow Qaf dwellers had done their level best to wash their hands of him all those years ago.

He was going back.

Miu twisted in his hold, a horrified look on her face.

"Done," she spat. "That's the end of our deal. Let me go now, Lierr, or I let the Doorway close."

He looked down at her, smoothing an errant lock of hair behind her ear. "Let the Doorway close," he said pleasantly, "and you'll regret it. I'll simply make you reopen it. After." Since her fingers twitched on the stones, she clearly understood the implications of his threat.

Good.

"Bastard," she accused. "You've got what you wanted."

"And now I should let you go?" His eyes swept regretfully over her face. It really was a pity to take her to Qaf, but without her he wouldn't be able to reopen the Doorway on his own. He'd be trapped there, until he found a Caller willing to overlook his very unfortunate status with the Qaf council. Since he rather doubted he was going to find such a Caller—the council kept very close tabs on them for a reason—he wasn't going to run the chance of losing Miu.

"Yeah." She glared up at him. "Thought you were a man of honor, Lierr. We had a deal. You're bending the rules and trying my patience."

What did she think she could do? Knowing Miu, she had a half-dozen backup plans. Unfortunately for her, she'd learned everything she knew from him. Which meant he was at least one step ahead of her.

He pulled her toward the Doorway.

"A man of honor." When she dug in her feet, he simply scooped her up and strode toward the dark, waiting shadow that separated this realm from Qaf. "You're forgetting, my dear. I'm no man."

She hissed something extremely uncomplimentary about his parentage. Her accusations could have been true, for all he knew; it was certainly true that most Ifrits were hardly discriminating in their choice of sexual partners.

"I'm an Ifrit." Saying it made everything seem so much more real. He had succeeded. He was going home. And he was—finally—going to have his revenge. He closed the distance between them and the Doorway. Gritting his teeth, he pushed his leg through the thick, dark curtain of air. Painful awareness tingled along his nerve endings. He could feel long-dormant desires awakening. Stirring. Yes, his sexual appetites were going to come back with a vengeance once he was exposed to Qaf's lunar pull again.

"Ifrit bastard," she growled, fighting against his hold. Her hands smashed up toward his unprotected throat and he fought back a snarl of his own. His right hand wrapped around her throat, seeking for the pressure points that would incapacitate her. Finding them, he pressed. With a choked cry, she collapsed in his arms.

"Sweet dreams, little thief," he whispered, cradling his burden in his arms. Unhesitatingly, he stepped through the dark sheet.

Chapter Twenty-two

The bastard had taken the bait.

Jafar struggled not to burst from concealment too soon. Watching Lierr wrap a fist in his mate's hair and expose the vulnerable column of her throat took more control than he'd thought possible. He'd wanted to leap toward the pair, rip his mate from the other male's arms. None of which was part of their plan to trap the thief master.

Mentally, he stalked Lierr, testing for weaknesses in the male's defenses. He'd surrounded himself not only by human guards, but by powerful *mazhyk*. Logically, Jafar understood that Miu had to go through all the motions of reluctantly cooperating with Lierr. He was too well protected and Jafar didn't like the odds of success if he were forced to confront all of those guards at once. To say nothing of the *mazhyk* the thief master might be wielding.

Lierr bent his head and whispered something to the struggling Miu. Edging closer through the shadows, Jafar moved up behind him. He was still too far away to hear what was being said. He forced himself to wait, not knowing how Miu's scheme was going down. He had to wait until the Doorway opened.

And then the entire plan went to hell in the proverbial handbasket. The Doorway opened, all right, but through it, Jafar could make out not the familiar tunnels of the catacombs, but the distinctive reddish glow of Qaf.

Hell, he never should have let his Miu come with him on this fool's mission. Neither of them knew enough about how the necklace worked to really control it.

With a savage growl, Jafar leapt from his hiding place. Already, Lierr was moving toward the open Doorway, his long stride eating up the ground with each step. Miu was draped in his arms, limp. Jafar reminded himself that her position was part of the plan—as was his reaching the pair before Lierr took her through the Doorway. But something had gone terribly wrong. It seemed fairly certain that Lierr had either traveled by Doorway before or understood the way the necklace worked far better than they. Obviously, he'd done something to direct the portal so it would open in Qaf. Whatever happened, Jafar could not let Miu go through that Doorway with Lierr.

Now he cursed himself as twice a fool for having agreed to her plan in the first place. Preparing to attack, he launched himself into a smooth, lethal run. Straight for Lierr.

Lierr spat a low curse and *mazhyk* lit the tea garden. Jafar didn't need to feel the blast of heat from the Doorway to know where Lierr wanted to go. Hell. The bastard *was* an Ifrit. He glowed darker with each step toward the open Doorway.

"Stop," Jafar barked, knowing that Lierr wouldn't, but hoping against hope. With Lierr possessing Ifrit

mazhyk, the fight would be closer than he'd anticipated. Sighting his target, Jafar threw his first blade.
Aimed for the heart.

Cursing, Lierr threw up a shield of hot air with the
flick of a wrist, then swung his armful of Jafar's female
around to use as shield. This was the part where Miu
was supposed to resuscitate. She did, coming alive in
the other male's arms in a lethal whirl of arms and
legs.

Lierr subdued her easily, and with too much pleasure. "I'll enjoy teaching her what an Ifrit demands of
the female in his bed. And there's not going to be a
damned thing you can do about it."

"Want to bet?" Jafar growled, taking a step forward.
He sensed rather than felt the guards across the tea
garden drawing their blades.

"Right. She's your mate." The Ifrit cocked his head
and stared at Jafar. "I should be concerned about that
bond you've got between the two of you." He shrugged.
"No. Not really. I've heard that the male can feel every
touch, every stroke the female feels. That true, Jafar? If
it is, you're going to feel me fucking her every day for
the rest of your life."

Miu sank her teeth deep into Lierr's wrist.

"Oh, not nice, love," Lierr growled. A thick fist
came up, snapping Miu's head back. This time, Jafar
knew, she wouldn't be coming out of it anytime soon.

Jafar shifted with a roar of rage. Pheromones were a
red wash of color obscuring his vision. He gave the
beast full rein. There was no time to stop and negotiate—he didn't think Lierr was in any mood for it anyway.

Pausing, Lierr smiled. "See me off, now, will you,

Jafar? Did you know Pho was my lover? Once again, here I am with a female of yours and, surprise, surprise—turns out she's not yours at all. I hear darling Pho had you wrapped around her finger, wanting her. The big, tough Guardian who couldn't believe— couldn't accept—that the female he wanted didn't want him. All she wanted was what you could give her: access to the temple. My Miu here is cut from the same cloth. She doesn't really want you, Guardian. No, what she wants is your necklace—so that she can please *me*."

Lierr's voice told Jafar that Lierr had planned this setup from the very beginning. It was no accident that he'd sent Miu down into the catacombs, to the necklace and the Doorways Jafar had always guarded. He concentrated on ignoring the sharp bite of shock. Miu wasn't Pho, although the taunting sneer on Lierr's face claimed otherwise.

"You chose a female over the Guardians all those years ago. And now you've done it again. Slow learner, aren't you?"

"Miu is not Pho," Jafar said through gritted teeth.

Miu wasn't Pho. Logically, he knew this. But on the surface, the two females shared the same story: both had been intruders in the temple, intent on personal agendas, and both times he'd let them go free.

Lierr shot him a look. "Are you sure about that, Cat? From where I stand, there are a whole lot of similarities. Guess who she'll choose—the master to whom she pledged herself as a child, or you, the male she's been fucking on the side?"

This was where Miu was supposed to roll free. Clearly, she wasn't going to be doing so anytime soon.

Lierr snapped his fingers. Large male bodyguards slipped out of shadows around them as Lierr stepped through the Doorway, taking Miu with him.

Rage poured through Jafar, struggling to break free of his skin as his Cat snarled in anger. Lierr had taken his mate.

Launching himself through space, he aimed for the rapidly closing Doorway.

Returning to consciousness was like swimming up through layers of thick, heated water that threatened to pull her down to some unseen bottom. Cracking an eye, Miu examined her surroundings and found her situation just as bad as she'd anticipated. Lierr had not only pulled her straight through the Doorway and into Qaf—he'd taken her afterward to a whole new part of Qaf. Instead of the hot sand plains that surrounded the cliffs on all sides, the damn male had dragged her into one of the shadowy caverns.

Now, he pressed his face against the side of her neck, tracing a hot, damp pattern on the exposed skin. She shoved at his arm, her head still swimming from his blow.

The bastard had hit her. Hard.

"Rise and shine, love." Sharp teeth nipped at her throat. "We're home."

No. Home was in another realm altogether. With Jafar. She forced the panic from her mind. She wasn't supposed to have wound up in Qaf. She was *supposed* to have been back inside the temple, with Jafar. Ready to hand Lierr and the necklace over to the Amun Ra. So, once again, things weren't going according to plan.

A hard finger stroked down her cheek. "I'm growing impatient."

Woozily, she opened her eyes all the way.

His dark eyes watched her. "You have heard stories about the Ifrits, love?"

"That women run screaming from them?" She smiled sweetly for his benefit, but her mind was racing.

"I'll have you screaming, all right." He dropped her onto something soft and she immediately shoved herself upright into a sitting position. Flat on her back with Lierr in the room seemed immensely unwise, and the massive bulge in his groin had her rethinking the word *immense*.

His eyes followed hers. "I'm looking forward to it," he said lightly. "I think you'll find I have some unfamiliar sides."

"Save it," she suggested, scooting to the edge of the bed. Somewhat to her surprise, he didn't stop her. Merely stood over her, looking smugly amused.

"At least admit that I won this round. Your little trick failed, Miu, and here we are. Just the two of us." He waved a hand at their surroundings.

The cavern to which he'd brought them held only the bed he'd dropped her on, but the enormous four-poster with its crimson hangings dominated the already impressive space. Flames roared to life in the fireplace with a flick of his hand, their shadows crawling across the thick fur pelts that covered the floor. She wasn't sure she wanted to know what animal had provided the rug. Since Ifrits liked to skin their enemies, she was probably treading on some poor wereprince who'd fallen afoul of the Ifrits and had sacrificed his pelt for their creature comforts.

Unfortunately, there were no windows. Just a single doorway, and of course, Lierr's large body was planted firmly between her and that escape route.

She needed moonlight to make the necklace work again: was the moon up here? If it were, she planned to do her damnedest to leave Lierr behind. Odds were high he couldn't move freely between the realms or he would have done so on his own. He *wouldn't* have been looking for the necklace.

She took a half step toward the cavern mouth. If she could make it outside, maybe she stood a chance of escaping. But first she'd have to retrieve the moonstone necklace. She put her hand to her throat. Lierr must have removed it while she was unconscious.

Lierr stalked toward her and she scrambled for the safety of words. She had to keep him talking. Had Jafar made it through the Doorway? Was he somewhere on Qaf, searching for her?

"Why?" She eyed him. Had he grown even larger since they'd arrived here or was she imagining things? "Why'd you come through the Doorway to our world all those years ago?"

"Looking for true confessions, a tell-all tale, Miu?"

"Humor me." Apparently he must have thought he *did* owe her something. Not only did he not backhand her for her curiosity, but he filled in the blanks for her.

"I fell in love, Miu." He bowed mockingly. "Like you, I'm afraid I chose someone a tad out of my social class. Pho was charming, talented, beautiful." He shrugged. "As well as bloodthirsty, passionate, and ambitious. Perfection in an Ifrit package with a bloodline that would have made a purist weep."

"Sounds fabulous." Had he placed the necklace in

his pocket? The material bulged slightly and, as unfamiliar as she was with Ifrit anatomy, she recognized concealed jewels when she saw them. How to get it back?

"Oh, she was." His eyes darkened. "Except for the princess bit. That part made *my* life infinitely more difficult. The rank and file don't court the nobility."

Not in any world. Yeah, that would have sucked all right. No point in throwing her abductor that bone though. "Didn't know that Ifrits had females." If they *had* females of their own, then why were they constantly marauding through the Doorways, making off with human females? Something didn't add up.

"A few." Lierr's eyes darkened. "Well guarded. But Pho, well, she was as restless—as *curious*—as I was. She'd laid hands on the necklace years before we teamed up; the bauble had apparently belonged to her mother. The necklace's powers made it possible for the wearer—and anyone touching her—to move through the Doorways as many times as they wished. So we explored."

"She was a moon daemon?"

"No, the necklace was keyed to her family's bloodlines. It worked for her and would have worked for her mother. It certainly didn't work for me."

"So why me?" She stared at him suspiciously. "Why am I able to make the thing work?"

He smiled patronizingly. "Apparently, when the necklace was created, moon daemon blood was used to seal the words into the stone. A loophole, a back door," he said impatiently, when she looked at him blankly. "In case someone besides the owner wanted to use the artifact, he'd have to know what kind of blood was used in the original ceremony—and he'd have to be able to lay hands on that kind of donor." He laughed, but Miu didn't think he found anything funny. "Ifrit society—our society—is terribly ancient. And rather Byzantine. My kind dotes on that sort of mystery and ritual. Creating a powerful artifact with secret keys would have been right up their alley. Easy access for those with the right family bloodlines—and a holy grail for everyone else."

Lierr stepped closer and, this time, there was no-where to go, short of hopping back up onto the bed, and there was no way she was issuing that kind of invi-tation. He stroked one long finger down her neck, test-ing the softness of her flesh. "Pretty," he said absentmindedly.

She stepped away from his touch, closer to the cav-ern mouth. She couldn't make a run for it though. He'd be on her in a flash. "Tell me more," she encour-aged. *Tell me more and forget about the lustful thoughts you're wearing on your face.* Hell, he could have written *gonna fuck you now* on his face and it couldn't have been much clearer that returning home was waking up the dark Ifrit needs he'd suppressed for so long.

"Well, eventually Pho's father found out that daugh-ter dearest was making unauthorized forays into the upper realms." He shrugged. "He wasn't happy. At all. He rather suspected that Pho was looking for a way to gain power. It's what most Ifrit princesses do, eventu-ally: supplant their sires. Take their places at the courts. Rule, if they're strong enough."

"Was she?"

"Maybe. It didn't matter. She was still very young

and Papa sent a pack of Ifrits after us while we were exploring Shympolsk. Without any Ifrits of our own and just a couple of human servants, we didn't stand much of a chance. He knew that."

"But you survived." And had somehow gone from inter-realm refugee to world-class thief.

"I did. I'm afraid I was too much of a rebel to give in and die quietly. While Papa's Ifrits grabbed my poor princess, I fled. She must have got away from them long enough to open a Doorway into that temple of your damned Cat, but then they killed her."

"She killed Guardians. And a mate."

Lierr shrugged, unconcerned. "It didn't matter. Not to me. She could have killed anyone she wanted, so long as they weren't Ifrit. The laws are different here, love. Your kind are terribly expendable."

"Right," she said tightly. "So your Pho was dead and buried in the Guardians' temple, and you were stuck in our world, with no way to open a Doorway back to Qaf."

Lierr nodded. "Until I found you. Then I knew I finally had a chance. Sure, the necklace was locked up good and tight in Pho's coffin and I couldn't see any way of getting to it right away, but I knew that eventually I'd have my chance. I waited, learning everything I could about the temple, grooming you to be the perfect thief, the perfect mate the Cats could not resist. I knew you would do anything I asked to complete the hundredth theft and gain freedom for you and your sister. You would bring me the necklace, and I would have my ticket home."

"But why did you want to get back to Qaf so badly?

You had everything you could have wanted in Shympolsk—wealth, women, power. Did you miss this place so much?"

"No." He withdrew the moonstone from his pocket. "Not precisely."

The Ifrit who stepped into the chamber answered the question for her. "He wanted revenge."

"Papa?" she asked lightly.

"Precisely." Dark satisfaction lit Lierr's eyes.

Chapter Twenty-three

Nothing had prepared Miu for the brutal reality of two Ifrits fighting it out, tooth and nail. *Mazhyk* to *mazhyk*. Each blow landed wetly, with the horrific crunching of bone. The chamber was awash in dark black blood.

Now would be an excellent time to get the hell out of the chamber.

Out of Qaf.

"I've been watching you," the Ifrit growled, flinging Lierr backward against the wall. "Every step you took, you bastard, I was there, I was watching."

Lierr spat blood and lunged toward his opponent. "Fat lot of good it did you," he sneered. "Lost your precious Pho, didn't you?"

"And you'll lose your female here," the newcomer snarled. "I sent a pack of Ifrits after her when she first laid hands on your necklace. Almost got her then, but instead, I'll have her now."

Miu edged away from the two Ifrits. This Ifrit was responsible for the deaths of Ebo and her men? Any sympathy she'd felt over the loss of his daughter died a rapid death. Papa jerked Lierr's arm impossibly high behind Lierr's back. With a wet popping sound, the bones dislocated and skin tore. Lierr howled, dropping the necklace to the floor.

"I'll use your little pet," the invader taunted. "Plow her hard while you watch. Not going to be much of her left after tonight."

Way to bring her into this. Lierr growled and shook his arm back into place, diving for the other man's chest with his clawed hands.

What had the other Ifrit said? Tonight? It was nighttime. Escape time.

The two whirlwinds collided before her in a rain of fire and sparks. Darting past them, she threw herself toward the necklace lying forgotten on the cavern floor. Just as her fingers closed over it, two large hands clamped brutally around her upper arms. Smoke blinded her. Where was Lierr? Something in the gloating look of Papa Ifrit's face as he picked up the necklace from the floor told her that her former Master hadn't fared too well. Deciding she needed to get away from this bloodbath, with or without the necklace, she lunged for the cavern entrance.

Outside, she found herself in a maze of tunnels and lava tubes that would have mystified anyone but a moon daemon. Drawing on her link to the moonlight outside, she began running for the surface as the chamber shook behind her.

In his Cat form, he was faster, so Jafar remained in it, ruthlessly pushing his body up the stone tunnel. Nothing was going to stop him from reaching his female. The Cat's paws devoured the distance, wicked claws clicking ominously against the loose stones. His female. His mate.

Judging by the din coming from up ahead, it wasn't going to be too difficult to find her.

If he were lucky, he'd kill two birds with one stone. He'd get his mate back—and he'd strike a devastating blow at the Ifrits. He didn't fool himself: even though he still was a Guardian at heart, he'd broken ranks. He'd turned his back on Amun Ra and the other Guardians. They might welcome any destruction he wreaked on the Ifrits, but they wouldn't welcome him back. In their place, he would have felt the same. He'd made his choice. And he hadn't chosen them. He'd chosen Miu.

Pushing thoughts of his mate hurt, broken—alone—from his mind, he let the Cat's drive consume him. The walls rushed past him in a furious blur. There. Up ahead. He'd spotted her. He fought back a sigh of relief and then wanted to roar. This wasn't like him. He didn't *feel*. Ever. He was a ruthless killer. A Guardian.

Well, it could rain Ifrits and he'd still want to pull the cursed female into his arms and rumble words of love and admonishment into her dirt-streaked hair. Fighting off Ifrits had left her distinctly the worse for wear. Long pieces of unruly hair stuck out of her haphazard braid and someone had dragged her face through the dust. Quite a bit of dust. She'd acquired a mud brown coating that made her look like a prickly Qevarian hedgehog.

Wait. His mind backed up, reeling. Mud was the least of his worries.

Words of admonishment. And love.

He understood discipline. And, hell, he was *made* for punishment. Heat sizzled through him as he considered the erotic possibilities of instilling just a *modicum* of sense into his mate. But love? The Cat chuffed in feral agreement and the man—well, the man knew when to admit he'd lost. Yeah. He closed his eyes briefly and wondered if his legs were really that wobbly. It would be embarrassing if he had to break off his pursuit and lean against the wall to catch his breath.

Love.

He loved his prickly, stubborn, gorgeous-inside-and-out *femi*. The Cat chuffed again and, this time, his mate finally looked behind her. Damn moon daemon eyes. They'd have picked him out even if his own eyes hadn't been glowing with the change, not to mention all that pent-up passion burning its slow, insidious way through his veins.

Yeah, he had it bad for her.

"Kitty?" She half turned, skittering to a stop. She reached out one hand to steady herself against the walls of the tunnel.

His Cat chuffed happily and didn't resist when he shifted.

"Moon daemon," he grunted, just to watch her eyes light up. Yeah, he definitely had it bad.

She took a step toward him—she was *coming*, to *him*—and then there was another loud, earsplitting explosion from behind her. Somewhere, an Ifrit shrieked with even more force than a cave banshee, and the smooth sides of the tunnel rippled with the expanding power. His eyes noted the red, abraded skin of her bare neck, but even the lost necklace didn't matter right now.

He wanted her to come to him. Willingly. More than anything he had ever wanted in his life.

"You *did* come for me," she breathed. There was something in her eyes, something he wanted—no, *needed*—desperately to see. And then the undulating waves of power rolled over them, shaking the surfaces and sending her stumbling.

Putting on a burst of speed, he lunged forward, reaching for her.

She shrieked as the floor gave way beneath her, sending her plunging down into a nearby lava tube.

The Ifrits were fliers by nature. Jafar doubted they'd put much time into cave maintenance. Sprinting, he leapt over fallen boulders until he was perched on the dark edge of the place where Miu had disappeared. He couldn't tolerate losing her. Not when he'd fought so hard to keep her.

Not when he needed her so much.

Distantly, he noted the whispers of love, fear, and rage pouring from him. Rough words, but hell, he'd never said he was a poet, had he? Although he knew that later, the raw sentiment would make him cringe.

"Damn female," he muttered, followed by, "Love her to bits, not in bits."

Flinging himself onto the edge, he peered down into the murk. The tube was a deep one, descending at a steep slant, with broken skeletons littering the floor. A floor that was a good forty yards beneath him. He swore.

"Did you mean it?" The voice came from his side; his gaze shot to the shadows and his heart stuttered foolishly. Miu clung to the side of the tube. One of the tube's previous occupants hadn't hit bottom at all, but had instead hit the side—and stuck. Miu hung there with him, clinging to the dead male's arm like a burr. Wise woman.

Jafar spared another glance for the bottom of the tube. Still too far to drop safely, he decided, even if she weren't plummeting downward out of control. He'd have to pull her up from where she was.

He only hoped the male who held her in his arms hadn't been dead long enough to fossilize. Brittle bones weren't going to be of much help here. He seemed to have been an Ifrit with bulky wings. He had probably died fairly recently: an unpleasant aroma reached Jafar's nose and he was fairly certain the stench wasn't coming from his mate.

Pulling off his cloak, Jafar dropped the leather over the edge of the tube. If she climbed up onto the male's shoulders—and the corpse didn't fall apart at her touch—she should be able to jump and catch hold of the material.

"Up," he said, waggling the fabric above her. And then, "Yes, I meant it," he grumbled. He did, too, but did she really want to discuss his feelings for her when she was dangling in midair over a pit of razor-sharp skeletons?

For a moment, he thought she might insist, but then she smiled, that small cat's smile of hers that made his cock throb and stir. "Guess that means I can trust you."

"Sure." He didn't bother telling her that love didn't mean he would necessarily do what she wanted.

"Jump," he said again.

"Better be sure, kitty."

He was. It was the only way he could get her out of her current predicament.

Miu eyed the dead Ifrit. First time he'd seen her look squeamish. "Ick. Can't really be worse than the snakes, though, can it?" Her expression said she thought the Ifrit-dead might actually be the greater evil of the two.

Another explosion rocked the tube, sending him half over the edge. He dug his heels in and scooted backward. They were running out of time. They had to get out of here. Now. "Speed it up, *femi*."

She glared at him, but started climbing. When her hand slapped the ground next to his head, he grasped her wrists and heaved.

Her body flew out of the tube. He caught a glimpse of wide, dark eyes as she sailed over his prone form; apparently, she'd been expecting a gentler landing because she grunted audibly when she landed. In a heap against the far wall. Well, if she wanted gentlemanly, she'd been running with the wrong crowd.

"Go," he growled, not bothering with apologies. Instead, he turned toward the tunnel, where it pushed upward in a steady, calf-burning drive toward Qaf's moon-blasted surface. They had big problems on their hands. The sounds of battle were escalating. It sounded as if the combatants were intent on blowing up all the tunnels and caverns in the surrounding area. He didn't need his Cat to tell him that anyone with an inkling of self-preservation would be hightailing it for the surface and an exit point to another world.

Miu shoved a handful of honey-colored hair out of her face and felt carefully for the leather thong that was supposed to be containing the mass. As if they had all the time in the world and the floor weren't shaking with bone-jarring force around them. She bounced slightly on her feet. "No," she said. "No leaving. No skedaddling. Not in that direction."

She'd obviously located the missing bit of leather because she jerked it toward the surface tunnel in unexpected punctuation. When she lifted her arms and began a hasty braid—maybe the noise was finally beginning to convince her that it was time to make a judicious exit—the thin silk of her tattered robe pulled over her chest. He was sick, he decided. All that pale, dusty skin gleaming through the tears had him fantasizing about pushing her back down to the floor of the lava tube. Mounting her right where they were and stroking some sort of carnal sense back into her.

"No leaving," she said again. "I'm not running this time."

He forced his jaw to remain where it was. No? She wanted to stay *here*? As if to prove his point, another bone-rattling explosion jarred the air around them. He thrust out an arm to keep her from falling.

"What," he asked carefully, "in Heqet's name would make you *want* to stay here?"

"The necklace, Jafar. I need to go back and get the necklace."

She hadn't brought the necklace out with her. It was still in the hands of an Ifrit. Lust vanished in an unpleasant flash of cold reality. If she wanted the necklace, she'd been running in the wrong direction when he'd caught up with her. When he pointed this out to her, she frowned at him.

"Details." Her hand waved vaguely in the air. "I had every intention of doubling back. Just as soon as I'd thrown a certain angry Daddy Ifrit off course." Another explosion made her grab his arm. Damn. The battle behind them was heating up. Pretty soon the entire tube system was going to come crashing down around their ears.

"Are you crazy?" His voice was low and tight. "The entire tube system is going to come down in a matter of minutes. We need to get out of here now." He'd have to come back later for the necklace—if Amun Ra left him alive long enough for a return trip.

"No." She dug in her heels when he tugged her toward the upward slope. "Appreciate the rescue, kitty—and the sentiments." She flashed him an evil grin and he fought the urge to groan. "But I'm going back. I'm getting that necklace."

She was crazed. He paused. Made her a good match for him, he supposed. Stubborn as a cat—or a mule. He cast another glance back toward the tunnel out of which they'd come. Dust was leaking from the darkness, swirling ominously around their ankles. In a few more minutes, it wouldn't matter who was right and who was wrong. They'd both be dead. Very, very dead. Not even shifting would fix the damage four tons of very sharp rock would do to his body.

"You don't need the necklace anymore. You're free of Lierr and so is your sister." He pointed out the obvious, deliberately swallowing his anger that she wouldn't give up. He knew she wasn't greedy—not really. So why wouldn't she let the necklace go? "Damn it," he roared, "let me keep you safe."

She paused for a minute and he almost thought he'd gotten through to her. "That's sweet, kitty." He closed his eyes. Gods give him patience. "But I want my necklace back."

"And you're my mate. I want what's best for you," he

said through gritted teeth. Crowding her against the tunnel wall, he pinned her beneath his heavy weight, reminding her of who was in charge here.

She shoved back at his chest but stopped wriggling. "Right."

Maybe she wouldn't argue with him. For once.

Then she continued, "We can go back together and get it."

"You were running for the surface before," he pointed out. "Seems to me that you've already admitted returning wasn't your best idea."

Stubbornly, she shook her head. "Got to go back," she insisted.

Oh, he really hoped not. Sounds of vicious fighting continued and the tunnel began to shake again. Orange light poured out of the darkness, accompanied by the familiar, heavy feeling of powerful *mazhyk* being unleashed.

"Lierr," he said tightly, "is not winning this fight."

"Good." She turned toward the downward slope. "All the better. I'll just grab the necklace and go."

He muttered to himself, "Should have left you in that tube."

Why not? Who was going to stop him? Miu couldn't; he had that much biology on his side. And, if he stashed her inside the tube, well, he'd know precisely where she was—it had to be safer than letting her return with him to the chamber where Lierr was engaged in mortal combat with one extremely pissed-off Ifrit.

Why not indeed?

Moving swiftly, he grabbed her off her feet and dropped her over the edge. She slid down the side with a satisfying shriek—hell, he had to admit it felt good to get a bit of his own back. She had him running in circles.

Curses drifted up.

He lay down on the side of the tube to check—yeah, she was snagged on that handy dead Ifrit once again. He got to his feet in a smooth rush of muscle and force.

"I trusted you!" Her voice echoed eerily off the rock that surrounded her. A small shower of ancient dust and rock crashed down the side toward her. She spluttered and swiped at her face.

"Good," he snapped. Being a knight in shining armor wasn't familiar territory for him. Usually he was the one stopping thieves—not striding off to *become* one. "I'm going to get your damn necklace. Hold on."

"Why?" she wailed.

Because if she let go, she'd die? He kept the words to himself, though. Both because he suspected sarcasm would have her launching herself for the surface and because the words were truer than he cared to consider. He couldn't let her go. Not now. She was too damn important to him. So instead, he settled for part of the truth. "Because you want that necklace. Because, for once in your life, you're going to have to trust me."

And he didn't even know why she wanted the damn thing.

As if she'd read his mind, her voice floated up toward him as she scrabbled at the sides. Surely, she wouldn't be foolish enough to try to *climb* out. Surely, she'd wait for him to come back.

"For you," she gritted out.

He stopped and stared down. Her face was a pale oval in the growing shadows of the tube. They really were running out of time. Conversation at this point was almost inexcusable.

Almost. He needed to hear what she had to say.

"Excuse me?"

"For you," she repeated. "I want the necklace for you."

"Why would I want the bloody necklace?" he roared.

"For the Amun Ra." Her face made it clear that she resented having to explain this. "You said he told you not to take the necklace out of the temple. Maybe if you bring it back, he'll remove the death sentence he put on you."

"Why, thief, anyone would think you *cared*," he drawled—and then he shifted, streaking down the tunnel she'd just exited.

Chapter Twenty-four

Miu sure didn't want the damn necklace for herself. It had already caused more than its fair share of trouble. In fact, it seemed to her that the people who tried to keep it had a nasty way of winding up dead.

Hell, she'd have begged *Lierr* to keep the thing, with her blessings, if it had meant that she could scoot on out of here in one piece—and take her Cat with her.

Problem was, the Amun Ra had put a price on Jafar's head when he had taken the necklace.

There was no way her Cat could return to his people without it.

If Jafar left the necklace behind, he would pay the price. He might anyway. The Amun Ra didn't strike her as the forgiving type.

Not a whole lot of wiggle room, and she was an expert when it came to getting herself out of a tight spot.

Speaking of tight spots, she'd landed in a bad one this time. Miu eyed the walls of the tube in which she was perched. Fifteen feet to the top, but it might as well have been a mile, for all the good it did her. There was no way she could get out until Jafar came back.

Another thunderous explosion rocked the tube, sending an avalanche of pebbles down on her head.

"You'd better be good and anchored, buddy." She eyed her dead companion thoughtfully. Not the worst date she'd ever had. Not by a long shot. The thieves who worked for Lierr weren't known for their charming manners—or any other stellar qualities for that matter.

Still, maybe her companion would be of some use after all. At the very least, he was a buffer. She'd thought she was the only living thing in the lava tube. Her mistake. The walls were alive, seething with minute insects she was certain were sizing her up for their next meal. That, or they were going to wait for her to season like Ifrit-boy. In addition, she was fairly certain she'd spotted movement on the bottom of the tube as well; she could only hope that whatever was down there couldn't climb.

"Sorry, lover." Just in case the dead guy still had feelings—or had been inconsiderate enough to leave a death spirit hanging about—she figured an apology wouldn't be amiss. Reaching around what had once been an impressively large male body, she snapped a long arm off at the elbow. Mountain climbers did it all the time, right?

Right. And who was she kidding?

Eyeing the razor-sharp end of the bone with some misgivings, she jammed the ivory shaft as far as she could into the smooth wall of the tube.

Which amounted to about two inches. Hell.

At that rate, she'd be an old woman before she got anywhere. Climbing, clearly, was out of the question. Wrapping her arm around the Ifrit's throat, she leaned backward cautiously, angling for a better look at her surroundings. Slick, steep walls. Yeah, she was in an old lava tube, all right. Qaf was nothing but one giant fubar as far as she was concerned.

Lovely.

This close to escape, and all she could do was sit and wait while someone else came to save her. Sitting and waiting—she shuddered. Not her thing. So—she tapped a finger against the Ifrit's moldering chin while she thought—what could she do? If she couldn't rappel upward and going down wasn't an option—there was *definitely* some sort of mass movement going on at the bottom of the tube—what *could* she do?

She could always wait for Jafar to come back.

Right. As if she'd be so foolish. Counting on someone else to come and rescue her.

But he did come all the way to Qaf, didn't he? a small voice whispered. It wasn't as if he'd let her go her own merry way and screw the consequences. No, he was still trying to *protect* her.

Acting as if he really were her mate. *Which he isn't. He can't be.*

She was a thief. He was a Guardian. *Opposites.* And she'd never really been one for the whole "opposites attract" thing.

Desperate times called for desperate measures. If she couldn't get herself out of here, all she *could* do was wait for the Cat to come back. If he decided she was worth bothering with—and she really didn't know. Perhaps she'd finally pissed him off one too many times.

Hmmm. If Jafar's cloak had been able to reach her, then she had to be within ten feet or so of the top. If she could gain a couple of feet, perhaps jumping would become an option. Right, then. Gingerly, she crawled up the Ifrit's torso, using his exposed bones as handholds. When she reached his shoulders, though, her luck changed.

And not for the better. With a sharp crack, the bone beneath her foot gave and she slipped. Straight down the dead man's torso. Frantically, she grabbed handfuls of his clothes, yanking her body against his. Ick. With a disgusting click, his leg bone left its socket. Fortunately for her—unfortunately for him—when he'd fallen, he'd impaled himself on a convenient spike of rock projecting from the wall.

"How in the hell do these things happen to me?"

She wasn't getting out.

Not on her own.

Since there was nothing else to do, she settled for rummaging through the dead guy's pockets. Perhaps, if she were lucky, he'd been packing some nice sharp climbing spikes or an extra rope.

"Whatcha got for me?"

Not much, was the answer. Pretty slim pickings. She'd done better rolling the drunks at the tea gardens. All her search turned up was a spartan handful of unfamiliar copper coins and a small, flat medallion that hummed faintly with *mazhyk*. That last was interesting. She slid the lot into her pocket and considered her next move.

Cat had better hurry up. Sand and loose rock were starting to pour into the tube from above. Eventually, she figured, she was looking at a cave-in. That, or, in about five years, there'd be enough detritus at the bottom of the tube for her to just stand up and step out.

The sounds of fighting grew closer.

And the dead Ifrit slipped an inch. Oh, hell. All the concussions shaking the ground were finally knocking the guy loose. From somewhere came the feral roar of a Cat in full attack mode. For some inexplicable reason, the sound made her feel safe, and wasn't that crazy, hanging from the wall of a lava tube in a dead man's arms? More sounds echoed from above her. Curses. Sounded like her ride was approaching.

Looking her dead Ifrit in the eye, she wondered if dead guys were any good at giving advice. Probably not.

"You think I should trust him?" She looked down at the pile of bones and old rags at the bottom of the pit. "Trust can be a bitch. Was that what got you into this?"

Not surprisingly, the dead guy didn't answer her.

Nevertheless, the answer had been creeping up on her for some time now, and since she couldn't run, all she could do was admit the truth. No matter how strange it sounded when she said it out loud.

"I love him. I love my damn Cat."

"Good." Jafar's face appeared abruptly over the side, and a rope hissed through the air to land by her face. "Delighted to hear it. Applaud your sentiments and the charming change of heart. Now move your sweet little ass. We're about to have company."

CHAPTER TWENTY-FIVE

A powerful emotion Miu wasn't quite ready to name swept through her as she climbed the rope. If she'd been the labeling kind of female, she might have called it elation. Or joy. Or any one of several deliriously happy sentiments that she wasn't going to acknowledge.

Not now. Not while it seemed pretty clear that their lives were in serious jeopardy. Buzz kill, that.

His hard hands wrapped around her forearms, yanking her out of the tube. The damn tube *he'd* thrown her into. Yeah, she owed him for that one. But he didn't stop pulling once he had her out of the tube. Despite the earthshaking concussions and a whole lot of uproar coming from the tunnel out of which he'd apparently just sprinted, he pulled her straight up against his hot, hard form. His mouth sought hers in a kiss that made liquid heat blaze through her veins. Gods, she'd missed him.

And he'd only been gone ten minutes.

Reality check.

So what if she'd had her doubts that the man was coming back for her? That he might have just decided to call it a day and leave her stuck in the tube? She'd done her level best to encourage that kind of thinking on his part.

His tongue licked along the seam of her mouth.

"Miss me?"

Oh, he had no idea.

"Had me a substitute male," she whispered, and then did a little plundering of her own. He tasted like hot, wild sunlight and the warmth of him was a welcome shock in the cool shadows of Lierr's caves. He tasted right. He tasted familiar. The part of her where his bells rested creamed in welcome, wanting him inside her. Now.

He'd come *back* for her. No one had ever done that before. Instead of thanking him, however, "Did you get it?" were the words that came out of her mouth. Never mind what she was thinking. Had he been injured? Was he hurt? She let her eyes run over him, checking for injuries.

He'd picked up a couple of slash marks on the side of his throat—made her wonder if the Ifrits had vampire blood in their family tree—and what looked like an alchemical burn on the side of his face. Someone hadn't played nice. You had to be real careful detonating those powders, particularly—she glanced up—when you were sitting in a cavern full of old, unstable rock.

"Here you go." A familiar weight settled around her throat. "Now I won't have to get you a ring."

"Wait, you were planning on getting me a ring?" A gift? Doing a quick mental inventory, she couldn't remember the last time someone had willingly given her gemstones. Lierr's little necklace didn't really count, since he'd planned on repossessing the stones—and her. Unexpected pleasure curled through her.

"Planned." He shot her a teasing look. "Past tense. You want this necklace? Fine. It's yours." He was dragging her up the slope now, pulling her inexorably toward the surface. Together they stumbled out of the caverns and into the otherworldly moonlight of Qaf. "Open a Doorway. Now."

She didn't have to look behind them to understand the urgency in his voice. Yeah, getting the hell out of there would be the wise and prudent thing to do. For once, she was happy to be agreeable. And look—her little fall into the tube had conveniently nicked a tender spot. She frowned at the crimson stain on her forearm. Hazard pay. That was what Lierr should have been giving her.

"Now, Miu," Jafar bit out. "Take stock of your damages *later*." The ground thundered around them. "There's an entire clan of Ifrits—really, really pissed-off Ifrits who might just be looking for a necklace—headed our way."

Right. She'd demanded he become a thief, she supposed, so it was up to her to get his back. And to hope that two out of three would be enough to placate the Amun Ra, because there was no getting around the sad fact that they'd lost Lierr.

For good.

She focused, pulling down the moonlight into the stone, channeling the *mazhyk* until she felt the air splitting open around them, and the Doorway exploded into existence.

"Nice," he commented, dragging her through the opening. "Glad to see you're finally getting over that whole not-taking-orders thing."

"You wish," she said, and snapped the Doorway closed behind them.

CHAPTER TWENTY-SIX

Miu stepped out of the Doorway—and into the temple. Right between the two pylons that marked the temple entrance. The stone Cats were still caught midshift, reaching out with their claws for the still-soundlessly-shrieking thief.

Probably a harbinger of what was waiting for her inside.

Don't think about that.

She didn't want to face the Guardians for a second time. But she knew, in her gut, that it was the right thing to do. Who would have guessed that she would end up doing the right thing? That she would *want* to do the right thing? She reached out a hand for Jafar, letting her fingers wrap around his thick wrist and slide over his warm skin in a small caress. He'd been willing to give up the Guardians, to give up his temple and his responsibilities there. For her. It was a sacrifice she couldn't let him make. If those terrifying moments in the lava tube had shown her anything, they had shown her all too clearly that Jafar was the one male she could trust, the only one she would love.

"Heqet's balls," he growled. His blade materialized

in his right hand, even as his left arm snaked through hers, pulling her back outside the temple.

"What do you think you're doing?" Jafar turned to his mate, his eyes glowing. "Why did you bring us here, of all places? You can't set foot in the temple again. Not without Lierr. The Amun Ra sent us after him and we're returning empty-handed."

"I'm turning myself in," she said.

"Excuse me?" Jafar's eyes shot to hers. Fur rippled over his arm as he began to shift. "I must have misheard you. I thought you said you were turning yourself in."

"I am."

"Over my dead body," Jafar growled.

Now that was precisely the problem. She didn't want to see his dead body—and the Amun Ra had all but promised that Jafar would be destroyed for choosing to help her. Heqet knew, she wasn't going to stand for Jafar being pulled to bits and sent back to that vortex.

If it took sacrificing herself to convince the Amun Ra that Jafar had not been derelict in his duty, she would do it. She'd tell the Guardians that *she'd* taken the necklace, that Jafar had only been protecting his mate.

The first Cat appeared in the entranceway. She'd known they'd be quick, had half wondered if they'd be watching for her. Easiest way in was through the front door, right? They knew how she thought. They were on to her.

Sanur was the first Guardian out of the entrance, his legs braced as he stood on the steep ramp that led up into the temple. Good. She remembered Sanur as the playful one, the one who would be most likely to show mercy.

"Make it quick," she told him.

"Now you're being noble?" Apparently, Jafar had figured it out. Then, turning to Sanur, he cursed. "Don't touch her, you bastard."

"I can kill her now," Sanur said, "or I can drag her back to the Amun Ra. Those are the only two choices on the table."

She twisted free of Jafar's grasp.

"Miu." Her name was a roar of agony. *Don't care for me*, she chanted in her head. *Let go. Just let go.* Couldn't he see that there was no other way out of their dilemma? No way were they both going free. So she'd chosen. And she'd chosen *him*. "You're a fighter." His eyes held hers. "You never give up. So why bring us here?"

"Because this is where we need to be," she said sadly. "This is where we need *you* to be. And this is where the necklace needs to be." She held the necklace out to him. "I got what I needed—you kept your end of the bargain and Lore is free." And Miu had something else even more precious: the knowledge that she was loved, that someone cared about *her*. Not for what she could do for him, but because of who she was. She trusted her Cat.

"You were right—Amun Ra was right—when you warned that taking the necklace out of the temple was dangerous. Lierr can't be allowed to get his hands on it. None of the Ifrits can." She still couldn't believe that Lierr was an Ifrit, that he'd masked what he truly was for so many years. "And the safest place for it is back inside your temple. With you watching over it. Just another piece of business, kitty."

"You spit in the face of the authority figures." His voice was an anguished whisper. "Why go willingly this time?"

Because she had to make things right. She had to take her lumps. Even if it killed her. She would be a real mate for once. She'd make sure he was safe. That he lived the kind of life he needed: watching over the Doorways and protecting their world. And if the Amun Ra was too pigheaded to see why he needed Jafar, she'd remind him.

"Quick," Sanur promised, his arms closing around her. "I vow to Heqet I'll make your death a quick one."

CHAPTER TWENTY-SEVEN

Déjà vu. If Jafar couldn't convince Amun Ra that his *femi* deserved life, his *femi* would die. And it was no damn consolation to him that her death would be quick.

That Heqet-cursed Ifrit princess had torn out his heart and trampled on it. Up until now, he'd been delighted that that organ had shown no signs of resuscitation. Lesson learned. Now, his chest ached for the woman currently residing in one of the small holding cells beneath the floor of the audience chamber. Somewhere, she was alone in the dark.

He had to convince the Amun Ra to let her live.

And if he couldn't do that, he admitted silently to himself, then they would fight their way out of this mess together.

He'd never been one for words. The need to speak—and speak convincingly—had his stomach in knots. In the distance, he could hear the rough murmur of Cats' voices, the faint, metallic music of shifting weaponry, and a feminine scream, abruptly cut off. He had to do this.

He was going to save her, he growled—and then he was going to kill her himself. How dare she take these sorts of chances with her life? Why had she been so foolish as to just give herself up to his fellow Guardians?

"Once a thief, always a thief, my brother." The Amun Ra lounged carelessly on the divan, the room's only piece of furniture. The massive divan had been covered with exotic pelts of long-dead mythical creatures.

Jafar began again.

"Not a thief. You know I was the one who took the necklace."

The Amun Ra's flat, silvery eyes met his. Deadly. Lethal. Jafar had never made the mistake of underestimating the male, as some of his fellow Guardians had. This being had called them out of the vortex where they had existed, had ruthlessly thrust them into the bodies of the dead and dying, to animate a warrior corps for his own use. You simply couldn't be surprised by anything a male like that would do.

Or the lengths to which he would go.

"Maybe so, my Cat." The Amun Ra's voice was as cold and flawless as the rest of him. "But she's a thief at heart. We both know the truth of the matter. I was willing to overlook it earlier. I wanted the master thief. As you yourself pointed out, there was no point in taking out the little guy when I could have the head of the operation. Now you tell me this Lierr is gone back to Qaf. Dead?" His voice was a delicate question.

Jafar bit back a growl. "Incapacitated," he rejoined. "Trapped. Imprisoned. And"—a hard grimace stretched his lips—"punished."

"Punished is good." Something savage lit the male's eyes. "You are quite sure of this?"

Interesting that the Amun Ra could put the Guardians' spirits into human flesh but not see for himself the truth of Jafar's words. Not all-powerful, despite the Guardians' perceptions to the contrary. Jafar filed that fact away for future examination and chose his next words carefully.

"Saw to it myself. Left him broken. Buried."

"Deep beneath the surface of Qaf." The Amun Ra's words were not a question, but a pleased recollection. Twice already Jafar had been through the history of what had happened on Qaf. He jerked his head in agreement. Lierr's injuries were no longer a concern. The heavy air inside the chamber stirred.

The female on the divan stretched sinuously, rubbing her pale flesh against the Amun Ra's arm. The male seemed not to notice.

"Broken rules, my brother," he said, not taking his eyes off Jafar. He was watching for something. But what? Jafar searched his mind for anything—*anything*—he could use as leverage to save his *femi*.

Amun Ra's long fingers stroked down the female's flank, dismissing the Guardian standing before him.

Jafar gritted his teeth. He was not going to fail. Not this time. He itched to loose his Cat, to lose himself in physical battle, even though he knew there was no winning against a creature such as the Amun Ra. The male was a bottomless lake of *mazhyk* and Jafar had seen what was left of the Guardians who thought to challenge Amun Ra for leadership rights. The Ifrits had left more of Ebo than the Amun Ra had of the males who had challenged him.

"Bent, not broken," he said desperately. Amun Ra's flat silver gaze swiveled back to pin him. *Save her*, he thought desperately. "Bent," he repeated carefully. "She's brought back the necklace."

"You leave me little choice," Amun Ra pointed out, almost gently, which terrified Jafar more than being on the pointed end of the male's blades. "Why do you defend her so doggedly? If it is a simple matter of wishing for companionship, other arrangements can be made." The female stretched out on the couch, drawing her white hands up her bared thighs. Reaching down, Amun Ra stroked the golden bells that disappeared inside the woman's vulva. The sound of soft wetness growing juicier filled the hushed room. "I could give you this one," he suggested.

That one was not his *femi*.

Jafar shook his head. "Not interchangeable."

"Right." The male made a shooing motion with his hand, and the female, shooting him a disgruntled look, sauntered off into the shadows. Toward the growing sounds of his fellow Guardians in the outer chambers. Hell, he hoped his *femi* was locked up far away from that lot. Lusty and uninhibited, they were.

He frowned. He only hoped Miu's capture wasn't the cause of their celebration. He tried again. "Valuable, she is."

"Really?" The Amun Ra looked down at razor-tipped nails. "Convince me of that."

"She opened a Doorway between our realm and that of Qaf. I was able to travel through it." He leaned casually against the wall, ignoring the dust that coated the gold bands around his upper arms. The Amun Ra wasn't much for housekeeping. None of them were.

"She *closed* her Doorway, I trust?"

"She did." What would have happened if she had

not? Was that where the first Doorways had come from—abandoned portals that a lazy or unwary traveler had left open? "We were trying to use the necklace to bring Lierr back to the temple," he continued doggedly. "But the bastard knew all about the moonstone. He had his own way of directing it, so the Doorway opened in Qaf instead, and Miu was forced to go with him."

"She did all this using *my* necklace."

"Not yours." Not to put too fine a point on it, but the necklace belonged to the temple. Didn't it? "It came from Qaf originally."

"My temple." Amun Ra shrugged in a lazy ripple of power. "My necklace. But," he conceded, "valuable information."

"Did you know she could do this, make the necklace work as it was intended?"

"Perhaps," his leader admitted, shrugging his powerful shoulders. The silver cape slipped from his shoulders as he rolled them. "Damned slippery," he said, eyeing it. "But it comes with the office."

Jafar went on the offensive. "So, if you knew what the necklace could do—what *Miu* could do—why kill her? Why not simply keep her here with us? Why should I turn her over to you *now*, for your cockeyed idea of justice?"

"She has got to you, hasn't she? Isn't there justice in punishing a thief?"

"You *let* me take the necklace and escape with her." He was suddenly sure of this. The whole thing had been an elaborate trap. Sparks of *mazhyk* glinted in the air around the Amun Ra as he pushed away from the divan in a smooth, serpentine glide. The Guardians might be raw power confined in powerful, male bodies, but the Amun Ra was something else altogether.

Something alien.

"Leaving the necklace untested—leaving it where it could fall into the hands of Qaf and be pressed back into its original service—no, I don't think that would have been terribly clever of me," Amun Ra scoffed. He hadn't drawn his blades yet. Perhaps there was still hope?

"Qaf had to be—has to be—stopped." Jafar had never disagreed with that sentiment. He'd seen firsthand the danger of the Doorways and Qaf's ability to open them. His Miu, however, wasn't a threat to anything other than his own peace of mind.

That, and his heart.

Somehow, though, he didn't think the Amun Ra was interested in that particular organ. Not unless it sprouted swords and a wicked aim. So what did the male want? Why had he stayed his judgment thus far?

"Take her from me and you'll have to send me back." He meant it, too. If the Amun Ra were going to kill Miu, he'd have to pay a steep price: the loss of one of his Guardians. Jafar was willing to be returned to the void.

As long as Miu walked free.

Amun Ra stared at him, not blinking.

"But you don't want to kill her," Jafar said slowly. "Not really. You wanted her to come back here. Why?"

Amun Ra said nothing, just steepled his fingers and waited, the asshole. "Because you wanted to see what she would do. What she *could* do." It was all beginning to make sense now. "She's a moon daemon and she can work the necklace, open the Doorways. You're not planning to wait for the Ifrits to come through. This way, *you* can take the battle to *them*."

Slow, methodical clapping came from the divan. "Precisely. Of course, since your mate's not a full-blooded daemon, there was a question of her strength. It seems"—Amun Ra examined the razor-tipped edges of his nails, a small smile playing over the corners of his mouth—"that the weakness was nothing a little sex and blood couldn't take care of. That *you* could take care of. If you're willing to cooperate, you could spare me the need to retrieve another spirit from that vortex of yours."

"Deal." Jafar strode toward the door. The sex he could certainly take care of.

And he would enjoy every minute of it.

Who knew violence had a smell?

All Miu's high-minded idealistic thoughts of taking her lumps and accepting the consequences of her actions vanished in a heartbeat. Pausing on the threshold of the temple's main chamber, she drew the stale, silent air deep inside her. Hot and dry, the air carried a smoky promise of too many powerful males caged in a small space. Waiting for her.

Wasn't she a lucky girl?

The long gallery of stone cats flanked them on either side; the only visible signs of life besides her companion was the less-than-straight path her bare feet had marked in the inches-thick dust of the gallery floor. *Just like walking on a thick, spongy carpet*, she thought, somewhat hysterically. Now she could feel the violent force stirring in them. Lust and heat. Curiosity and anger. *Don't think about that.* Instead, she focused on the doorway ahead of them. Why had she had the harebrained idea that doing the right thing was the right thing to do?

"Mental," she grumbled. Sanur's hand reached out and clamped onto her waist.

"Keep walking," he said.

"Don't trust me?" she asked.

He shook his head slightly. "No farther than I can throw you."

"That's the thanks I get for doing the right thing?" She frowned.

"Too little, too late," he rumbled in his deep bass.

She had to be insane to even think of doing this. She just wasn't cut out to be a martyr.

But for Jafar, she could do anything. So he could stay here with all these Cats, where he belonged. Sucked that she wasn't going to be receiving accolades for this particular sacrifice, but there you had it. Probably build her character, make her stronger—right up until the point where it killed her.

Lifting her chin—really, there was no point in appearing cowed—she stepped forward, her bare feet slapping against the cool granite slabs of the floor. How in the hell the temple's original builders had managed to finesse the immense stones into place was a mystery; she could feel the vast cold weight stretching away below her into the shadowy depths of the temple. Thick swirls of dust clung to her feet, painting her toes a less-than-attractive shade of grimy gray. Really, if she made it out of here, she needed to point out the availability of cleaning services to these guys. A sneeze tickled her nose and she fought back the urge.

"Faster," Sanur growled. He drew his blade in a sharp hiss of steel. Lovely, and here she was with her hands tied. Literally.

Don't screw this up. Simple, right? Give herself up, let the Amun Ra take his revenge—*try* to take his revenge, she thought grimly—and then Jafar's obligations were met. Of course—she eyed the massive bronzed door in front of them—getting out of the Amun Ra's private chamber would probably make climbing that escape shaft look like a visit to the petting zoo.

Yeah, death was looking more certain by the minute.

The chamber they entered contained the same half-naked female lounging on a divan. Didn't that sort of splay-legged posture get old? Miu eyed her. Seemed cramp inducing, but Sanur was stiffening up behind her, so she figured he'd appreciated the eyeful he'd just received.

She let her eyes run around the room: it was crowded with Guardians. Good sign or bad sign?

Jafar stood on the far side of the room, his face impassive. When Sanur brought her in, however, a shadow flickered across his face. Regret? Concern?

Apparently, Sanur was running behind schedule. They entered in midsentence. Amun Ra was already in full swing, pontificating with lazy ease about the hideous, death-deserving crime she'd committed—really, you'd think no one had ever stolen something from the temple before. "And I thought he'd cut me some slack for returning voluntarily," she whispered to her companion.

Sanur didn't bother to reply.

Across the room, Jafar was tossing his blade up and down, his eyes not moving from the Amun Ra's. She had to give him credit: he hadn't tossed so much as a wayward look at the other female. Which was good. She was turning over a new leaf here. Ripping his head off was not going to demonstrate what a good mate she could be.

Jafar swiftly crossed the room to stand by her side. A man with a mission—and she was it.

His hands closed on her shoulders and he swung her about to face the room.

CHAPTER TWENTY-EIGHT

"What do you have to say for yourself, thief?" the Amun Ra demanded. "You have stolen from the temple. Is there any reason we should not put you to death for it?"

She spluttered, but words weren't getting Miu out of this mess. Not this time.

"Shut up," Jafar whispered tenderly into her ear. For good measure, he licked the delicate shell, letting his tongue trace the curve with wicked intent. She squirmed. "Just let me handle this." He didn't wait for her to answer, but turned to the assembled Guardians.

Cats pressed in around them. "Thief," the Guardian nearest them said, his blade leaving its scabbard. To her surprise, Jafar placed his body between the male and his mate. She wasn't alone. He was going to stand with her.

"It is true: my mate came to the temple to steal," he began. "Yes, she took the moonstone necklace, but she has brought it back." He swung her body in front of his, so that everyone could see the silver necklace about her throat. "She has sworn to turn over a new leaf. The moonstone necklace is her last theft, the hundredth stolen artifact she needed to free her from the thief master."

"All well and good," the Amun Ra drawled. "If what you say is true." His cool eyes examined her. "I do not wish to see Jafar lose another female. He needs a loyal mate to settle him down. Since Pho's betrayal he has been a bit too bloody vicious for my liking." He glanced at Jafar and her Cat looked down. "Doesn't leave much of the Ifrits he captures," Amun Ra added, when she looked confused. "No one to ask questions of. And," he added meaningfully, "it's the questions that tell me so much."

She had to say the right thing. And she had to say it now.

"I'm done stealing. And I have other skills," she pointed out. Jafar's hands tightened on her shoulders.

"Think, *femi*, before you speak." Right. As if a little well-considered forethought had ever really changed her path.

"Already thought," she whispered back. And she had, too. She wanted this man—and she was beginning to suspect that he really, truly wanted her.

"Skills such as picking pockets?" the Amun Ra asked slyly.

Behind her, Jafar stiffened. "You picked someone's pocket, *femi*?"

She remembered the dead Ifrit, the items she'd lifted from his pockets. How did the Amun Ra know about that? This male's power constantly surprised her.

"Granted," the Amun Ra mused, "he was a dead man. I suppose that might be a mitigating circumstance. Couldn't use what he had in his pockets."

She kept her mouth shut.

"But still, you took something that didn't belong to you." The Amun Ra approached, put his hand into her pocket. Metal clinked and behind her, Jafar groaned. The flat metal disk she'd taken appeared in the Amun Ra's hand.

"Recovery," she said boldly, and Amun Ra looked at her, leveling the dark power of that gaze on her. "*Mazhykal* artifact that seemed better off in your hands than in some dead Ifrit's."

"You were bringing *me* the artifact."

Keep the act together. Make it seem like she didn't care if seven feet of *mazhykal* aggression was toying with her, probably before killing her.

Jafar poked her in the ribs and muttered, "Answer."

"You want the Qaf dwellers to have it?"

"Right." He lifted her chin and regarded her, all smooth, towering male. Maybe challenging him had been hasty. "Not particularly, no."

"I concede that you could be useful to me. Your ability to use the necklace to open Doorways might be very helpful. And I have no wish to send Jafar back to the vortex." He met the Guardian's hard gaze. "If I were to kill you, I believe I would have no choice but to do that."

Jafar merely growled in response.

"So it is settled." He smiled darkly. "By my reckoning, you're a female in our temple and the summer moon is rising over the Valley even as we speak. Surely, my little daemon halfling, you know this." It was true. She could feel the silvery plucking of the moon deep inside her. "So," he growled, "you will run again, and your mate will hunt you. These are my orders, and for once . . . You. Are. Damned. Well. Going. To. Follow. Them. I can't have a Guardian," he added, when she looked surprised, "who doesn't know how to take orders when the time is right."

"A Guardian?" she repeated, as Jafar's hands closed on her shoulders. "You want me to be a Guardian."

Amun Ra nodded.

"Why, A.R.," she said, and someone groaned audibly at her shortening of his name, "I didn't think you cared." And she'd never considered gainful employment before. Maybe it would make an interesting change.

"I can recognize talent when I see it."

Right. "And I thought you only created Guardians from that creepy vortex of yours. Yet here you are. Offering me a deal. A job," she added with some surprise. "Do I get a paycheck?"

He ignored her last question. "Well?" he demanded of Jafar. "Are you just going to stand there?"

"Enough talk," Jafar said sternly. "Get going, my Miu. I figure you've got a whole lot of running to do."

She knew a threat when she heard one.

And a promise.

Blowing him a kiss, she turned and ran.

Pho's tomb seemed like the right place to confront her Cat, so she sat there waiting for him, swinging her feet. Being naked as a jaybird might have gotten the point across more clearly, but that seemed a bit too blunt. Just in case she'd misunderstood that raspy declaration of love while she was stuck in the lava tube.

"You said this was your last job," he said carefully, as he came through the door. His eyes scanned the chamber, but she could have told him that all was safe. No treasure daemons or death spirits. No traps. Not now. "The hundredth theft. End of the contract. I don't know if I can stand to have you facing danger again. And the Amun Ra *will* put you in danger. You do realize you're trading one impossible master for another?"

Her eyes met his. "Yeah. But I'll be facing danger with you. We'll be together." She slid off the coffin with a squeak as he stalked toward her.

"There is that." He reached out a hand and slid the tunic from her shoulder. The ball of his thumb stroked feather-soft over her skin, skimming the sweat-slicked hollow.

"It's actually kind of a turn-on to be in the middle of the action," she admitted in a rush.

Jafar's eyes snapped up. His hand fell from her shoulder, grasping her by the elbow.

"Say that again?" he asked, in a deceptively quiet voice.

"I'm not the stay-at-home, mind-the-fire kind of a female. I enjoy danger, a challenge," she admitted.

"But now you've got a partner. Someone to watch your back." He said it cautiously, as if he weren't completely sure she would accept his role in her life.

"Yeah." She smiled. "You."

"You're really going to be my mate this time?"

She looked deep into his eyes. "I trust you, Jafar. You're the first."

"Say it," he insisted.

"I love you," she admitted, still a little hesitant to speak the words out loud.

"And I love you, my *femi*," he growled. "Never doubt it."

He prowled toward her as if to remind her of the sensual bond between them, of his unique ability to satisfy her secret needs and desires. She loved his body, large and aggressive and—*hers*. "We have unfinished business, you and I."

"We do?" She stared at him, confused.

He sat on the edge of the coffin and pulled her down onto his lap. "Spread your legs," he said darkly. "You've had this coming to you for days now."

"For what?"

His large hand was already shaping her ass, finding the slit in her leather pants. The titillation of his teasing touch made her cream. Oh gods, he knew what she wanted. What she needed. One large hand bluntly traced the seam of her ass and slipped inside her creaming entrance.

"Yes," he demanded. "You need *this*. Mate." His finger gently stroked the opening, testing her slick readiness.

"Yes," she panted. She did. And he needed to give it to her.

His other hand descended, delivering a sharp crack to the leather that faded into a stingingly erotic burn. Each sharp smack drove her farther onto his impaling finger, making her ride him deeper, stronger.

"For thieving," he said gently, paddling her harder. Orgasm coiled inside her, building. "I would not want you to forget. And," he added, his voice a low, dark whisper promising unspeakable pleasures, "because *your* ass is *mine* and I would not want you to forget that, either."

"Is this what mates do?" she gasped. Gods, she could not hold back the pleasure. It rippled through her in long, hot waves.

"Yes." He smoothed the leather over her ass. "They do this, and whatever else they can think of. I love you, my Miu."

"And I love you. Look, I can say it without sounding surprised. I'm thinking of it as an adventure." She rolled over and pulled his head down to hers. "You're part merck, after all, Jafar."

He tested the word. "Merck. Thief." The words no longer seemed so alien.

"Yes. Stealing females, breaking hearts." She stared up at him hopefully and then wriggled, offering him a tantalizing glimpse of her pink, glistening sex.

"Plundering and pillaging," he offered. She raised one leg to his shoulder and let her legs fall apart. He gasped, unable to bite back the sound. Gods above, he wanted her.

"Yes," Miu agreed, "starting with the mate you've carried off from beneath the master's nose. What penalty do you think such a theft might merit?"

"If she loved me?"

"Yes, if she loved you?" Which she did. "Which I do."

"A very stiff one indeed," he agreed solemnly, and then proceeded to show her that he was more than able to pay the price.

New York Times Bestselling Author

C. L. WILSON

"A brilliant, sensual must read." —Christine Feehan

QUEEN of SONG And SOULS

Only together could their souls be complete.
Only together could they survive.
Only together could they unlock the secrets of the past
and unleash their greatest magic.

TAIREN SOUL

As war rages all around them, and the evil mages of Eld
stand on the brink of triumph, Rain and Ellysetta must
learn to trust completely in their love and in themselves,
and embrace a forbidden power that will either destroy their
world or save it.

"C. L. Wilson's exquisitely written romantic fantasy debut
will dazzle readers with its richly imaginative story."
—*Chicago Tribune* on *Lord of the Fading Lands*

ISBN 13: 978-0-8439-6060-0

New York Times Bestselling Authors
Katie MacAlister
Angie Fox
Lisa Cach
Marianne Mancusi

My Zombie Valentine

FOUR WOMEN ARE ABOUT TO DIG UP THE TRUTH

Tired of boyfriends who drain you dry? Sick of guys who stay out all night howling at the moon? You can do better. Some men want you not only for your body, but your brains. Especially your brains.

It's true! There are men out there who care—early-rising, down-to-earth, indefatigable men who'll follow you for miles. They'll take the time to surprise you, over and over. One sniff of that perfume, and you'll have to use a shotgun to fight them off. And then, once you get together, all they want is to share a nice meal. And another. And another.

Romeo and Juliet, eat your hearts out.

ISBN 13: 978-0-8439-6360-1

NINA BANGS

"No one combines humor
and sex in quite the way Nina Bangs does."
—*RT Book Reviews*

The Castle of Dark Dreams is just part of an adult theme park, right? The most decadent attraction in a place where people go to play out their wildest erotic fantasies. Holgarth isn't really a wacky wizard, and Sparkle Stardust doesn't actually create cosmic chaos by hooking up completely mismatched couples. And that naked guy chained up in the dungeon? No way he's a *vampire*.

Wrong . . . dead wrong, as botanist Cinn Airmid is about to find out. It's up to her to save the night feeder's sanity, but to do that she'll have to get close to the most dangerously sexy male she's ever encountered. And one look in Dacian's haunted black eyes tells her close will take on a whole new meaning with someone who's had 600 years to practice his technique. Even a girl with a name that conjures up images of forbidden pleasure has a few tricks to learn from . . .

My Wicked Vampire

ISBN 13: 978-0-8439-5955-0

DEB STOVER

Blood . . . Rivers of it.

The visions are overwhelming. They come every time
Beth visits the scene of a murder. She lives the victim's
last moments, feels the pain, sees the perp. And it's
driving her mad.

*A flat tire . . . A deserted country road . . .
A man too hot to be true.*

Trading life as a Chicago homicide detective for
a job as a nomadic insurance inspector was supposed to keep her safe. Ty Malone is anything
but. What isn't he revealing about the missing
person's claim on his 'runaway' wife? What really
happened to beautiful Lorilee Brubaker-Malone?
And just how far will Ty take his seduction of the
one woman whose gift can uncover the terrifying
truth?

ISBN 13: 978-0-505-52606-9

LEANNA RENEE HIEBER

What fortune awaited sweet, timid Percy Parker at Athens Academy? Hidden in the dark heart of Victorian London, the Romanesque school was dreadfully imposing, a veritable fortress, and little could Percy guess what lay inside. She had never met its powerful and mysterious Professor Alexi Rychman, knew nothing of the growing shadows, of the Ripper and other supernatural terrors against which his coterie stood guard. She saw simply that she was different, haunted, with her snow white hair, pearlescent skin and uncanny gift. This arched stone doorway was a portal to a new life, to an education far from what could be had at a convent—and it was an invitation to an intimate yet dangerous dance at the threshold of life and death . . . .

The Strangely Beautiful Tale of Miss Percy Parker

"TENDER, POIGNANT, EXQUISITELY WRITTEN."
—C. L. Wilson, *New York Times* Bestselling Author

ISBN 13: 978-0-8439-6296-3

INTERACT WITH DORCHESTER ONLINE!

Want to learn more about your favorite books and authors?
Want to talk with other readers that like to read the same books as you?
Want to see up-to-the-minute Dorchester news?

VISIT DORCHESTER AT:
DorchesterPub.com
Twitter.com/DorchesterPub
Facebook.com (Search Pages)

DISCUSS DORCHESTER'S NOVELS AT:
Dorchester Forums at DorchesterPub.com
GoodReads.com
LibraryThing.com
Myspace.com/books
Shelfari.com
WeRead.com

☐ **YES!**

Sign me up for the Love Spell Book Club and send my
FREE BOOKS! If I choose to stay in the club, I will pay
only $8.50* each month, a savings of $6.48!

NAME: _____

ADDRESS: _____

TELEPHONE: _____

EMAIL: _____

☐ I want to pay by credit card.

☐ **VISA**   ☐ **MasterCard.**   ☐ **DISCOVER**

ACCOUNT #: _____

EXPIRATION DATE: _____

SIGNATURE: _____

Mail this page along with $2.00 shipping and handling to:
Love Spell Book Club
PO Box 6640
Wayne, PA 19087
Or fax (must include credit card information) to:
610-995-9274

You can also sign up online at **www.dorchesterpub.com**.
*Plus $2.00 for shipping. Offer open to residents of the U.S. and Canada only.
Canadian residents please call 1-800-481-9191 for pricing information.
If under 18, a parent or guardian must sign. Terms, prices and conditions subject to
change. Subscription subject to acceptance. Dorchester Publishing reserves the right
to reject any order or cancel any subscription.